Alan Carmichael

The Writers' Group

First published 2013

© Alan Carmichael   2013

All rights reserved

No part of this publication may be reproduced, stored in a retrieval system, or transmitted in any form or by any means, without the prior permission in writing of the author.

This book is a work of fiction. Any resemblance to actual persons, living or dead, is purely coincidental.

ISBN 978-1-493-53521-7

www.thereluctantthief.co.uk

By the same author

The Reluctant Thief
The Gift

contents

part I
part II
part III

Part I

"Everyone has a novel inside them. And that's where it should remain."

Literary Agent

"But the part that is good is not original ..."

*H*e knows without looking that the house is the one on the left. He has counted down, two by two, from the street corner. He knows it's the right place, though his eyes remain on the pavement ahead except to look once at his watch. He swears. Despite his careful timing, it is still five minutes before the hour.

He does not stop, does not look up to examine the house, or the door, or the curtains which he assumes are closed, but instead walks on. At the corner of the next street he looks at his watch again and sees that exactly two minutes have passed. He crosses the street, a further ten seconds, counts fifteen paces, turns a half-circle and begins to walk back. There is a woman in the far distance coming towards him, and it occurs to him that his nerve will fail if they pass outside the very house he is seeking. But she crosses the road well before.

Two more minutes have elapsed. It is, finally, three o'clock exactly. He turns, pushes a wooden gate, and walks up a short path. Rings the bell. It is done. The waiting is over.

Someone opens the door a fraction. A woman's face is in shadow. The eyes are tired. Hostile.

He thinks something is wrong, he thinks of walking away. But he says, 'Is Isabella there?' The old woman shifts her weight and pulls the door open a touch more. The man breathes in, takes a step forward and squeezes through. The front door closes behind him and she points to a room down the hallway on the left. He moves towards it and presses against the door handle. The room is empty. He looks back. The woman knocks on a second door and vanishes behind a third.

The man walks into the centre of the room letting the door swing shut. He takes off his coat and looks around. There is subdued lighting. A large double bed with a green spread. A chair, and a dressing table with a hairbrush, a lipstick and what appear to be plastic handcuffs. The blinds are drawn. A teddy bear is propped up on the pillows. A wardrobe is half open. Inside he sees a nurse's uniform and other outfits in leather and plastic. He lays down his coat and leans against the frame of the bed. He waits, absolutely still. His nervousness has gone. It has been superseded by another *kind of tension. An expectation. His hands are shaking. And then the door opens and she strides in.*

Long black hair, centrally parted. Very straight and glistening. A black, see-through something, boots with silver heels. She is smiling. She is very beautiful.

He starts to speak. 'Hello I'm ...' She watches him but does not react. He reaches into a pocket and extracts an envelope. She accepts it though she does not check the contents. Instead she places the envelope on the dressing table. And then she does something which surprises him, and which he will remember for days ahead.

She walks up and kisses him on the lips ...

I know what she's going to say, Peter thought. The pause lengthened. *I just know ...*

'I think I'll leave it there,' said Harriet. Peter sighed. There was a rustling of papers, a few coughs and then silence.

'Yes -' another pause '- well ...'

'Hmm ...'

'So what happens next?'

'You're not writing from experience, I hope?'

'They never kiss.'

'Who says?'

'That's what I've heard. Kissing's too intimate.'

'How much was in the envelope?'

'That shit.'

'Who?'

'The man.'

'Why?'

'Well it's ...'

'What?'

'Exploitation.'

'How much *does* one pay?'

Peter, who had said nothing, glanced across at Shelley, also silent. Her eyes met his and she smiled before turning to the other two men in the group. Ben, the younger, was staring at his copy of the manuscript, as was Art, a generation older. Both gripped pens in their right hands. Both had crossed their legs.

'Well, what do our male members have to say?' said Shelley.

'Boo-boom.'

'Now, now,' said Virginia, around whose living room they were all seated, and who rather presented herself as the matronly voice of moderation. 'This is a piece of literature. And a good one, I think, Harriet.'

Harriet, the only one of them whose city job demanded a certain formality of dress, extended her stockinged legs and, with her left foot, detached the stiletto heel from her right. 'Ah,' she sighed. 'That's better.'

Lucy and Kath, occasional attendees who, when they did show, turned up together and sat next to each other, were giggling over something.

'What's the joke?' said Ben.

'Two hundred pounds.'

'We were just checking it out,' said Kath, holding up her phone. Ben leaned forward and she passed it to him.

'Two hundred pounds an hour. It took ten seconds to find. Just google "London" "escort" "services".'

'These new phones,' said Art. 'Bloody marvellous. 'Ere, let me see.' And he put his reading glasses back on to peer across. 'Blimey, she's not wearing much.'

Virginia got up and walked over to a side table where she refilled her glass with water. She stood there, drinking and frowning, with an imprecise sense of disapproval at what seemed the frivolous nature of the discussion so far. At the previous meeting she had told them in the pub afterwards how sober and ordered the atmosphere at home had become, now that her youngest son had finally been packed off to university. 'Right. Harriet,' she said firmly. She walked back to her seat and picked up the manuscript. 'No thanks,' she said as the phone was passed her way, 'I don't want to see.'

'Yes, well. Harriet. It's just about there,' said Ben. 'It just needs a bit of tightening up.'

'Curtains and blinds …'

'What?'

'First para. The room has curtains. Later, he notices the blinds are drawn.'

'Let me see …'

'And towards the end, he's "absolutely still". Yet his hands are shaking.'

'Where are we now?'

'And you tell us about "another kind of tension".'

'So?'

'Do we need to be *told* if you've *shown* us already?'

'And - "superseded" - it's a "c", not a second "s".'

'No it isn't.'

'I'll spellcheck …'

'No need, Ben,' said Harriet briskly. 'It's correct as it is.'

'Ahem. Point-of-view?'

'What about it?'

'Second paragraph. He doesn't look up. But he knows about those curtains. How? Remember, the reader sees the world through *his* eyes.'

'That's nitpicking.'

'Either it's right or it isn't.'

'Omniscient POV?'

'Too many *he's*,' said Art. 'The first two paras. *He* knows. *He* has counted. *He* knows. *He* does not stop. I'm always telling the junior subs to watch out for this.'

'Come on, this is not *The Guardian*.'

'I like it,' said Virginia. 'Short sentences. He *does* this, he *does* the other. It generates tension. We sense something is about to happen.'

'If you want Dan Brown tension make them shorter.'

'Dan Brown?'

'It's not a thriller. It's not *genre*.'

'Well, perhaps it is. Harriet?'

'I …' It occurred to Peter, looking at her at that moment, that he could not recall ever having seen Harriet smile. Perhaps in these economic times it was considered not quite appropriate behaviour for fund managers and private equity specialists. 'Well, I don't read thrillers,' she said. 'My taste is literary. That's what I read, that's what I aspire to write.'

'Haven't we gone beyond that?' said Ben. 'Fiction these days is beyond labels.'

'Is it? I wonder,' said Virginia. 'Tell us, Harriet, what happens next?'

'Well, I want to show …'

'Does he have a name?'

'… that he's got a long way to fall, that there is an ugly underbelly to our society, even at what appear to be its most successful levels …'

'How do you define successful?' said Art.

'Well, the Bentley, the sylph-like wife, the private schools for the children. These things are just not enough.'

'Don't you think -' said Virginia, ' - I'm not saying these things are not worth writing about - but - how original is that? Don't we know that already?'

There was a keen intake of breath. Harriet looked up and glared at her.

'Nothing wrong with repeating it,' said Art. 'These yuppy scumbags need to find out what the rest of us think of them.'

'Some might call *me* ' - Harriet was whispering - ' one of those yuppy scumbags.' Her voice rose. 'Although my bank did *not* get a government bailout.'

'I didn't mean ...'

'Can I ask something?' said Shelley. She coughed. 'Sorry, can I ask you men a question ...'

Lucy and Kath giggled. 'I know what you're going to say,' Lucy chirped.

'Art. Ben. Have you ever done it?'

'What?' said Art, and Peter saw Ben reach for his glass of water as a rash of colour came to his cheeks.

'Have you ever done it with a prostitute?'

Peter watched Ben's face, now recovered, and vowed silently that he would never reveal himself in a similar way. He turned his blandest stare towards Shelley, knowing that he would be next.

'Peter?'

Art broke the silence. 'What do you take us for? Blimey, we're not all like that.'

Kath was giggling again. 'Come on, lads. What about those stag parties to Amsterdam? Ben, don't tell me you've never been tempted by that kind of ...'

'I'm always too drunk,' said Ben.

Virginia breathed in and was about to speak, but said nothing. She usually took it upon herself to keep the discussion focused on literature, at least until they moved to the pub, but it occurred to her that this was a question worth exploring. She had aired her concerns, often to her girlfriends and even once or twice to the writers' group, about what exactly her sons got up to at university. Could they ever, would they ever ...? She looked at Ben, only a few years older than the three of them, Ben, with his self-consciously precise movements, his pale blue v-neck sweater and white t-shirt, and she decided that he was not the type of person who would ever let himself be seduced into that kind of behaviour, despite his reddening just now. She could not see him even drinking too much - despite his protestation - or ever losing his temper. And she simply could not imagine him indulging in something so sordid as ... 'Tell me, Harriet,' she said, 'did you do any research for this?'

And then she thought, reflecting on her ex-husband, the trouble with men was that you never knew.

'Just the usual. The blogs. The kiss-and-tell stuff. *Callgirl this..., Highclass hooker that ...*'

'Will there be loads of sex?' Kath asked.

'In my book?'

'What does he do next?'

'Do?'

'Your hero. Does he, well, do it with Isabella?'

And then Harriet smiled. Peter gaped. 'Sex and literature don't mix,' she said.

'But there has to be a bit of ...'

'Of what?'

'The two of them, like, fucking.'

'My dear, I don't want this book to win the *Most Egregious and Gratuitous Act of Fornication in Literature Prize...*'

'You mean the *Bad Sex Award*?'

'Wouldn't complain if mine did.'

'So, Hattie,' said Art, 'what does happen next?' Peter saw Harriet's face tighten very slightly at the diminutive. The thought came to him that Art was getting his own back at the women, that this was payback for the suggestion that all males might stoop so low as to consider the services of a call-girl.

'I see him' - Harriet turned to look at Virginia - 'I see him leaving that house feeling smugly pleased, elated even. He resolves to do it again. And again. But then, over time, he becomes obsessed, addicted, he even, dare I say it, falls in love ...'

'You can't let him off the hook in that way.'

'Boo-boom.'

'What do you mean?'

'Well it suggests he's the victim, not the villain.'

'That's what I want to show, that none of us are entirely innocent, but that we all suffer one way or another.'

None of us IS innocent, Peter thought, and then he wondered whether his pedantry really mattered, whether it was usage alone which defined what was correct or not.

'I used to know a couple of women who worked as prostitutes.' Shelley was speaking. 'Two girls at university. They did it one day a week.'

Peter looked down at his copy of Harriet's manuscript and listened to Shelley's light Australian accent. Her voice, low and slightly husky, would be perfect for radio, he thought. As he listened, eyes averted, he pictured her in his mind, her blonde hair over black sweater and black jeans. A blue woollen scarf, which she continued to wear indoors, knotted at the neck. She described how one of her friends had been approached outside the senate building, how her friend was horrified at first, even if secretly flattered, and yet, once she learned how much money she could make, had allowed an unadmitted fascination to be indulged. It did indeed turn out to be considerably more lucrative than working behind the bar at the students union, and soon she had persuaded a girlfriend to join her and then later, though here for some reason Peter suspected she was stretching the truth, a gay male friend to act as a ladies' escort.

Peter allowed himself to be mesmerised by the very slightly rasping tone of Shelley's voice, and as she presented her tale, it seemed to him that her story had something of the sense of remove from the hard physical world that Harriet's fiction had, a dissociation which came from the failure to pin down how and why it is that people do the hard things they do. He tried to imagine Shelley's friends as they were faced with their first clients. Or Harriet's protagonist when he picked up the phone to book his assignation. Wasn't fiction supposed to place him there, *just there*, on the cusp of that leap into the unknown? Or did it offer something entirely different, a means of glossing over the real struggle of any such leap? Perhaps this soft option was the voyeurism it really provided, a cheap prurience and not the real thing.

And as Shelley continued to talk, he looked up and stared at her pale and beautiful face, now lit up by the animation of her storytelling.

At that moment, Virginia raised her eyes as well, though in her case it was from her wristwatch as she reflected on whether to call time on the meeting and move on to a pub nearby. But she paused as she caught sight of Peter gazing at Shelley. With one hand he was caressing a cheek, as if he might shield his own face from other eyes. Virginia sighed. She had sometimes wondered about the possibility of some romantic entanglement emerging from the group, indeed she had wondered whether it might be a subject for one of her own bitter-sweet literary confections.

She sighed again and smiled. *She's out of your league, my friend,* she thought.

*

Three of them remained in the pub.

Lucy, Kath and Ben had made their separate excuses as the meeting ended. Harriet had stayed for one quick glass of wine, citing a seven o'clock breakfast conference the following morning. Art had in quick succession consumed three pints of Guinness before his daughter showed up - with a scowl at the line of empty glasses in front of him and a look, if not up to the heavens, then at least to the high stucco ceiling - to drive him home.

The group had met Art's daughter a few times before. And he had spoken of her on many occasions, usually to complain, either about her teetotalism or her political views now that she occupied the post of senior op-ed writer for a midmarket tabloid.

'Come on Rosa, one more,' he pleaded as she waved the car keys.

'Dad, that old rag you work for needs you at your desk tomorrow morning. All bright and bushy-tailed.' She presented the others with her brightest smile and took his arm.

Peter, Shelley and Virginia watched them lurch out the pub.

Virginia had remained because she was curious - curious as to whether her intuition about Peter and Shelley was correct. But both were behaving with impeccable reserve. Instead Shelley was asking about what had just five minutes before become the talking point of what was left of the evening.

'So, Peter, you've been very quiet about this.'

'Well, I ...' He sighed. 'I wasn't going to tell anyone until I had had replies from them all. But, it just came out.'

'Which ones did you write to?' Virginia asked. Peter had been telling the stragglers that he had submitted samples of work to a number of literary agencies.

He shrugged. 'Half-a-dozen I picked from the internet. Some biggies, a couple of one-woman-bands.'

'Any replies?' said Shelley.

'One' - he smiled broadly - 'by return of post.'

'Don't they email?' said Shelley.

'Some agents are not very technology literate.'

'What did it say?'

'You know, the usual pre-printed stuff. *Thank you for considering our agency. Now fuck off.*'

'It didn't.'

'The exaggeration is only slight. ... *could not see a market ... did not love your work*. There wasn't even a signature.'

'Why do they need to *love* a person's work? Sounds a bit dopey.'

'It's agent-speak.'

'Well I think what you've done's very brave,' said Virginia.

'But Peter. You …' Shelley was gazing at him. She breathed out. 'Your novel's not ready yet.'

'It kind of is,' said Peter. 'I've had a working draft for a while now. As you all know.'

'When do you expect to hear from the others?' said Virginia.

'I sent in the submissions a few weeks back,' said Peter. 'Anytime, I guess.'

'That's so exciting,' said Virginia. 'You're so brave.'

'You think?'

Peter was wondering whether he had been wise to tell even the two of them. He had been careful to keep his hobby hidden from everyone apart from his wife Janice and immediate family. And - with the exception of the agency submissions - the writers' group, of course. His colleagues at work, and friends he knew in every other capacity, he hoped to surprise only when he had achieved success as a writer and his hobby had somehow, miraculously, become his trade. He had a fantasy that he might be walking down the street with his boss or a mate from five-a-side, and they would pass a bookstore. The two of them would pause, stare at the hardbacks stacked in the front window display, and his companion would turn to him, open-mouthed, wide-eyed - 'That book. It's your name on the cover. That's YOU.' And Peter would turn away self-deprecatingly and perhaps blush slightly. 'Just something I've been working on in my spare time.'

Because somehow the alternative - to set his friends up with the knowledge that he was slaving away at this enterprise evenings and weekends, to bore them with the intricate details of the hows and whys of the publishing industry, and then to fail - was not worth thinking about.

Some in the group disagreed.

'Would you call yourself a writer?' someone had once asked. 'Even though you're not published yet?'

'Not me,' said Kath.

'Me neither,' said Lucy. 'It would be like, so fake.'

'But why?' Ben had argued. 'If you play the piano for fun, a bit of Bach and Mozart, you call yourself a musician. If you hang your watercolours on the living room wall you call yourself a painter. Why shouldn't we call ourselves writers?'

Peter had been embarrassed by the conversation. It went against the grain to be so aspirational. It smacked of an American type of forwardness, a modern but, to him, misplaced concept of self-esteem - that phrase so loved by social workers and self-help gurus - an idea that something wanted was the same thing as something achieved. But it wasn't. Some people failed. Would-be writers too. It seemed more in character, perhaps more British, to hold off until the quarry was bagged.

And yet, as he waited for the yes-or-no from the agencies, as if his success were to be defined in these binary terms, by the flip of a reader's coin, the tension became unbearable. He expected the letters at any time. Every evening as he returned from work he would riffle through the mail, he would ask Janice and the children whether they had opened anything for him, or, worse, in the case of the children, used it for drawing or cutting and pasting. Every morning, as he left, he wondered whether his d-day had come. It was this tension, plus the two glasses of wine, that led him to let slip his news to the hangers-on at the pub.

'Well, you're the first,' said Shelley. 'The first to take the plunge.'

'I'm not sure I'd be brave enough,' said Virginia.

'Brave?'

'I'd be mortified by the rejections. I don't think I'd ever have the courage to open their letters.'

Peter did not tell her he felt the same dread, that opening the first letter had been exquisite torture. But as they finished their drinks and prepared to leave, she touched him on the arm and said again, 'I think what you've done is brilliant.'

'We'll all be doing it soon enough,' he said.

'That's for certain,' said Shelley. 'I mean, one of us must, must, *must* make it.'

'Make what?' said Virginia.

'Make it,' said Shelley. 'Get the agent, the deal, the Guardian review, the prize.'

'Get the megabucks,' said Peter. 'I hope Shelley's right. Someone in our writing group will surely do it.'

'Don't you think, Virginia?' said Shelley. 'One of us? Over the next year?'

'Why year?' said Virginia.

'Why not?' They gathered up jackets and scarves. Virginia still looked doubtful. 'Don't you agree?'

'You sound like Harriet,' she said. 'With her business plans, milestones, action points and … all that nonsense.'

'Think of it like a …' Shelley paused, perhaps as she searched for a better analogy.

'… a narrative arc?' said Peter.

Shelley turned to him. 'That's the one.' She reached across and patted him on the arm. 'Well, you've just fired the starting gun. Well done.'

And then she leaned over, put a hand on his shoulder, and kissed him on the cheek.

"... and the part that is original is not good."
attrib. Samuel Johnson

There was a metallic rasping, the sound of envelopes fluttering, and two dull plops as one parcel and then another fell to the floor. Even upstairs everyone could hear it.

Sleep would be impossible now.

Peter pulled the duvet over his head, drew his knees up to his chest, and thought to himself that a mere sixty seconds ago he did not know what he knew now. Could he re-create that moment, that cosy warmth, could he re-think it into being? Just for a minute or two?

Could he make what was, not?

Seconds later, he felt small legs climbing onto the bed.

'OK, Katie,' said Janice at his side. 'Mummy will be up in a moment.'

Another small head appeared round the door.

'Daddy's got two big letters,' said Emily.

'Daddy's being a sleepy head,' said Janice. 'Come on, you horrors, let's go make breakfast.'

Thank you for letting us see your material, which we have read and considered. Despite its qualities, it is not something we feel that we could successfully represent ...

Peter tensed as Janice rested a hand on his shoulder.

'Here,' she said, laying a mug of coffee on the table in front of him. 'What does it say?'

'Hmm. It's not good'

His eyes moved down the page.

... Please note that this is a personal reaction ... and we wish you luck elsewhere.

He breathed in deeply. After a few seconds he picked up the second envelope and re-read the contents.

Please forgive this form letter. Due to the number of submissions we receive ...

'Do you think they actually read it?' said Janice.

... we regretfully consider this is not a project we could successfully handle ...

'Here, look at this.' Peter pointed at the last paragraph.

... and if you haven't yet seen Phyllida Fowst's SELL THAT BOOK! (£16.99 from most booksellers), you might wish to buy a copy from us for £12 inc postage and packing (£9.99 on Kindle). It tells everything you need to know about presenting your work to agents and publishers ...

'The cheek,' said Janice as she moved around the table.

He withdrew a fat pile of loose sheets from the crumpled brown paper.

'Daddy, look at all those stamps,' said Katie. 'Can I keep them?'

He turned to the last page of the three sample chapters he had submitted and read the final few sentences. Sentences which he had believed - quite insanely - would leave readers thirsting for more. He looked up to catch Janice staring at him.

Later, as they unpacked the weekend's shopping from the back of the car, Janice broke the silence.

'So how many replies have you had now?'

'Two emails earlier in the week. And now these letters.'

'Plus the one by return of post?'

'A couple more still to go.' He picked up the last of the bags.

'You guessed it would be bad news, didn't you?'

They walked into the house.

'What'll you do now?' Janice continued as they drank tea at the kitchen table. The children played in the garden.

Peter sighed. 'What do you think? Is my stuff any good? Really?' He had shown his wife a full draft of his novel only a few weeks before. He had let her see the whole manuscript with a certain reluctance, a reluctance she seemed to share when it came to the reading. She told him it was pressure of work that prevented her from finishing it. Peter was, it pained him to admit, sceptical.

Yet a part of him was secretly thankful that it remained unread, or that if she had read it, had just skimmed. She had asked him the other night, as she so often did, why it was that he wrote. He thought but did not say, *I need to speak about the things I can't say to you.* And it came to him later, *And that truth is one of those things*. He wondered now whether this was apparent from a close reading of the text; or whether - more damningly - any presumed psychological depth was not in fact there. Was his material shallow? Unengaging?

Janice said, 'You must persevere. Who was it - who's that boy-wizard woman - who had thirty rejections …' Peter gritted his teeth as she spoke. '… before she got that first contract?'

She poured more tea, and then walked round the table, placed another cup in front of him, and started to rub his shoulders. 'What does your writers' group think?' she said.

He closed his eyes and imagined that it was Shelley applying the massage. His breathing slowed.

'Eh Peter? What do they think?'

He flexed his shoulder muscles and got up. 'I didn't actually tell them until last week.'

'Why not?' She looked quizzical. 'Isn't that what they're there for? To encourage, support? Provide the odd nudge in the right direction?'

He did not reply for a few moments. 'I've been telling them the last few months that it was still only in draft. That it still needed loads of editing.'

The kitchen door burst open. Katie and Emily charged in, ran around the kitchen table exactly two times, screamed at the top of their voices and ran out again.

'Hey,' Janice bawled. 'You two.'

Peter said, so quietly that she did not hear, 'Let them be.' *I like kids to be noisy*, he thought.

She turned back to him. Her scowl remained. 'Peter,' she said. 'You've never introduced me to the group.'

'You've never asked to meet them.' This was not strictly true. And he knew that even if it was, it was really up to him to extend the invitation.

'Are they …' She scratched her head for a moment. 'Look, I don't mean to be rude. But are they any good?'

'What do you mean?'

'Are they really a help?'

'Of course they are.'

'You mean … it's not just an excuse to get out the house and have a drink.'

'Janice.'

She looked at him. Her eyes narrowed. 'Why don't you do another course. Sharpen up your skills.'

'The one I did was enough. Anyhow, that's how the group came about.'

'So? Is that an excuse?'

In a strange way he felt it was. 'I'd have to leave the group.'

'What? You make it sound like a marriage.' Peter said nothing. Even he recognised the absurdity of the non-sequitur. 'You're not that close,' she said. 'Are you?'

He had met them at a Creative Writing lecture series held in a dingy hall with fiendishly uncomfortable wooden chairs and located somewhere off the campus of the London School of Economics. For two terms he had spent two hours of every Tuesday evening discussing such subjects as *Point-of-View*, *Show-not-Tell, The Secrets of Good Dialogue*.

Their tutor, whose careless appearance and sunken eyes rather belied the glamorous photograph Peter had spotted when googling the two minor novels she had written, was encouraging as they sipped a farewell glass in the pub to which they had all decamped after the last lecture. 'Well, at least you lot can write,' she told them. 'That's more than I can say for last year's lot.' There were twelve class members at the bar, all the attendees except one, but that pleased Peter as he did not have to make conversation with the class bore, someone who had on two occasions reduced a fellow student to tears with his clunking and quite misdirected criticism.

'So what are you all going to do next?' their tutor asked as she accepted a second glass of wine from Peter. 'I mean, let me tell you, it's a difficult game, getting published.'

'In fact, a few of us plan to carry on meeting.' Emails had been swapped the week before.

'We're forming a Writers' Group.'

'You can join us.'

'Only if you want to, of course.'

'We're just amateurs, after all.'

'Not that we wouldn't welcome …'

And so it began. Although their tutor declined the invitation, citing a battery of excuses not one of which implied that she was just glad to see the back of them.

They started meeting after the summer, and, as autumn and winter came and went and another spring arrived, numbers gradually got whittled down to eight. They rotated venue at each other's homes, though they never met at Peter's in Finchley - his house was not considered close enough to the centre of town - and the routine had become well established. Two or three of them would submit samples of a couple of thousand words a few days before. During the meetings, which began at seven, the author would read a section and then they would discuss the emailed passages, up to one hour per author. After this they would retire to the pub to chat, sometimes about literature, more usually about anything and everything besides.

Some of them continued to do other classes. He knew this was true of Ben and Harriet. This seemed a bit sad to Peter. It wasn't as if he felt that there was nothing left to learn, it was more that there had to be some sense of progression, measurable over time, and it seemed defeatist to retrace old steps and repeat those tedious exercises the tutors loved to prescribe - *Describe a smell, Describe a room from childhood, Describe a moment of pleasure or pain.* The scales and arpeggios of writing, those tutors insisted. As Virginia remarked, Horowitz never practised, though perhaps she might have foreseen the class bore's riposte, that she was of course no Horowitz.

Instead of a further course he had set himself a timetable, precisely as Virginia had accused Harriet of doing, with milestones and critical-action-points, and whose final goal - publication - was to take place exactly two years after he first opened a document and typed his first word. But that two years was almost up, and he had no clear idea how long this whole process was going to last.

The day's rejection slips were not making this question any clearer.

'I want to meet them.' Janice prepared papers at his side for her case the next day. The television was off, the children in bed.

'Who?'

'The group. The writers' group.'

'Why?'

'Why not?' She turned to him. 'Are the girls good looking?'

Peter snorted. 'Average.'

'So what are they like? Tell me.'

'I don't know. Just ordinary people.'

'Ordinary?' She sighed.

'What's your case tomorrow?'

'You're changing the subject.'

'I'm serious.'

Janice sighed again. 'Assault charge. Nasty piece of work.'

'Think you'll get him?'

'Depends on the jury. And my marvellous summing up, of course.'

'I'm sure you will.'

'You know, perhaps I should write a book. With my experience of the courts. What is it they say, *Write about what you know?*'

Peter turned away as he winced at the cliché. 'My dear, I'm sure you could do a very fine novel.' This was more than a casual compliment.

'You think?'

In fact, he had seen a few of her written legal opinions, and they were fluent and, to him, a non-lawyer, free of unnecessary jargon. No purple prose. And it worried him just a touch that she might in fact make a better job of writing fiction than him. Despite his course. Despite his plan.

Despite the group.

Later. In bed. Peter had just switched off the lights.

'I'm serious, you know.'

'What?' They lay side by side in the dark.

'I'd like to meet them.'

'Who?'

'The group. Your blessed writing group.'

Peter turned over on to his side. He opened his eyes and stared into the pillow. 'When I'm published,' he whispered.

"Trust the tale, not the teller."

DH Lawrence

'*M*ate, she said she's sorry.'

It has occurred to Tony once or twice in the past that Stan is a useful bloke to have around. Stan is talking now. His left hip leans into the bar, his arms are folded in front of him and his left foot is hooked around the right, while a young guy facing him flicks drops of liquid from a leather jacket. Megan is fumbling in her bag for tissues. Her glass is on its side, while the ice and lemon drain away onto a beer mat.

Tony has only been away for a couple of minutes, and already things are looking bad. At a cracked sink in the gents a tap with a bad case of the hiccups sprayed boiling water onto the crotch of his trousers. There had been no wipes, and the loo paper just seemed to make the stains worse. He had buttoned up his jacket, the grey one, the smartest one he's got, to give himself some protection from people's stares.

And now this.

'Megan, what happened?' he says.

'Your bird needs to be a bit more careful,' the guy in the leather jacket says.

'I said -' and Stan straightens up '- she's sorry.'

'Megan, let me get you another ...' Tony says. His voice sounds squeaky.

'Don't worry, mate,' Stan says. 'Sorted.' And already he has the barman's attention. It had taken Tony five minutes to get served earlier.

'Thanks, Stan,' Megan says. 'That's really kind.' She smiles sweetly. Tony does not like that smile. The guy in the leather jacket slouches off.

Two hours ago, he had high hopes for the evening. Megan, just started at school, is by common consent in the staff room the best looking of this year's newbies - though Tony is careful not to take part in these conversations after the deputy head was heard to complain they were downright sexist. More important is she doesn't yet know about Phoebe and the kids. Best not to talk about the ex at this stage of proceedings.

Tony is amazed as anyone that she accepted his invitation for a date. He has planned a quick drink, and later paella at that La Vieja Cabra just round the corner. But then, seven-fifteen, Stan had rung.

'Fancy a pint, mate?'

'Well, Stan, actually I'm meeting someone.'

'Bring him along.'

'Her, actually'

'Ooh, I see.'

Trouble is, Tony still owes Stan a tenner for that Moroccan blow. He finds he just can't get through the weekends these days without a bit of weed, especially now that he's lost the right to the kids Sundays. It's that bloody solicitor Phoebe is screwing.

So here they all are. 'Umm, Megan,' Tony says. But she is listening intently to Stan as he talks about his days as a Hell's Angel. 'Megan.' She looks vaguely annoyed as she turns to him. 'Time.' He taps his watch. 'The table's booked for eight-thirty.'

At that moment his head pitches forward into her blouse. His skull feels like it has been cracked open, and his ears are ringing. A second bottle lands close by and smashes on the floor. Over Megan's shoulder, in the mirror behind the bar, he sees the guy in the leather jacket propping the exit door open and lobbing things at them. He shouts, 'That's for fucking spilling your bird's drink over me.' A third bottle sprays beer over Tony's jacket as it hits his back. His head lurches forward again. 'Tony,' Megan screams.

The barman is out from behind his bar in a flash. Another bottle sails by. 'Cunts.' The kid scarpers. Megan looks horrified. He extricates himself from the contours of her perfumed silk and rubs the back of his head. 'What are you doing with your face in my chest?' she shrieks.

Stan is laughing. He thinks it's hilarious.

It's a disaster, Tony reflects. But at the same time he can't stop thinking about Megan's breasts.

Art breathed in. 'I think I'll leave it there,' he said.

'Carry on,' said Harriet. 'You've still got a page or two.'

'Nah.' Art was scribbling notes in the margin of his text. 'Anyway, it's crap.'

There was a rustling of pages and then a silence, which Virginia eventually interrupted.

'No. It's. Not.' She punctuated each word with a wave of her forefinger.

'It's good, Art,' said Ben. 'And … it's funny. Hard thing to do in fiction.'

'One thing,' said Peter. 'Third para. You use the *pluperfect*. Yet you're writing in the *historical present*. Do they really work together?'

'What's the pluperfect?' said Lucy.

'Look, can I say something?' Kath spoke up. She sat right up close to Lucy. They were sharing the same manuscript. 'Why do we read at all? I mean - nothing to do with your reading, Art, it's great - but shouldn't we have read the pieces beforehand?'

'Yeah,' said Ben. 'We'd have more time for discussion.'

Harriet grimaced. 'Sorry, sorry. I haven't had a chance this week. Too busy.'

Peter looked up at Shelley who was running the fingers of her left hand through her hair as she scanned back through the text. He narrowed his eyes as he gazed, and then turned away sharply. *I'm ogling*, he thought. He felt he had to say something. 'I don't know. I just think … -' he improvised '- it gets us into the rhythm of the prose.'

'But it's the text that matters.'

'It's not just the text,' said Shelley.

Peter said no more. In fact, the truth was he found the act of reading oddly soothing. He liked the sound of his own voice. And yet to say that would just come out so wrong.

'The trouble is' - Ben was speaking - 'you mask the weaknesses. If a sentence doesn't work, you unconsciously supply the emphasis to make it work.'

'Well, have someone else read.'

'I don't want to read someone else's stuff.'

'I don't want to read my stuff,' said Art.

'Hey, that's …'

'… a bit extreme.' Kath's and Lucy's voices echoed.

'It just comes over as so crap,' said Art. 'Just so … so …'

'Don't be silly.'

'So what, Art?' said Shelley.

'So lightweight.'

'What's wrong with that?' said Virginia. 'Nothing wrong with lightweight. Think Wodehouse. Amis.'

'Amis *Père.*'

'Come on, that Wooster stuff's not me.' Art rubbed a hand over his close cropped head. 'I'm more kebabs on the Old Kent Road.'

'There's humour to be found everywhere,' said Ben. *How banal*, Peter thought, and he noticed Ben redden, as if he realised what he had said. Peter had to suppress a smile.

Art scowled. 'There's got to be something more. Some grit.'

'Well ...' Shelley was again twirling her hair through her fingers. 'What's it about? What's the high-concept?'

'You what?'

'What are you writing about? Could you sell it to us in ten seconds.'

'I'd bloody well need more than ten.' Art scowled again. 'It's ... well it's about redemption. Tony's redemption. I know he comes across a bit of a klutz. And this thing with Megan looks as if it's dead in the water. But she offers him - eventually - the possibility of retrieving something out of all the fuck-ups. Some shred of dignity.'

'Good. That was brief enough,' said Shelley. 'And I'm sure the redemption bit will come out. We're only on chapter three.'

'What do the rest of you think?' said Art. 'Lucy? Kath?'

Peter saw Harriet frown. She was wearing her customary black business suit. She opened her bag and took out an elegant silver case. The act of extracting and then putting on her reading glasses was, he guessed, something of a defensive gesture. She had once confided to him that she was not especially fond of Art's work. 'Too blokey,' she told him. 'And that Tony. I just want to grab him and ... shake him.' To an extent Peter agreed. It was not the kind of literature he himself would pick up at the local bookstore. Not that he ever bought anything except online these days.

And yet the prose had a certain easy readability. He had a suspicion that agents, fed up with the anguish and earnestness of so much that arrived on the slush pile, not least the stuff which might be submitted by some in this room, would sigh with relief at a few pages which, quite simply, made them giggle.

'Kath? Lucy?' Art said again.

'I like it.'

'It's good.'

There was a pause. 'Anything else?' said Art.

'Who says *bird* these days?'

'Well, Kath, when I was a *nipper*, you took your *bird* to the *flicks* on a Saturday night. That of course may have been before you were born.'

Virginia was suppressing a smile. In fact, she was trying to recall what term, or terms, her sons used these days for the girls they were chasing (and, a subsidiary question this, why was it that the Writers' Group led her so often to reflect on her family). She had been wondering to herself recently whether her younger son might - might, just possibly - be gay. How could one tell? It seemed to be one of those problems that parents, for the first time, in this generation, were forced to address as a matter of course. Would her parents or their parents have asked the question? And was she being prejudiced - she supposed there was an 'ism' of which she was guilty - was she being prejudiced by even considering it?

Was there someone she could ask? She began to think of a colleague of her ex-husband, one of the barristers at his chambers, a middle-aged man with a beautiful collection of suits. She remembered that it was known he shared a smart flat in Chelsea with his male companion, and yet this fact was simply taken as the state of affairs. She had of course met similar men, many of them valued friends, in the course of her charity work. But it would surely be indiscreet and forward to approach one of them. And what would they discuss? Whether the young man had a stash of Playboy magazines under his bed? Whether its absence proved something? And anyway all the pornography was on the internet these days. Or so she was told.

'Virginia?' Art was looking at her.

'Yes?'

'You were saying?'

'Was I?' And it came to her, with a faint and ghastly horror, that she must have been speaking her thoughts out loud. Was this incipient senility? 'So …' she improvised, 'what do you call them these days?'

'Call what?'

'*Birds*.'

Lucy and Kath looked at each other, and then at Ben, as if the three were the group representatives not of a certain demographic but a separate species. As if the oldsters had stumbled into their midst rather as David Attenborough might chance upon a tribe of gorillas.

'Don't look at me,' said Ben. And, in an insight, it occurred to Virginia that he, Ben, might be the perfect person for that hypothetical conversation about her son.

'Well, would you chaps -' Art pointed at him and Kath and Lucy '- you three, would you ever read something like this if it wasn't for the group?'

'Of course we would. Why shouldn't we?' said Kath.

'You don't think it's too, well, old?'

'In what sense old?'

'Well …' Art got up, stretched, and began to pace around the room. He paused on every right step, as if there was some soreness there. 'Does it seem written by old people? For old people? I mean, my mug's never going to appear on *Hello* magazine. Is that a problem for anyone under thirty?'

Peter looked at him and then at Virginia. He wondered how they might appear on the back flap of a novel, and whether their mugshots might not be improved by some discreet photoshopping. For Art, a seventies rock star-turned-national treasure look, the type who receives the *Légion d'Honneur* in his dotage. In Virginia's case, with her strong bone structure and managed grey hair, academic. Or, better, retired chief of MI5. 'If it's on looks alone,' he said carelessly, 'none of us here is going to land that publishing contract.'

'Manners,' said Virginia.

'Thanks,' said Kath. 'That makes my day.'

'You know how to charm the girls,' said Harriet.

'I'm sorry, I only meant …' Quite suddenly he felt ridiculous.

'Anyway. Speak for yourself.' Shelley was looking directly at him. She had a wide smile on her full lips.

Ridiculous, and in her case, of course, quite wrong.

From: Arthur Redknapp <arthur1727@speedymail.com>
To: Shelley <shelley.banks@calbxer.co.uk>
Cc: Peter Pindar <peter.pindar@thegateway.gov.uk>;
Harriet Spence <h.spence@collingwoodmorley.com>;
Ben Jacobs <ben.jacobs@centurydesign.com>;
derek.frost@harbottle-swire.com;
Virginia McCorquindale <virginia44@wazoo.com>;
Lucy Boland <lucy@miaow.com>;
Kathryn Kenton-Jones <Kath@miaow.com>
Subject: Literary Competition

Dear all
Just come across this -
www.thewriterslaunchpad.co.uk/literary/contests

New competition for wannabe authors. Anyone interested?

Lots of prize money and stuff.

Cheers
Arthur

From: Kathryn Kenton-Jones <kath@miaow.com>
Subject: re: Literary Competition

Cool. Winner gets £1000

> New competition for wannabe authors. Anyone interested?

From: Peter Pindar <peter.pindar@thegateway.gov.uk>
Subject: re: Literary Competition

But do you get a deal?

From: Ben Jacobs <ben.jacobs@centurydesign.com>
Subject: re: re: Literary Competition

> You get an "introduction" to a "top" literary agency.
>
> > But do you get a deal?

From: Peter Pindar <peter.pindar@thegateway.gov.uk>
Subject: re: Literary Competition

> But do you get a deal?

From: Harriet Spence <h.spence@collingwoodmorley.com>
Subject: re: Literary Competition

> ' … no guarantees of a publishing contract are promised, implied or otherwise to be inferred by this or any other …'
>
> Pete, scroll down to the small print

From: Lucy Boland <lucy@miaow.com>
Subject: re: Literary Competition

> *The* small *print ...??*

From: Arthur Redknapp <arthur1727@speedymail.com>
Subject: Literary Competition

> F***king cheapskates !!!

From: Lucy Boland <lucy@miaow.com>
Subject: re: Literary Competition

Hmm. Mentoring by pro authors for 5 runners up, I see.
Lucy xx

From: Ben Jacobs <ben.jacobs@centurydesign.com>
Subject: re: Literary Competition

>   Who's funding it?

From: Virginia McCorquindale <virginia44@wazoo.com>
Subject: re: Literary Competition

> *Don't think my material's quite ready yet*
> *Best*
> *Virginia*

From: Arthur Redknapp <arthur1727@speedymail.com>
Subject: re: re: Literary Competition

>   Arts Council, isn't it?
>
>   > Who's funding it?

From: Shelley <shelley.banks@calbxer.co.uk>
Subject: re: Literary Competition

>   How do you enter?

From: Derek Frost <derek.frost@harbottle-swire.com>
Subject: re: Literary Competition

>   Dear Writing Group members
>
>   So glad to hear you are still going strong.

And - Art - SO SO sorry about that punch-up last time we met.

But may I suggest you take me off your CC list (my poor secretary is getting inundated!)

Very best wishes
Derek

PS Let's meet for drinks sometime. Christmas?

From: Ben Jacobs <ben.jacobs@centurydesign.com>
Subject: re: re: Literary Competition

> How do you enter?

… First 20,000 words, plus 300 word pitch

From: Shelley <shelley.banks@calbxer.co.uk>
Subject: re: re: re: Literary Competition

>… 300 word pitch

How gruesome !!?!
S

From: Peter Pindar <peter.pindar@thegateway.gov.uk>
Subject: re: re: re: Literary Competition

>… 300 word pitch

Sounds like an ad campaign

From: Arthur Redknapp <arthur1727@speedymail.com>

Subject: re: re: re: Literary Competition

> ... 300 word pitch

The whole literary scene is so f***king commercial these days.
Cheers, Art

From: Harriet Spence <h.spence@collingwoodmorley.com>
Subject: re: re: re: Literary Competition

> ... scene is so f***king commercial

Come on, Art, put yourself in their shoes. They'll be ploughing through thousands of entries.

Most of which are probably tosh (not ours of course).

Harriet

From: Shelley <shelley.banks@calbxer.co.uk>
Subject: re: re: re: re: Literary Competition

I see that one of the judges is Phyllida Fowst. She exec-produces BooksCorner.

From: Arthur Redknapp <arthur1727@speedymail.com>
Subject: re: re: re: re: Literary Competition

You mean that crappy TV book group?

From: Shelley <shelley.banks@calbxer.co.uk>
Subject: re: re: re: re: Literary Competition

> What's that phrase of hers?
> "Agents only choose what's good. And if you're not chosen …"

From: Ben Jacobs <ben.jacobs@centurydesign.com>
Subject: re: re: re: re: Literary Competition

> "…YOU'RE NO DAMN GOOD."

From: Shelley <shelley.banks@calbxer.co.uk>
Subject: re: re: re: re: Literary Competition

> Oh God. Suppose that means Boy wizards, Chick-Lit, Bodice rippers.

From: Lucy Boland <lucy@miaow.com>
Subject: re: re: re: re: Literary Competition

> *Fifty shades of vampire ...*

From: Kathryn Kenton-Jones <Kath@miaow.com>
Subject: re: re: re: re: Literary Competition

> … Misery memoirs !!

From: Arthur Redknapp <arthur1727@speedymail.com>
Subject: re: re: re: re: Literary Competition

> White-slave trading anyone?
>
> PS Why is this worse than Black-slave trading?

From: Lucy Boland <lucy@miaow.com>
Subject: re: re: re: re: Literary Competition

We need ishoos!

From: Arthur Redknapp <arthur1727@speedymail.com>
Subject: re: re: re: re: Literary Competition

Can't stand that Daily Mail stuff

From: Virginia McCorquindale <virginia44@wazoo.com>
Subject: re: re: re: re: Literary Competition

I must say, whatever happened to the simple desire to write beautiful prose?
Love
Vxxx

From: Derek Frost <derek.frost@harbottle-swire.com>
Subject: re: Literary Competition

Ladies, Gentlemen

Help! My in tray is full.

Thanks, Derek

From: Harriet Spence <h.spence@collingwoodmorley.com>
Subject: re: re: re: re: Literary Competition

So is anyone going to enter?

From: Arthur Redknapp <arthur1727@speedymail.com>
Subject: re: re: re: re: Literary Competition

Nah.

From: Shelley <shelley.banks@calbxer.co.uk>

Subject: re: re: re: re: Literary Competition

> I'm not ready yet.

From: Peter Pindar <peter.pindar@thegateway.gov.uk>
Subject: re: re: re: re: Literary Competition

> Next year.

From: Ben Jacobs <ben.jacobs@centurydesign.com>
Subject: re: re: re: re: Literary Competition

> Not sure they'd go for my stuff.

From: Virginia McCorquindale <virginia44@wazoo.com>
Subject: re: re: re: re: Literary Competition

> *How on earth do you write a pitch?*
> *Vx*

From: Lucy Boland <lucy@miaow.com>
Subject: re: re: re: re: Literary Competition

> *Not for me.*

From: Kathryn Kenton-Jones <kath@miaow.com>
Subject: re: re: re: re: Literary Competition

> Me neither.

From: Harriet Spence <h.spence@collingwoodmorley.com>
Subject: re: re: re: re: Literary Competition

> Anyone? No?

From: Arthur Redknapp <arthur1727@speedymail.com>

Subject: re: re: re: re: Literary Competition

Blimey. So much for that then

"If I like the first sentence, I read the second. And if I like that, I read the third. And if I like that, I read the fourth."
Literary Agent

Of course, Peter did enter. The very next day.

He had a prepared manuscript, edited and formatted on his PC for the agents he had already written to. The competition merely required the addition of the pitch. He had discreetly followed the email exchange during the day at work. At home the following evening he made a copy of the one-page synopsis he had prepared - six hundred words - and considered how he might halve its length. The task turned out to be more difficult than he had imagined.

'What's that you're doing?' Janice asked him. They both sat on the settee, two feet apart, laptops on their knees. The children in their pyjamas lay in front of the TV channel hopping. 'Emily,' Janice turned and barked. 'Volume. Mummy's trying to work.'

Peter stared at his computer screen. He had not typed a single character in twenty minutes.

'Pete?'

'Oh, nothing. Something for the book.'

'Let me see.'

'Later.'

Janice sniffed. She returned to her case notes.

The problem was the nature of the pitch. It had been tough enough slimming the synopsis down to the three hundred word target. Minor character sketches had been taken out, and the paragraph describing the development of the middle section scrapped. He was getting there, the count stood at just ten over. Yet something else was needed. On top of the word cull he needed to alter the tone. It had to be different from a synopsis.

Your pitch is more than just a summary, he read on the competition website. *It must grab the attention and explain why your reader should continue reading.*

The exercise depressed him. He had read in a Sunday Times article, some how-to section in the magazine on writing your first novel, that research showed how browsers in bookshops made their decision to buy within two minutes of opening the book - or was it after reading the first two paragraphs? Or even the first two sentences? The message was clear: capture your target's interest from page one, and pages two and three will follow.

The trouble was, he thought, it's bollocks. He put his laptop down, walked over to the bookshelves at the far wall, and pulled down novels by Philip Roth, Sebastian Faulks, and Will Self. He looked at the first lines of each. Then, picking a number at random, he turned to the sixty-ninth pages and read the first few paragraphs. This was the thing, he could see no discernible difference in style, tone, or punchiness. The openings seemed as languid - as *flabby*, his tired eyes told him - as the bloated middles. Indeed in the case of Self's book, with its lack of punctuation and paragraphs, the pages might have been swapped in some printer's error and no one would have noticed the difference.

Was there anything in any of the beginnings to entice a reader in?

Yet these books secured contracts, their authors commanded huge advances. A comment came back to him from their tutor in the Creative Writing class. *Martin Amis could write a shopping list and still get a publishing deal.* He supposed that that was true. And he, Peter, was not Martin Amis.

He pulled down a recent Amis and read the first page.
And thank god for that.

*

'Dexter, my dear, how does one write a pitch?'

Virginia had not spoken to Dexter Amiss for, she guessed, a couple of years. In fact not since a charitable reception a friend had organised at the Royal Opera House. Not that Dexter could ever, she estimated, be regarded as a suitable recipient for the largesse this particular charity provided - it was aimed at distressed musicians and actors. This estimation was based partly, of course, on the wealth he had accumulated in running a string of advertising agencies, but also because it would be stretching matters, surely, to argue that his campaigns, though witty and eye-catching, could ever be described as art.

Though Virginia was sure that, with a glass of champagne inside him, he could persuasively argue the opposite.

'My dear Virginia, long time no see. When are you going to invite me back to your beautiful *gîte* in Bordeaux?'

The place in Bordeaux, her cottage by the Dordogne, was where Dexter and his then-wife had stayed for week at the invitation of Virginia and her ex-husband. The holiday had been a disaster. Or, more properly, the suitable subject for a French farce. The bed-swapping that occurred had precipitated the ends of both their marriages.

'Dexter, stick to the question.'

'My dear, why do you want to know?'

Why did she want to know? Perhaps a more important question was, did she have a novel for which one might write a pitch? Since the flurry of emails about the competition she had been wondering to herself whether in fact she did.

'What's it for?' Dexter added.

'Not telling.'

'I see. Well. Hmm.' And he hmm'ed some more.

Virginia had always been attracted by the short story form. Certainly this was the case when she started the course which led to the group, and on every occasion when she had read excerpts, it had been a thousand or so words from one of her Chekhovian fables (dare she describe them thus?). And yet the stories she wrote often featured the same characters, or at least characters who were generally similar by class, age and preoccupations. And it had occurred to her with some force, as she examined the competition website, that it would not be too much of a task to string her stories together into a - well - a single loosely structured narrative. She had laboriously totted up the word counts of half-a-dozen of her little tales, and the total comfortably breasted the fifty thousand minimum requirement.

Change a few names. Add a beginning and ending. A few connecting passages. Why not? The deadline for entry was still a few weeks away. She could easily manage this over a few mornings.

All that remained was this damned pitch.

'Well,' said Dexter, 'What's the USP?'

'Please, none of this awful jargon.'

'What's your proposition? Why should your customer choose you over someone else?' He added, 'What's unique about it?'

'Unique?'

And she looked across at her bookshelves. At the hundreds of titles. She had read most of them, at some point in her teenage or adult life, many more than once. Some she had forgotten, some she had given up on after fifty pages, some she had consumed in an alcoholic haze when her marriage was falling apart. All those authors, all that sweat and effort, all that heartache. And there were thousands more. She thought of her local independent bookshop, and then of the multi-acre warehouses - our era's *dark satanic mills* - that Amazon maintained. Had she not read that one hundred thousand new books came out each year? In *Britain* alone

'Let's imagine it's a new type of beer …' Dexter was saying.

Who wrote these books? Who edited them and published them? Who cut down the trees, shipped the timber and built the presses?

'… or a car, or a mousetrap, or a can of beans …'

And who sweated and slaved over them, who got up at 6 or stayed up till 2? Well, perhaps she didn't. But many did.

'… there's so much product out there already …'

And it seemed to Virginia that for all the mass of stuff available in the shops and on the websites, there was still an individual story in each case, there was an individual's desire to make sense of something.

'… so how does one cut through the white noise …'

Whether that something was how to lose weight, or why the Big Bang banged, or how one's own precarious life led one to where one was.

'… how does one differentiate oneself from the rest …'

And that individual struggling to make sense of things was, in her case, well - it was her.

'… how does one -'

'Dexter,' she broke in,' What was that unique whatsit?'

I know what it is, Virginia thought. *I know what makes this particular product different.*

'The USP?'

It's me.

*

This whole pitch thing, Ben thought, *it's a doddle*.

He had imagined it would be hard. But it wasn't. He had already written five.

'His trade was murder. And his next assignment was his partner in crime.'

He looked again at the opening sentence of the most recent of them, and wondered whether it was not a shade too close to cliché. But this was an appetiser, a teaser, a blurb. You could regard it as a loss-leader. And, anyway, the next sentence did have something of a postmodern twist - 'But it all goes wrong when he is caught up in someone else's narrative.'

Despite that it was the most *pulp*-ish of the five. The others were more literary. The question was, which should he choose.

He wondered what Jim Thomson might have gone for. Carver? Auster? Cormac McCarthy?

He already had feedback from a couple of the creative writing forums he subscribed to. His Facebook page had some interesting comments, while a few blogs maintained by States-side indie publishers offered their own slant. Most interesting was a site with a literary text generator - youfakeme.org - which he was already addicted to. Last night he had spent hours on it, propped up in bed with his iPad the only source of light in the room. *And how easy was that on the eye*, he thought.

But the site ... he wondered whether he should tell the others.

You had to input your characters' names, the length of text you wanted to generate. Then you selected from the various pulldowns - and here's where it got interesting.

Style: Literary, Bestseller, Oprah (Oprah?), SF, Romance, ...

Plot: Quest, Adventure, Pursuit, Love, Revenge, Transformation, ... (Hadn't he read that there were only seven basic plots? Or was it eight? Or twelve?)

Influences (optional): Hemingway, Nabokov, Austen, Roth, Archer (Archer?), ...

Hit Go, and there it was. The text in front of his eyes. It needed some tweaking, a quick run-through with the spell-checker - *note to self: US or UK?* - and you had your pitch.

He wondered whether to tell the Group. Or rather, the Groups, he corrected himself. He felt he could not mention anything to Virginia and Peter and Harriet. After all, he had taken part in the email exchange where they had each of them rather pooh-poohed the competition. No, not that Group. But the other one? This was where things got tricky.

Virginia, Peter and the others knew that, when he met them on the Creative Writing class, he had already done that very same course, with the very same tutor, the year before. What he had not mentioned was that, as with them, a few of the students this first time round had swapped addresses and determined similarly to carry on meeting. They met every fortnight - the weeks of the two Groups alternated - and two or three of them read extracts of their works-in-progress. Although, unlike the other mob, they met in a public space in the centre of town. The Royal Festival Hall was the location they chose, since it had a bar, it had tables and chairs scattered over a wide area on the ground floor, and it usually emptied out once the concert got going.

The arrangement worked well, in its own way. The attendance was more sporadic, the group members might make consecutive meetings and then disappear for a month, but it seemed to suit them. The question remained - and he repeated it to himself now - why had he gone to such lengths to keep the Groups secret from each other? It was one of those things he had failed to come clean over at the beginning, and which after a while became too embarrassing to explain. Like when the host serves up steak at a dinner party and you forgot to say you're veggie. Just go with the flow. Keep shtum.

And anyway, suppose they wanted to meet each other? Suppose then they did not get on?

There was one other reason why he remained protective over the *other* Group. And that concerned one of its members.

There were two Americans, and a good part of both of their novels focused on the clash of culture they experienced in London. And this meant that Ben felt more relaxed that his book was set in the hardboiled streets of the US. Some had questioned why he needed to base his story over there, whether he would even be able to get the vernacular right. Marcus and Mary were more sympathetic. Especially Marcus whose book explored his African-American heritage through the eyes of a young woman caught up in the upheavals of the sixties, from Notting Hill to Harlem to Haight-Ashbury. His book Ben found unutterably intriguing. In Marcus's writing there was a power enveloped in elegance, a combination which Ben saw in everything he did, from the way he moved to the way - sharply and sympathetically - he corrected Ben's occasional misuse of American slang. His demeanour was, to use a word today considered not quite correct, *manly*.

He remembered meeting Marcus for a drink after one of the group's get-togethers. Ben had gone on ahead to the pub and ordered the round. At a window table he had observed Marcus negotiating the traffic as he caught up: watching alertly, then skipping forward a few paces to the central reserve as a van seemed to miss him by a whisker. And then doing the same again, with a twist of his long body, as he reached this side of the road.

'Do you know any basketball teams around here?' Marcus had asked as he joined Ben inside.

'Haven't a clue,' said Ben with an admiring smile on his lips.

They had talked that evening about their respective literary projects, and Marcus discussed the problems his parents' generation faced in the America of LBJ and Vietnam, Malcolm X and flower-power. Ben had considered, and then decided against, counterpointing Marcus's reminiscences with his own family's flight from the shtetls a century and half before. It was simply too distant. And anyway, to engage in that kind of one-upmanship could sound a little bit tacky.

So Ben had just listened. And he had watched Marcus's long fingers grip and caress the neck of the single bottle of beer he consumed in the hour they talked.

All eight of them sat in the pub. They were all there because Kath had something to say, and she had told them she wanted to say it. Peter had news as well but he had not yet decided how and when to tell the others. His news was good. In fact he was asking himself whether anyone might have noticed he was feeling chipper. During the meeting, just finished, he had spoken frequently and positively about the short story that Virginia had read. He had not always done so in the past. Her work had for him a quality of being too finely wrought. Its prose was too delicate and oblique, the concerns of the characters, usually ladies of a certain age and class, too isolated from the experiences of the broad mass of readers. He had told her once that her stories were like rich fruit cake. She had taken his words as complimentary, and yet the barb, which, perhaps fortunately, had not struck home, was that they could only be consumed in small doses.

But such reservations did not seem appropriate today. Not since a certain emailed communication had plopped into his in-tray at 3:34PM that afternoon.

He had read it so many times he could recall the wording. He repeated it silently to himself now.

> *'The three chapters you sent me read well and are sufficiently intriguing for me to ask you for the rest (by post, please, with sae if you want it back).*
>
> *I'm not yet convinced of its saleability, as your theme is a difficult one to dramatise in a fresh and compelling manner; and while I understand your ambition to examine the psychology of your protagonists in greater depth there may yet be a danger of making stereotypes of them.*
>
> *But I won't know till I read more, to which I look forward.'*

He breathed out, a long sigh, picked up his glass of wine, took a small sip, and said, 'Hey, everyone, …'

But Kath was tapping the top of her glass. 'Guys. Excuse me.'

'Kath, what's up?'

'What's this "*guys*"?'

'Is this important?'

'You're not pregnant?'

'Art!'

'Sorry.'

'Hang on. I need some ice and lemon.'

'Kath.' Virginia looked around the table, pausing for a moment at each face and then waiting for Harriet to return from the bar. She returned to Kath. 'Go ahead.'

'Umm. I just wanted to say … well, we spoke about this in the past … umm .. are we still looking for new members?'

There was a collective intake of breath.

'Depends.'

'On what?'

'Who it is.'

'And whether they can write.'

'And whether we like what they write.'

'Who is it, Kath?'

'Yeah, who is it?'

'It's this guy I know.' She paused for a second before continuing. 'Well, actually we're going out together.'

'Ooh. How exciting,' said Virginia.

'Should make for some interesting debates,' said Art. 'What if you hate his stuff?'

'I don't,' said Kath.

'It's good,' said Lucy. 'I've seen it.'

'What kind of material does he write?' said Ben.

'He's South American. He's from Chile.'

'Ooh. Magical Realism.'

'What language does he write in?' said Peter. Immediately he realised the question was daft.

'Well, English of course.' Kath glared at him.

'I'm sorry. I only meant to say …'

'Does he write in Spanish as well?' Ben's question seemed to defuse the momentary tension.

'Yes. I think so. I've never seen anything he's written in Spanish.'

'Well, everyone -' Virginia again '- what do we think?'

They had had this discussion before. They had discussed the possibility of friends of friends joining, or people met on other creative writing courses. Someone had proposed setting up a website, which seemed to Peter a strange thing to do given that they had nothing to sell or advertise or in any other way to impart to the world at large. Ben disagreed. 'One day we'll have to market our books.'

It had seemed in the past one of the curiously pointless arguments in which pros and cons were so finely balanced that no resolution was possible. And as it started again Peter knew that the opportunity for informing the others of his own news was fading. Perhaps for the best, he thought, he might be letting slip too much of a hostage to fortune. He would instead present them all with the details once he had written his signature on the end of a fat and comprehensive contract.

But there was another question which troubled him, a question related to this one, and that was whether to inform his wife. The idea of refraining was in a strange way attractive, and yet he knew it presented a path which might cause problems down the line. If, for example, his economy with the truth was discovered at a time not of his own choosing.

And he found himself immersed in a sense that his writing project was taking over his life in a way in which nothing else did. It had assumed centre stage.

'Well are we decided?'

Peter returned his attention to the question of Kath's boyfriend.

'Do we have enough people already?'

'What's enough?'

'If there are too many, we won't get time to read.'

'One more isn't going to make that much difference.'

'Yes, but what about the next, and the one after that?'

'If you really feel like that,' said Kath, 'I'm not sure I want to …'

'I'm sorry, Kath. But you must agree there have to be limits.'

'It's just a writing group.'

'We're not discussing immigration policy.'

'What's his name?' said Shelley. 'Kath, what's his name?'

Kath looked irritated by the conversation. She paused before answering. 'Raúl. His name's Raúl.'

'Well, Kath,' said Shelley, 'I'd love to meet him.' And collectively the group appeared to shift its position.

'So would I.'

'Do bring him. Next time.'
'Yes. It'll be a real change.'
'I think it will be good for us all.'
'So. It's unanimous?'

*

Lucy was driving Kath home.
'You know,' said Kath, 'this evening I almost decided to call it a day.'
'Why?'
'You heard how they dissed Raúl.'
'It wasn't that bad'
'Yes it was.'
'Are you going to bring him next time?'
'I don't know.'
'Well you have to now. After all that.'
'He may be busy.'
Kath sensed the sidelong glance from her friend. 'You've got that look,' Lucy said. 'I know you. You're still pissed.' And then, 'Come on, you have to bring him. If only to show them.'
'I think I'll set my brothers on them all.'
'Your bro's?'
'Six-four. All three. Rugby players.'
'Yeeaah. That's the spirit.'
'Don't tell the others I said that.'
'So - how's your own writing going?'
'Same as ever.'
'I.e. nowhere?'
'Just been so busy.'
'Same here.'
They were silent as they watched the road ahead. The two women lived out east in Stoke Newington, half a mile from each other. Halfway through the first term of the Creative Writing class, at some point between week 5 - *Harnessing the creative urge* - and week 6 - *Playing God - Characterisation*, they had met by chance very late one Saturday night at *The Blue Room*. Kath had been out with girlfriends from work, the four of them vampirically dressed up after a Halloween party.
'Oh my God.'

'It's you.' Lucy had been pub-crawling.

'What are you doing here?'

'Love your outfit.' Lucy's friends were staring open-mouthed at the spike heels, fake fur and red lipstick as Kath's group sashayed towards the bar. As the two of them huddled together later with their *mojitos*, and after they had admitted they would never read the mid-list books of their tutor, now slumming it with would-be amateurs like them since she had been let go by her publisher, they discovered that their middle names were the first names of the other.

'So you're Catherine?' said Kath.

'And you're Lucille?' said Lucy.

'I never use Kathryn,' said Kath.

'I just HATE Lucille,' said Lucy.

The coincidence still seemed kind of weird. But a good kind of weird.

They lived in flatshares, and never invited the group to their places for meetings as there was always too much coming and going: too many people, girlfriends, boyfriends, friends from university, friends from work. Sometimes you just tripped over the sleeping bags. And Kath had this vision that Virginia would take one look at the wine stains on the carpets and, well, just leave. Much better to meet in the living rooms of the ones who could actually afford new furniture.

'So, Kath,' said Lucy. 'Tell me. Is he any good?'

'Who?'

'You know.'

'At what?'

'You know.'

'In bed?' And they both burst out laughing.

'No,' said Lucy, 'I meant …'

As Kath wiped her eyes she said, 'He's brilliant.'

'… the writing.' They both began to giggle again.

'Well truth is,' said Kath, 'I've not had time to read anything he's written.'

'How come?'

'Too busy.'

'Doing what?' There was pause. And then once more they cracked up.

*

The following day Peter spent half-an-hour during lunch composing a reply to the agent. He knew the email had to be brief, but was unable to figure out what tone to adopt. It should be respectful but not obsequious. It should be grammatically correct and yet not too formal. This was, after all, an email. It had to be artfully artless. He would be sending in the manuscript by post. Or - a thought - should he fork out to have it couriered? Either way, would it be presumptuous to include in the email a request for an acknowledgement once the package had arrived?

But after he had pressed the 'send' button he spent the next half-hour re-reading the text and cringeing. Apart from anything else, how could a literary agent have a name like that?

> *Dear Mr Booker*
> *Thank you for your email, I'll endeavour to get a package sent out as soon as possible.*
>
> *Fingers crossed, though I understand and respect your caveats.*
>
> *Kind regards*
> *Peter Pindar*
>
> *PS May I request that you confirm by email the receipt of the manuscript?*

But the sending of the package was delayed by the fact that the task of printing out the damn thing - three hundred and nine pages, single-sheet, twelve-point, double-spaced - would take the best part of an hour on his crappy home printer, and now that he had decided to hide this small success from Janice he needed to wait for her to make herself absent for a few hours.

The opportunity did not arrive until the weekend, when she took the children to see her mother.

'You're not coming?' She frowned at him.

'Got something from work I need to get out the way.' He lied. 'A bit of peace and quiet would do me good.' At least that part was true.

The printer had already been going more than an hour when the cartridge ran out of ink and he had to cycle to the shops for a refill. And then he had to start again as he had forgotten to include the page number on the first sixty pages. And then he decided - a minute after the re-start - to print out in *Best* rather than *Draft* quality. And looking at the speed at which it spewed out the first few pages, he knew it was likely to take the whole afternoon.

He was relieved when Janice rang to say she was staying overnight.

'Are you OK?' she said. 'You sound flustered.'

'Of course I am. You go ahead.'

'What'll you do this evening?'

'I'll just ... get a DVD and a curry.' He did not tell her the printer was still only on page one hundred and twenty-seven.

'Do you want to speak to the girls?'

'No, I'm ...'

'What do you mean, you don't want to? What's up with you?'

'OK ... sure, go ahead. Quickly.'

'I see.' He heard that tone come into her voice. 'I see.'

In fact it took him the rest of the evening, first of all to wait for the full manuscript to be printed, then to re-print those pages which had got scrunched up, and then to skim through a few of the chapters which even he had to admit were slightly weaker, just very slightly, than the others.

He agonised over whether to make a few final changes - just one or two. But then he reasoned that changes might put the page throws out of sync, and he would have to print the whole thing off once more.

The previous day he had bought a number of heavy-duty envelopes of various sizes, and he now tried each and every one in turn to see which provided the best fit. Not too small - it might rip open en route. Not too large - the pages might get jumbled up inside.

And then, of course, he needed an accompanying letter. Damn, he had forgotten about that. *Why don't they bloody well take email?* he thought. And one answer came to him immediately. They had no intention of doing themselves what he had wasted an entire evening on.

It was midnight before he had the thing packaged and addressed in front of him on the kitchen table. He had not sealed the envelope. He knew he had better do so, or else the temptation to take it out, review, change, edit, reprint, might be too great. But the tiniest doubt remained. What had if he had forgotten something? And of course he did not have the stamps. He would have to wait until Monday before he could get to the post office. That would be a nightmare in itself, queueing behind the pensioners and the tourists.

An hour later he was drunk. He had carried the envelope into the living room with a bottle of scotch and a tumbler in his other hand, placed all three items on the coffee table in front of the TV, and sat there, dividing his attention between the brown package and a late-night football re-run. After the second glass, he sealed the envelope. After the third he decided to sellotape it as well in case the seal came undone.

'What a palaver,' he shouted out, staring at the thing with its asymmetric patchwork of tape. 'What a fucking palaver.'

He knew his daughters could have done better.

'It's OK, Raúl,' said Virginia. 'We won't bite.'

They all sat in the living room of Art's semi-detached in Shepherd's Bush. The seats - a sofa, one armchair, and half-a-dozen fold-away garden chairs - were arranged around a low wooden table upon which was laid one jug of water, a stack of plastic beakers, and a plate of digestives.

Art's wife had died five years before.

'We're dying to hear a sample of what you've written,' said Shelley.

Raúl sat straight-backed between Lucy and Kath. The young women looked nervous.

'Did you bring anything today?' Peter asked.

'No, he didn't.' Kath answered for him.

'That's all right. We're reading Shelley and Ben anyway.'

'Tell me, Raúl,' said Harriet. She grunted as she reached forward for a biscuit. And then again as she grabbed two more. She had not found time to eat the sandwich she carried in her handbag between leaving work and arriving at Art's. 'What kind of stuff do you like?'

'Stuff?' he said.

'Books.' She munched as she spoke. 'What do you like? What do you read? South American?'

'He reads everything, really,' said Kath. 'Don't you?'

'Well,' said Art, 'I like that Gabriel Garcia whatsit. *One Hundred Years of Cholera*.'

'And Mario Vargas Llosa,' said Virginia. 'What a romantic name. And that *Aunt Julia* book of his, what's it called? …'

'You know he's a fascist?'

'… *Aunt Julia and the Kite Runner*, it's just one of my absolute all-time favourites.'

'Borges.'

'Puig.'

'Paz.'

'And Roberto Bolano of course. What a find.' Quite suddenly, as he finished saying these words, Peter had an attack of quite excruciating cramp. He caught Shelley glancing up at him. His cramp, he knew, was just plain embarrassment. The thought welled up, somehow, from some ghastly corner of his mind, *Just imagine if he'd been Black*. He pinched his arm with his nails. A second later, he saw that he had drawn blood.

The previous Christmas a friend had bought him Bolano's *2666*, all nine hundred pages of it. He had not yet started the book. He doubted whether he ever would. He wanted to shout out loud to them all, *Let's rewind, let's start again*. Shelley came to his rescue.

'Well, I've not read any of those chaps,' she said. 'In fact, I've not even heard of some of them.'

There was a silence for a few seconds.

'Same here,' said Kath.

And then Raúl said, 'And for me as well.'

Everyone stared at him. He began to grin, and then they all burst out laughing.

"The writer has paid her dues when she has faced the silence of the infinite; when she has stared unflinchingly at anguish and has stood resolute in its embrace; when she has gazed into the soul of another and has grasped some faint inkling of the depth of its mysteries; when she has laughed in despair and cried in ecstasy and has finally grasped that love and hate are two sides of the very same coin.

On the practical side, …"
Advice on *The Writers Launchpad* Facebook page

Peter had arranged to meet Shelley and Ben outside Earl's Court tube station at nine-thirty on the Saturday morning. They would walk from there to the exhibition centre to catch the lecture for ten o'clock, with perhaps a moment or two to spare for coffee and chat beforehand.

Peter was on time.

Punctuality was a virtue he admired in any circumstance, but on this morning there was another reason he had made sure he would be present at the ticket desk by the main entrance on the Earl's Court road at least five minutes before. He wondered whether Janice had noticed. She often seemed to have uncannily good instincts when it came to his motivations, whether open or hidden.

'You're up early,' she had said. 'Do you really have to go?' She was still in the shapeless M&S pyjamas she favoured since the children were born. Katie and Emily had been up for two hours, and Janice looked exhausted already. Her chance for a Saturday morning lie-in was over.

'It'll only be till midday. No, make that one o'clock. Perhaps two.'

She sighed. 'What's the conference about?'

'Advice for first-timers. The lecture's part of a series to coincide with the Book Fair.' Janice looked doubtful. 'It's a real chance for me to meet publishers and agents,' Peter said.

'Well, perhaps we could meet for lunch.'

'Mmm. Might be difficult.'

'Why?'

'Thing is, I …' He hunted around for a suitable reason.

Janice held his eyes as she shook her head. 'Well, just phone,' she said.

But Peter had turned his phone off as soon as he got on the tube. It remained off at Earl's Court as he stood the other side of the barrier and waited with a copy of *The Times*. He was wondering whether he could get away with keeping it off for the duration of the lecture when he saw Shelley coming up the escalator. He waved, but she seemed to be in conversation with someone just behind her. As they rose he noticed the man's white cane and dark glasses. Peter lowered his hand and observed her as she helped the man over the last step and guided him to the gate. She was wearing skin-tight jeans tucked into soft leather boots. White t-shirt and a grey cardigan, a couple of the lower buttons casually fastened. Trademark scarf, leather jacket, shoulder bag. And - a black beret. As he stared, as she went through the barriers and spoke for a moment with the woman who was waiting for her blind companion, a question which had been bugging him resolved itself in his mind.

That seventies film, he thought. *That legendary philanderer*. He had seen the film late night on Channel4 the previous week. *Warren Beatty.* It came to him then. *Shampoo ....* And, of course ...

Shelley turned, waved, and skipped over towards him. 'Hi, Peter.'

Julie Christie. 'Shelley.'

'Been waiting long?'

From a certain angle. 'No, not at all,' he said. *With her hair the way she's done it.* 'Who's your friend?' *Under that beret.*

'Oh, just some guy I met. You heard from Ben?'

'Why?'

'He can't make it. Check your phone.'

'It's been off.'

'He said some work thing's come up. So it's just the two of us.'

Peter felt an access of elation. He had to resist the temptation to take her arm. 'Well, let's go then.'

*

There were four people on stage. A publisher; an agent; a writer in middle age who had had some success when she wrote her first novel - a fictionalised life of Lady Mimi Jex-Harding, jazz-age flapper turned Colombian brothel-keeper - after a distinguished career in the Ministry of Agriculture and Fisheries. Chairing was the founder and chief executive of Writers Launchpad, a consultancy offering critiques and advice for authors and which claimed to have discovered four out of the five shortlisted entries for the Radio 2 *Snuggle Up to a Jolly Good Read* competition. Trailing purple cashmere and ersatz third world jewellery, whose jangling Peter could hear from his fourth row seat, she strode across the stage challenging the audience to find their authentic inner voice.

But Peter's mood would have remained as elevated had she been relaying an exhortation for eternal vigilance from Kim Jong-un. It was the first time that he had been alone with Shelley for any lengthy period of time, the first time he had been with her at an event not strictly related to the Group, and after about half an hour he had the sudden insight that he might look back at this moment, this precise moment, as one of those very few in his life where for a brief time he was happy. Just, quite simply, happy.

'What do you think of her then?' Shelley leaned into him and whispered into his ear.

'Not sure I'll be taking her advice on the inner me too seriously,' he said, equally softly.

He sensed Shelley's neck twisting. 'Not sure the audience agrees.'

Peter turned himself and looked. It struck him how many people there were. All of them crouched forward and listening intently. Not merely hundreds, A thousand perhaps. Mainly but not exclusively white, mainly but not exclusively Peter's age or older. Was the entire middle class population of London trying to get that first book off the ground?

This thought seemed to be echoed by the line the agent was taking in his speech.

'We get hundreds of submissions,' he said, and went on to describe how precarious was the whole process of finding the occasional diamond in the chaff. The hall fell silent as he suggested that the best advice he might offer would be to - 'well, give up now'.

The two other speakers tried, with only partial success, to sound more encouraging. The publisher, apparently bored, checked his iPhone as he spoke. The writer described at length the thirty-seven rejection letters she collected before striking lucky.

But the mood lightened as the meeting ended with a question-and-answer session. A cordless microphone was handed to a headphoned assistant who prepared herself to race up and down the steps as questioners with their hands raised were picked by the panel.

'Please be brief,' the chairwoman said. 'We want as many of you as possible to get the chance to speak.' And initially the questions came thick and fast, the type of questions he had discussed in bars and pubs all over London. *Will e-readers replace books? Is plot more important than character? Do you need an agent? Do you need to be young and beautiful?* ('It helps!') *What's next after Potter and the 52 shades?*

'Next. You, Sir.'

'Is the novel …'

And then there appeared to be the sound of something like a struggle in the rows far up at the back.

'Please, can I …'

There was a thunk as the mike was dropped.

'No, Madam, not you.'

Or perhaps snatched away.

'Please, can I …'

'*Madam.*'

'Please, can I …'

'Ok. Ok. Madam, go ahead.'

'Thank you. Can I address my question to Eddie Macklin.'

This was the agent on the panel. 'Me?' He pointed to himself, his mouth open.

'Yes you, Eddie. Can I ask why you haven't replied about my manuscript?'

'Well, have you sent it to my office?'

'Four times.'

'Did we ask to see the whole thing?'

'You promised you would read it.'

'Did I?'

'Everyone says it's marvellous.'

'Do they?'

'You made a commitment.'

'Did I?'

'Your secretary said …'

Eddie Macklin looked across at the chairwoman and raised his eyebrows. 'Next,' she shouted.

'I'll be waiting for you,' the woman said. 'By the exit.'

'Next.'

'I'll be waiting ...' The microphone was snatched away.

Peter turned to Shelley to find her staring at him and giggling. His happiness was complete. But there was to be more.

'Time for one last one,' the chair called out. 'You sir.'

'Thank you.' A male voice. 'Thank you. I would like to ask the panel what they think of the prevailing thesis of postmodernism - one might mention Lacan, Derrida, Self and others -' a clearing of the throat '- that the gap between signifier and signified has become a chasm that can never be bridged. Or, rather, that to do so is to subscribe to a pre-Joycean ...'

'Look, Peter -' Shelley was nudging Peter in the ribs. '- it's that guy from the course, it's ... I can't remember his name.'

'Derek?' Peter turned to look.

'... and, furthermore, that the English language novel, by failing to recognise that there is no such thing as character, but instead only shifting realities ...'

Indeed it was. Derek, the only one on the creative writing course who had, with the universal agreement from the others, not been invited to join the group. Derek, who, with his criticism, had on two occasions reduced Lucy to tears.

'Excuse me.' Someone from the panel interrupted. 'What exactly is the question?'

'... if plot, circumscribed as it is by beginning, middle and end, fails to get to grips with the unmediated randomness of human existence *as it really is*, then should we not reject the bourgeois tropes favoured by so much of the literary establishment ...'

Peter turned to Shelley with a groan. 'My God, you're right.'

'What's he saying?' said Shelley.

Someone in the audience began to boo. Another shouted out, 'Next.' There was a general sound of shuffling on the panel as the forum members began to gather up papers and open their bags.

'...what I'm trying to say is ...' The booing increased.

The chairwoman stood up. 'Well it's been a great pleasure for us all to be here. Thanks to my panel, thanks to you the audience, to the Book Fair ...'

Eddie Macklin was sprinting for the exit.

They spent ten minutes looking at the tables and the stands just outside the conference room. They picked up flyers and brochures, put their names down for a lucky dip offering a free critique from The Writers Launchpad, though they declined to purchase the new novel by the panel's one author. They considered having a look at the Book Fair proper, but decided against when they realised that their lecture tickets, at twenty pounds a pop, did not include entrance.

'Lunch?' Peter suggested. *Please say yes.*

'Hmm. Any idea where?'

'Chelsea's not far.'

'Could be crowded.'

She was right. There was a game on at Stamford Bridge.

Instead they wandered down Old Brompton Road looking for the first halfway reasonable gastropub. The sky had cleared and it had warmed. Peter carried his jacket over his shoulder. He knew he should have been looking for the right place to stop but felt immersed in a sense of the moment, so trapped in the here-and-now that any willed deviation seemed impossible. It was Shelley who spotted a place on a side road which advertised food and a beer garden at the back.

'You lead,' said Peter. 'I'm following.'

The pub was a spacious Victorian building with a long bar, high mirrors behind, at which a mildly shabby couple in middle-age seemed out of place as they opened bottles of Pinot Grigio for a young and affluent mixture of tourists and West End shoppers. Peter wondered if what he felt might be described as grace, especially when the barman, an unreconstructed Cockney with a line bordering on mild offence and what in Islington would pass as racism, referred to Shelley, as Peter paid up and she found the Ladies, as the *missus*. He felt somehow re-defined, re-branded within a new world of coupledom. And he loved it.

When she returned they ordered food and went out back to the crowded garden where they found seats at the end of a wooden table.

'Cheers,' Peter said. He took a mouthful from his pint of beer.

'Cheers.' Shelley was drinking beer as well. He approved.

Peter did not really know very much about Shelley. Perhaps Virginia, generally more sociable, who indeed had something of the air of a professional hostess, had got her range. And yet he doubted it.

He knew she came from Melbourne, though her accent, as with Kidman and Blanchett and the current crop of Australian actresses, had lost its hard edges. She had arrived in London while still in her teens, then spent time in South Africa where, it seemed, there had been a long-term relationship. It had ended abruptly, though he apparently followed her to London - occasionally she would sneak off to a corner to take a difficult call, where she could be heard whispering in exasperated tones. Her work, as far as he could make out, involved fundraising for charities. And this conjunction of opposites - huckstering amongst the City's elite on behalf of NGOs staffed by unworldly innocents - had a fascination for him. When she was on 'the money trail', as she put it, she would turn up for group meetings in black suits so sharp - minimally accessorised with the perfect shoes, handbag and pearls, her blonde hair pulled back in a tight ponytail - that everyone, first time, had stared.

'Been to a funeral?' Art asked, misreading the situation.

The book she was writing was a child's-eye view of a disintegrating family. It was written in faux-naïf style. Peter thought it lacked polish, and yet undeniably had charm and a sinister undertone.

'Do you think it helped?' he asked her now.

'The talk?' A cat perched on a brick wall stared down at them with slit eyes. Shelley stretched and took a sip from her drink. 'I suppose.' She looked at him with a smile.

'What?' he said.

'Guess what. You know that competition? Writers Launchpad?'

'First twenty thousand words?'

'Plus pitch.'

'Phyllida Fowst.'

'I've entered.'

'You haven't.'

'Yep.'

'But your book's not finished.'

'They don't know that.'

'So what if you win? And you need to send in the whole thing.'

'I'll cross that bridge when I get to it.'

Peter had to laugh. 'Well, so have I,' he said. The day seemed to be getting better and better. 'So what was your pitch?'

'There was *"a dizzying journey into a dark centre"* in there somewhere, plus *"an uncompromising portrayal of deception"* if I remember correctly.'

At around Midday that same Saturday Virginia sat in the café at the Sadler's Wells Theatre waiting for her friend Martha. As she waited she skimmed through the Arts Review of *The Guardian*, the only section of that newspaper she read with any frequency. She checked her watch. Martha was late, as usual. As usual this rather irritated Virginia. Nevertheless the thought came to her that she might fold the paper away into her bag before her friend arrived - *Virginia, you're not reading that socialist rag? Please!*

Her eye was caught by an article on the London Book Fair. She began to read, then to wonder whether she might have enjoyed herself ever so slightly more if she had joined Ben, Peter and Shelley at Earl's Court. In fact she was the one who had spotted the publicity for the lecture series and who alerted everyone in the group by email, yet she had quickly ruled herself out of attending when she found the date clashed with one of her regular lunches with her best friend. But, as she waited and waited, she knew that this was an event that could easily have been postponed a week.

Too late now.

She wondered how the boys were getting on with Shelley. Australian Shelley. Mysterious Shelley. And Virginia decided, there and then, that she would invite her out for lunch.

The act of having lunch with a girlfriend was, she knew, something more than a simple opportunity to share ideas, or to see and be seen. It was also something of a ritual which defined a boundary upon the other side of which lay - lay, what? Something which she could only describe as intimacy.

It did not matter whether it was with a business associate, the current partner of her ex-husband, or even the girlfriend of one of her sons. When what Gareth, Luke and David mockingly described as *the summons* actually came, the two women would not discuss work, or any intervening man, or money or politics or the weather. Yet the things they did discuss, while on the surface trivial - the décor of the restaurant, the recent *Verdi* at the Opera House, the young's lady's family - would, Virginia believed, bind the two women together.

As she considered the idea, and increasingly warmed to it, she realised that it was something of a surprise that she even contemplated going through this ritual with the Writers' Group, people who, she had initially feared, would bear the same relation to her social circle as might have done her hairdresser or solicitor. But two things had made her change her mind. The first was that, quite simply, she had come to love and value their company. The second concerned Shelley herself. She was something of an enigma.

This realisation had come suddenly, the evening when she saw Peter's moment of naked desire and realised that he was infatuated with her. Later, in the pub, as the others had discussed the recent Booker prize nominations, she had reflected that, yes, it was obvious, she was beautiful, why weren't all the men in love with her. Beneath the carelessly brushed hair and the trainers and t-shirt, there was a freshness which, in Virginia's eyes, seemed reminiscent of a hippy innocence of the 60s.

Why weren't Ben and Art in love with her as well? Well, perhaps she was a touch too old for Ben. And way too young for Art - if he still thought about such things. *If Ben ever thought about such things*, it came to her as an afterthought.

There were other mysteries as well.

While she knew pretty well what the others did, how they earned their money - Ben with his trendy job in design, Art hanging on at his paper - there were blanks in the narrative with Shelley. Virginia knew she had once freelanced as a journalist, that she now fundraised for charities. But it was never clear whether these things actually earned her money. She was never short, she was generous buying rounds. Although she still rented.

And her friends. She did not have a partner, rarely spoke of past relationships. She was rarely interrupted by mobile phone calls during their fortnightly sessions, though once or twice the ensuing whispered conversations had been fraught. But occasionally - and this was done without artifice - she might namedrop a connection, someone in the news, someone with power and influence. *Oh, I know his daughter*, she might say of an infamous businessman. *I was talking with him at a party last week*, this about a firebrand MP.

And then there was her book. Now just what was that about?

*

The following morning Art's daughter Rosa knocked at his door, at exactly ten in the morning, to take him over to hers for the day.

'You can stay tonight if you wish,' she told him as they drove to her house in Fulham. 'Do you really have to be at the office on Monday?'

Art said nothing. It had been enough of a struggle to make sure he was ready, shaved and showered and properly dressed, at a reasonable hour on a Sunday. Not that he had been up especially late the night before. It had been the kind of evening he had enjoyed innumerable times in the past - drinks at a couple of Soho pubs with a bunch of cronies from the old Fleet Street days, pasta at *Angelo's* in Wardour St, the evening rounded off with a few nightcaps in the basement bar of the Burlesque Club run by old friend Annie (formerly Andy) - the kind of evening which, in dark moments, he knew to be the only experience he still unconditionally enjoyed in this, the final stage of his life. The kind of evening, which, in still darker moments, he knew he might not enjoy for too much longer.

He wondered in the car whether it was possible to tell his daughter about these feelings, or these fears. When she actually began to speak to him, after four consecutive calls on her handsfree, it became clear that at least on this day it would not.

'Stay at ours,' she repeated. 'It might be a good idea. We need to talk about something. You and me.'

'What's that?'

'You'll see.' She said this with the tone she had acquired at perhaps the age of fourteen and which meant that whatever he, or, in earlier times, her mother might say, Rosa's mind was made up. So he said nothing else for the remainder of the journey, concentrating instead on how he might endure the rest of the day in the company of Rosa's two young children and the man she had married.

It was a matter of amusement and, to some of his oldest friends, disbelief that his son-in-law was a man called Rupert. It was true that he and they had once imagined a world where all such class-based judgments might be rendered things of the past, and where any father, any ordinary bloke, might call his son Tarquin or Jeremy out of simple love for the name and not because of any category signifier. But this world had never materialised. And when his daughter had informed him that she was to marry a banker he had almost wept. When the grandchildren arrived he had known it would be his duty to provide some form of balance to their view of life - and to be fair to Rosa they did, at this pre-teen stage, still attend state schools. Was now the time to discharge that duty?

Could he, would he, take them aside, this very afternoon, and talk them through the things he had seen - the abandoned mines, the broken communities, the mounted charges of the pigs - the things he had reported on, once, during what was the highpoint of his journalistic career? Would they understand if he told them he had once hurled a flour bomb at the armoured car carrying the Australian plutocrat who was now their mother's ultimate boss? Could they ever comprehend how absurd it was that their Dad was called *Rupert*?

There was at least one thing, however, that this blond-haired, chinless wonder did provide, and that was a supply of decent wines to his guests. And now that Art's hangover was finally receding the prospect of an afternoon whose hard edges were softened by a palette of Burgundy whites and Bordeaux reds was enlivening. And his mood was rising when he was plonked down on their living room settee with a large glass of something which was pink and sparkling.

'Just relax for a mo',' his daughter said, 'while I check the roast.' Which meant, for her, checking the Latvian teenager who actually did what one might call the domestic heavy lifting. 'Johnnie. Sarah.' Rosa screamed. 'Granddad's here.' And as he heard the sound of feet pattering light and fast down the stairs he began to lay out in his mind a few of the subjects which he might just raise with the youngsters: Oz Magazine, Blodwyn Pig, Wapping, Blair Peach, John Lydon, the Poll Tax riots.

'So what do you think? Dad?'

Art snoozed. The sunlight fell gloriously on his left cheek. They all sat out in the garden.

'Dad, are you listening?'

The truth was that Art did not want to agree with his daughter, and yet there were one or two things that were attractive about her suggestion. His Saturday evenings in Soho would become less frequent, he might have to re-consider whether to take his retirement and claim his pension - he knew that some in the office would be glad to see the back of him. But on the other hand he would be living on a street where he would not get jostled and spat at by the local teenagers whenever he walked from the tube station to his front door.

'You'll be living close by, rent free. Isn't that right, Rupe?'

Rupe grunted. 'The flat's an investment for us, so we're buying anyway,' he said. 'And rather you than four twenty-somethings partying every night.'

Art could not bear to tell his daughter - or the police - that he had been mugged twice in the last six months as he got cash from the ATM. He could not tell her because for thirty years he had instilled into her the precept as an article of faith that the war against racism was as important as the class war itself. But he had to square this with the fact that though he got on swimmingly with his neighbours, the Idowus and the Husseins, his was now the only white face on the street he lived in.

'You'll make a packet from selling your flat.'

'You can baby-sit the kids.'

'We're just two minutes away.'

'Lydia can do your housekeeping.'

Something in him stirred. He had noticed the young woman's supple thighs wrapped in those tight jeans as she bent to pick up the toys from the living room floor.

And then the dream shattered - 'I'm sure Mum would have approved' - Art opened his eyes and stared at his daughter.

'Hazel? I'm not bloody well doing anything that woman agrees with.'

He saw his daughter sharing a glance with her husband. With *Rupe*. 'Dad, I only meant -' and then more softly -'Mum's dead.'

'So what?'

'What do you mean?'

He knew he was on shaky ground. And yet it seemed to him that anything Hazel might theoretically have approved of was therefore and necessarily a bad idea.

'I mean the answer's No.'

The Literary Agency

One thing they all knew was that one day, eventually, they would have to deal with agents. They would have to phone them, write to them, email them, plead with them.

They knew the names, they had surfed the websites and checked which authors each had signed.

They knew that agencies came in all shapes and sizes, they were large and small, highbrow and lowbrow. They knew they covered the English Civil War, sci-fi and cookery. Most were in London, but not all, though all professed to love both literature and the bottom line.

They knew some agents were mercenary, some unworldly, some friendly, some intimidating, some eccentric, some buttoned down.

And they knew that the Hephzibah McCracken Literary Agency was just plain daft.

> *We seek writers who are ludic, inventive and eloquent fabulists ... who eye a needle in a literary haystack and glide the camel through it. ... writers with burning curiosity and a searching mind, a desire to help people and improve the world, with appreciation of simplicity and complexity ... and excellent spelling ...*

They crowded around Ben's iPad and gasped as he paged through the website. Lucy said she did not understand what on earth it was going on about. Virginia, charmed by the sentiment, wondered nevertheless what the ship of the desert had to do with writing.

> *... what fills us with joy is the writer with a palpable love of language, who eschews cliché, handles pacing with the skill of a dancer, who conjures up mood and atmosphere with an apparently invisible wand, ...*

'I think I can just about manage all that,' said Art, 'except the dancing.'

> ... *my assistant, half Burmese, half Mancunian, speaks Cornish and Hebrew, is provocative and probing, skilled in a variety of deconstructionist techniques ...... and has travelled extensively through Sub-Saharan Africa.*
> *She is also a double bass player...*

'Ben, just where did you discover this?' said Shelley.

'You haven't submitted, have you?' said Peter.

And as the glasses of wine were passed around they hatched a plan.

'You know what we must do ...'
'What?'

> *... Please provide with your submission,*
> *>A handwritten copy of your CV.*
> *>An essay analysing why you will never be a finer writer than Jane Austen.*

'A spoof.'
'A spoof what?'

> *>Attach also a piece of bad writing, which may be your own, and provide a summary of its faults ...*

'A spoof submission.'
'A fiction. A romance.'
'A tale. A fable.'
'A ludic fabulation.'
'... eschewing cliché of course ...'
'... exquisite and refined ...'
'... and deconstructed ...'
'Boys, don't be silly.'
'Just make sure,' said Lucy, 'it's spelt correctly.'

"Literary authors envy us. We can do what they do, but they can't do what we do."

Lee Child

*T*he two men looked down at the woman in the chair. Her mascara was smudged. She did not think to fix it.
— *I guess it's always the same at the end.*
— *Guess that's right.*
The men did not wait for the woman to respond. Her face was tilted towards the floor.
— *I remember the first one.*
— *First one?*
— *Woman as well. Screaming and hollering like it was party time.*
— *Screaming and hollering.*
— *Laughing as well. Big belly laughs. Like it was the best party in town. Like it was one of those moments when you jes forget all the crap. 'Cause you know those moments are pretty well all you've got in the world and you might jes as well take 'em as they come.*

The younger man was silent. He had had a first one as well.
— *Truth was I didn't know what to do. Shut her up or what. Noise was threatening to get out of hand, what with smartass neighbors and all. I was with ol' Sharkey at the time. We were a team back then. We were partners. Hard to imagine now. But we were. Toughest moment of my life when he turned and they sent me after him. Toughest moment. But those days he was still something. He jes looked at me and shook his head. Let it run, he said. Real quiet.*

The older man smiled. He walked to the window, raked his hat back a shade, and began to close the blinds. One after the other. When he was done he walked back to the center of the room.
— *He was right I guess. Ol' Sharkey. After a while she jes stopped and stared down at the ground. Like this one here.*
— *What do you think she's thinking?*

Neither man thought to ask her.

The older man moved towards the door and tested the lock. He walked over to the dining table and placed the briefcase on top.
— *What time's the car coming?*
— *Three.*

— *What time you got?*

— *Ten before.*

The older man nodded. He thought for a few moments. After a while he said,

— *Well I guess if I was sitting in her place I'd be thinking of all those decisions I made which didn't turn out so right. Or the ones which did. And maybe thinking how five times it was one, five times the other, but you could never figure which was gonna be which. I guess I'd be thinking 'bout my sister that I ain't seen since I was a kid who wrote me when she buried my Ma and who's married to some kyke dentist up in Seattle. I'd be thinking how she was real pretty even when my Pa did those things and that's what led to the bust-up, me and him, and I never saw none of them again. I'd be thinking about ol' Sharkey and how it never sat right with me when he was layin' in that same chair and I was standing over him after I'd traced him to that basement in Harlem. Ugly. Real ugly. And I guess I'd be wondering whether it could have been any different, any different at all, by the meanest amount.*

The older man laughed softly. He looked down at the briefcase and opened it.

— *You or me?*

— *Hell, you're the boss.*

He took the contents out of the case and handed them to the younger man. The woman did not look up. The younger man took the metal tubes in his hands and fashioned them into a single piece. He squinted his eyes and peered at the workings of the assembled object. His movements were practised and sure.

When he was done he looked across at the older man.

— *Say, how old were you when you tracked down ol' Sharkey?*

— *I guess your age son.*

For a second a shadow hung between them. The younger man narrowed his eyes. At that moment the woman gulped. She gulped again.

— *We got a taxi coming.*

The younger man nodded. He walked to the side of the woman in the chair and he pointed the gun at her head.

Then he shot her.

'I think I'll leave it there,' said Ben.

After a five second silence Art said, 'Ouch.' There was another silence, and then - a sharp cry from Virginia - 'Ben.'

'Some dark stuff in there,' said Art.

'Creepy.'

'Is she dead?'

'BEN ...'

'Where does Sharkey fit in with all this?'

'Do we need to know yet?'

'BEN.' Everyone looked round at Virginia.

'What?' said Ben, his voice defensively soft.

'How can you write stuff like this ... about these ... these ghastly people ...'

Shelley was smiling. Peter caught her eye. He had a sense that Virginia was wondering what kind of mother could bring up a son to have such thoughts. And whether her own sons might think similarly.

'Ginnie,' Art said patiently. 'That's life today. Gritty, real, raw, ...'

'40s *noir*, I should say,' said Harriet. 'I can just see James Cagney ...'

'Lee Marvin.'

'More like *Grand Theft Auto*,' said Lucy.

'Hmm ...' Ben scratched his head. 'Is that what you think? Is that how you see it?'

'Much better than *Grand Theft Auto*,' said Kath. 'Miles better.'

'Like these guys have seen it all,' said Art. 'It's just another day's work.'

'Well, perhaps it's just not my cup of tea,' said Virginia.

'Tell me -' Shelley was leafing through the manuscript '- how did you decide on the vernacular? I mean, the American slang - it is set in America, isn't it? I'm not sure it's totally realistic - I don't know ...'

'We need a yank in the group.'

'Come on,' said Art. 'Brits can do US slang. Half the villains in Hollywood are Brits. Did you know ....'

'Shelley,' Ben said sharply. 'This didn't just come out of thin air. I thought hard about the location. It just didn't seem right in London.'

'Tough market to crack,' said Harriet. 'You're taking them on on their own turf.'

'Well, as my friend Marcus says ...' said Ben.

'Who's Marcus?'

Ben felt himself reddening. 'Just ... a friend.' He smirked. He had to be careful. The truth was, there *was* a Yank who had seen it. Marcus, of course, who had seen the manuscript, who liked it, had made suggestions and had told him frankly what felt right and where it just did not work. Marcus. From the *other* Writers' Group.

'What's so funny?' said Virginia.

'Er -' he knew one or two of those in the room might be a bit miffed if they found out he was two-timing '- nothing.'

Virginia sighed. 'It must be my age.'

Ben watched her as she sipped from her glass of water. She had been queasy once or twice in the past over his material.

He had had this kind of reaction elsewhere. It had come as a shock when his mother told him she had to abandon the sample chapters he had given her because of the violence.

'Ben, where does all this come from?' she had asked him one weekend when he was up in Leeds.

'Where does what come from?'

His mother scowled. 'You're not like that, are you?' She held up the sheets of paper from the manuscript. 'These characters, these men ...'

'You never read Cormac McCarthy?' he countered. 'Or even Irvine Welsh?' His parents looked blank. He knew there was no point in mentioning Elmore Leonard or the two Rays, Carver and Chandler, pulp writers whose reputations had been catapulted into the literary canon. 'What about *Cold Mountain?*' he said, struggling. 'James Bond?' And then, in a whisper, 'Midsomer murders?'

They were not convinced. The looks on their faces seemed to suggest there might be something inside him which was not quite healthy. Like a taste for porn.

'It's part of the modern world,' he said.

'Not part of yours,' his mother said.

Later, alone in his room, kept precisely as it was from his student days seven or eight years before, these thoughts came back to him as he fiddled around on his XBox. And especially as he blasted Pink Tony with his double-barrelled on a Miami shore-front. Blat. Blat. And blat again. The graphics on this game were exceptional. He knew one or two guys who had worked on them. And it came to him that some in the Writers' Group, in both groups, would never have played XBox. Or Playstation. The cartoon violence of the games, more realistic with each technology evolution, was something outside their experience. As would be flashmobs or paintball. Or all-night Tarantino re-runs at the Scala, stamina hiked up by nips of vodka and the odd tab of E.

Perhaps these things split the generations more than music or attitudes to sex. After all, his friends went to gigs with their Dads. And this division was defined by technology. Or - as he thought about it - by the dates when technologies became available. No one over forty played computer games. No one under forty did not.

Perhaps it was a good thing. Despite his parents' hang-ups he was not a violent person. Nor were his friends. It was as if the capacity for aggression had been excised - scooped out of them - by this fetishised interest in its depiction on screen and page.

But the line of thought broke down. He was not knowledgeable about Shakespeare, but knew enough to be aware that both the plays and the times he lived in were cruel and brutal. The dramas were no safety valve back then.

And then he shot her.

And here was another problem. He suspected that Virginia regarded his violence as specifically directed towards women.

And then he shot her. Her.

He remembered discussing *Blade Runner*, one of his all-time favourite films. In that headmistressy voice of hers she pronounced herself repelled by its misogyny.

'The women all die in such orchestrated, *balletic* ways,' Virginia had said. She loved her artistic metaphors.

He thought about her words now, as Shelley argued with Harriet about the ending. 'Does it need that final sentence?' Shelley was saying.

Ben looked up at the two women. *And then he shot her.* He wondered, should he make it *him*?

'What do you mean?' said Harriet.

'Well, leave it hanging,' said Shelley. 'Pump up the tension. Will he, won't he? End the scene with the man and the woman eyeballing each other. A kind of deadly embrace.'

A whisper, or more accurately a growl, emerged from the space on the sofa between Lucy and Kath. Lucy giggled.

'Speak up,' said Harriet.

Raúl coughed. It was the first full meeting he had attended. 'Not so deadly for him,' he said.

'That's right,' said Kath, squeezing his arm.

'Getting back to the slang,' said Shelley, 'You've got *layin'* ' - she emphasised the lack of the 'g' - ' but *standing*; '*jes*' but then '*out of hand*'. Why not '*outta*'?'

Ben wondered why she was always on his case. 'I'd be shortening every second word,' he said.

'You need to be consistent.'

'Pah. That's just editing,' said Art.

'You need to get these things right,' said Shelley. 'Agents want to see the finished article.'

'Every last comma and full-stop?'

'You have to get these things as good as they can be.'

'But that's why you have editors,' said Art.

'If there's something that can make it better,' said Harriet, 'do it.'

Art was scowling.

'Another thing,' said Virginia. 'Why no speech marks?'

'It's the fashion,' said Art.

'No it isn't,' she said.

'For thrillers it is.'

'Ben?'

He reflected a moment. He stared at the screen of his iPad. 'I don't know. I guess that's the way it flowed.'

'At least it's better than modernism,' said Virginia.

'Pre or post?' said Kath.

'To say nothing of the French,' said Art.

'Modernism?'

'No punctuation at all,' said Virginia.

'That's unfair,' said Ben, a fan of David Foster Wallace and Will Self.

'What've the French got to do with anything?' said Peter.

*

Peter accepted his change and tested the edges of the tray with both hands.

'You manage?' the barman said.

'Yep. Thanks.' He grunted as he lifted.

The tray contained a pint of bitter, a pint of Guinness, a bottle of wine with five glasses, a *San Miguel*, and a mineral water.

Full house, Peter thought. For once all of them had come to the pub after the meeting. He stepped carefully over to the table where they all sat, and laid down the tray.

'Ben, which one's yours?'

'It's OK. I'm drinking wine.' Virginia was pouring.

Peter picked up his pint. He felt slightly sorry for Ben. The discussion just finished - it had been at Harriet's in Clapham - seemed to have become a bit tetchy. They had not had time to discuss general issues like tone and readability.

'I really enjoyed your piece,' he said. And that was true. He did not normally like 'tough guy' literature - the endless lone adventurers, ex-Special-Forces chaps, the men with no name who live by a different moral code. Or at least never paid parking tickets. But there was a spare quality to Ben's prose. And it did leave room for characterisation in a manner which was neatly accomplished through dialogue. 'I like the way you differentiate between the two killers.'

He took Ben's grunt to be a *thank-you* of sorts.

'A hint of backstory,' Peter continued. 'And of future conflict between them.' It seemed to him also that there was a striking visual element. Someone had mentioned *film noir*. 'Ever thought of doing it as a screenplay?'

'Well …'

'Or graphic novel?'

Ben paused just long enough for Peter to think he had but was hiding it. 'I guess if I could find an illustrator.'

'How far have you got with the manuscript?'

'Close to a first draft.'

'Got an ending?'

Harriet was leaning over to re-fill Ben's glass. 'What's that?' she said. 'You've got a first draft?'

'Almost.'

She leant back. 'If only I had the time …'

'You know what we need?' said Shelley.

'What's that?' said Art. 'Apart from another round.'

'A writers' retreat.'

'Like Arvon? The place in Devon that does those courses?'

'What a racket,' said Art. 'Six hundred quid for a week of literary bullshit.'

'It's a business, Art,' said Harriet. 'Those who can't do, teach.'

'Shel, what are you getting at?' said Kath. 'Shel?'

'We should hire a place ourselves. All pitch in. Somewhere in the wilds of Scotland.'

'Too cold.'

'No phones,' said Shelley, 'no booze …'

'Steady on.'

'A week of just writing.'

Peter felt something stirring. He liked this idea. 'What about partners?' he said.

'No partners,' said Shelley. 'No distractions. We'd be there just to write. One whole week.'

'Raúl could come,' said Kath. 'Wouldn't you, Raúl?'

'Of course he could,' said Shelley. 'He's a writer.'

Virginia had been at the bar scolding the staff about the inadequately cleaned wine glasses. She sat down heavily, smoothed her trousers and looked around at the others. She had caught the end of the conversation.

'Virginia, what do you think?'

She looked at Shelley. 'Well, it's funny you should mention that. Are any of you partial to the Dordogne? …'

"Remember, Jack Kerouac *wrote* Doctor Sax *in a toilet."*
      www.writerslaunchpad.co.uk/faqs#*where-and-when*
"It shows."
                                  Posted response, later moderated

Virginia spent the next few days wondering whether it had been wise to make the offer to the group in the pub after the last meeting. But Shelley's idea of a week on writing retreat seemed so lovely she had been unable to resist. It seemed to solve a number of problems, not the least of which was that she was beginning to feel her holiday home in Bordeaux, while charming and beautiful, was underused now that the children were grown.

In fact she had been wondering recently whether it was time to sell up.

Her youngest son David was at Manchester University - to read PlayStation studies, as she maliciously put it to her friends - and, although she was sure he would be dropping in at the hols, with two or three or a dozen friends in tow, it was likely that his horizons would be extending to Thailand and Patagonia rather than the sedate comforts of the Dordogne.

She had come moreover to have a somewhat nuanced appreciation of the holiday home. It had been the location for frequent vacations, weekends and longer, with her husband and their friends for five years before the split. The first three years were quite blissful, the last two increasingly bitter. And the memory of that woman in her bed could still make her physically sick. Yet, after they divorced, she had had the place extensively remodelled - at his expense and to her exact taste. And it had provided some sense of continuity for the children as their parents' lives self-destructed.

But her life was now changing. She did not relish holidays in the South of France alone, where the only conversations would be with the housekeeper and the local mayor.

She had, perhaps surprisingly, discussed the matter with Tony. They did meet from time to talk over children business - universities, trust funds, wills - always at a neutral space, sometimes at his Chambers, where she did, despite everything, enjoy the company of the head of practice and the other silks, and where

Williams, the chief Clerk, still remembered her and offered her a glass of sherry as she waited.

'My dear,' Tony had said, 'it's entirely your decision.'

'But where should I holiday instead?'

At which point, leaning back, he rested his hands - he did have well-boned and elegant hands, she reminded herself - on his waistcoated paunch. 'As I said, Ginnie, it's for you to decide.'

Later, in the cellar bar to which they retired, he asked her, 'Ginnie, do you still love it out there?' He drawled, '*He who is tired of France is tired of* ... I paraphrase.'

Execrably, she thought.

She discussed the matter at lunch the next day with her friend Martha. It was bright outside, despite a May chill in the air. Bright inside the restaurant as well, with its white walls, the white linen on the tables, the dazzling *chemises* worn by the twenty-somethings who directed her to her table.

'Darling -' Martha did not take off her sunglasses until they had kissed and she was seated '- what's up?'

After leaving university the two had worked together at the same firm, a small agency specialising in opera and classical music and situated in Holborn. It sometimes pained Virginia to recall that she had left after eight years upon the birth of her first child. Martha, childless and currently husbandless, had gone on to set up her own enterprise, and spent as much time in New York and Paris as in London. She had diversified, and was as likely to represent a Rolling Stone as a fourth tenor. Virginia had resisted repeated calls to join her, especially after the divorce came through, although she retained strong connections within the profession, and sat on the board of trustees of a London orchestra and a charity which ran music schools in South America.

She still received invitations to Bayreuth and Milan, and never missed Glyndebourne. But, as she had come to realise over the years, it was as much the personalities, the passion and the drama surrounding the world of opera that attracted her as the music itself.

She did not reveal this to Martha - but suspected that it might be true of her friend as well.

'So you want to sell up,' her friend shrieked over the Caesar Salads. 'Where would you go instead for weekends away? Brighton? Lower ... Lower Pewksbury?'

Virginia knew she was right. Martha had in fact appeared, as had many of her colleagues, under various guises, in a couple of her short stories. Her holiday home was the setting for a few. If Virginia sold up, what would she write about?

There was now another reason for keeping it, a reason which she did not explain to her friend. It was the Writing Group itself, that quixotic band of hopefuls, the type whom Virginia feared Martha might characterise as *little people*; that group whose company she had come to value as much as any other. She was cautious about name dropping in front these *little people* - she suspected they might disapprove if she rollcalled those of the great and the good whose phone numbers she had in her address book - but this was precisely because she valued their approval so highly.

She reflected, as Martha continued to gush about her latest signing, that these Thursday evening meetings were as valuable to her as any other event in her social calendar. She did not understand why. They just were. That they might hold their meetings in the bright kitchen or amongst the dusty mahogany of her living room in the village of *Etoile-sur-Dordogne* was as persuasive a reason for holding on to the place as she could think of.

From: Virginia McCorquindale <virginia44@wazoo.com>
To: Shelley <shelley.banks@calbxer.co.uk>
Cc: Peter Pindar <peter.pindar@thegateway.gov.uk>;
Harriet Spence <h.spence@collingwoodmorley.com>;
Ben Jacobs <ben.jacobs@centurydesign.com>;
Lucy Boland <lucy@miaow.com>;
Arthur Redknapp <arthur1727@speedymail.com>;
Kathryn Kenton-Jones <Kath@miaow.com>;
Raul.Olivera@yahoo.es
Subject: Writing Holiday

So are we agreed?

One of 2-9, 9-16, 16-23 Sep?

Best
Virginia

From: Ben Jacobs <ben.jacobs@centurydesign.com>
Subject: re: Writing Holiday

Is that Sun to Sun?

From: Arthur Redknapp <arthur1727@speedymail.com>
Subject: re: Writing Holiday

I'm easy. All are good.

Cheers
Art

> One of 2-9, 9-16, 16-23 Sep?

From: Harriet Spence <h.spence@collingwoodmorley.com>
Subject: re: Writing Holiday

> Will have to check with work. May do just a long weekend.
>
> Harriet Spence
>
> > One of 2-9, 9-16, 16-23 Sep?

From: Peter Pindar <peter.pindar@thegateway.gov.uk>
Subject: re: re: Writing Holiday

> > … May do just a long weekend
>
> Ditto. Kids and family holidays and things

From: Kathryn Kenton-Jones <kath@miaow.com>
Subject: re: Writing Holiday

> Gosh, Virginia, that's kind of you. I'd love to come.
> Can I say yes for Raul as well? Is there room?

From: Virginia McCorquindale <virginia44@wazoo.com>
Subject: re: re: Writing Holiday

> *Of course you can my dear.*
> *PS 3 bedrooms up plus 2 down plus sofabed in lounge.*

From: Kathryn Kenton-Jones <kath@miaow.com>
Subject: re: Writing Holiday

> We'll draw lots!

From: Lucy Boland <lucy@miaow.com>
Subject: re: re: re: Writing Holiday

Where's the nearest airport?

From: Virginia McCorquindale <virginia44@wazoo.com>
Subject: re: re: re: re: Writing Holiday

EasyJet to Bordeaux. Easy as pie.

Shelley, are you in?

V xx

From: Ben Jacobs <ben.jacobs@centurydesign.com>
Subject: re: re: re: re: Writing Holiday

Got it on google maps.
I'll email refs.

From: Arthur Redknapp <arthur1727@speedymail.com>
Subject: re: re: re: re: Writing Holiday

What's the local plonk like?

From: Harriet Spence <h.spence@collingwoodmorley.com>
Subject: re: re: re: re: Writing Holiday

The 'plonk', my dear Arthur, will be to die for.

From: Virginia McCorquindale <virginia44@wazoo.com>
Subject: re: re: re: re: Writing Holiday

I have a Saudi friend who's bought a local vineyard. He can lay on a case.

V xx

PS Shelley?

From: Arthur Redknapp <arthur1727@speedymail.com>
Subject: re: re: re: re: Writing Holiday

It just gets better.

From: Harriet Spence <h.spence@collingwoodmorley.com>
Subject: re: re: re: re: re: Writing Holiday

Steady on, Art. It's a WORKING holiday.

From: Virginia McCorquindale <virginia44@wazoo.com>
Subject: re: re: re: re: Writing Holiday

Ooh, I can't wait.
V xx

PS Shelley?

Kath was sitting alone at the bar in *The Blue Room* with a hardly touched bottle of *San Miguel*. She stared at pages 115 and 116 of her stained copy of *Pride and Prejudice and Zombies*, hoping that her obvious concentration would be enough of a hint to the barman to preclude any chat.

She was furious with Raúl who had abandoned her for the evening to meet up with his South American cronies. God knows what they were up to now. Watching football in one of the Latino sports bars in Soho, cavorting to some basement band playing *Salsa, Soca, Samba, Mamba* - she loved the music, she could just never get the names right.

Luckily Lucy was free. There were a couple of things Kath needed to talk about, not least the planned writing holiday. And would Raúl actually come? He had said yes, but she couldn't be sure.

She returned to the Bennet family mayhem - a guilty pleasure this, one of which her family would no doubt disapprove. Kath was taking a break from *Madame Bovary*, which she found somewhat heavy going in the re-reading, her school-copy *Penguin Classic* currently lying open at the halfway point on her bedside table.

But after a few seconds she put her new book down.

Raúl.

Just what was it about South American men?

At Uni she had dated an Eduardo, a Carlos, and a Fidel. How could a mother call her son Fidel? But, then again, how could she not? Kath had spent a summer in Havana - Ibiza with a social conscience. And the men she met were so delicious and mysterious, so athletic and yet vulnerable. And they had smooth dark skin and perfect teeth.

Kath had met Raúl at a Latin dance class which a friend from work had taken her to. She just watched that evening. Indeed she knew she would never get the steps right. She didn't have the long legs for it. And there was some inbuilt resistance to the rhythms even though she adored them - it must be the pituitary gland or some part of the brain with a posterior and an anterior. But afterwards Raúl invited the two of them to a bar where he sometimes worked, and they drank rum cocktails and chatted about the band leaders and the sounds from Cuba and Puerto Rico right down to his native Chile. It was after he said his great uncle had been interned by the *junta* back in the bad old days that her heart melted.

When they started going out there was still a lot she did not know about him, some of it because the language barrier made the sharing of personal information precarious at times. Her Spanish was pretty wonky. She knew he had studied literature, but it was a while before she realised that he wrote as well. Perhaps he had once told her - when they were out and she had had a drink or two. Perhaps not. But when she saw a few printed pages -

'Here's the Spanish,' he told her, 'I'm working on the English as well.'

- and understood what he was trying to do, a decision she needed to make became clear.

She had sometimes wondered whether she was actually cut out for writing. In honest moments she recognised that she taken the creative writing course to prove something not only to herself, but to others. To her family, her mother, her oh-so-high-achieving brothers. (Although now that middle brother Max, a captain in the Infantry, was being posted to Afghanistan, she wished, like her mother, they had aimed a bit lower.) Writing was one of those activities that seemed fun and inspiring when you sketched out the opening lines in the heat of that first moment of creation. It felt like drudge when you were on page nineteen and had to figure out what happened next.

She enjoyed the classes. And she made a new friend. Lucy was so much fun. Kath had signed up for the group, though - say it softly - she had read only sporadically since school. And she had been coming to the point where she was ready to tell the others that it wasn't working. They were all great people, but ...

And then - Raúl. If he could write in two languages, she could in one. They would explore literature together, this would be her new adventure.

'You know I write as well?' she told him. 'Not very much,' she added. 'But I've been on a course.' And she mentioned the Writers' Group.

'So that's what you get up to on Thursdays,' he had said.

And now he was part of it. So why wasn't he here tonight?

She looked up as the barman wiped the space around her *San Miguel*. He smiled at her. The moment was coming when she might need to be rescued.

'Hey, LUCILLE.' A high voice above the pub noise.

'Hey, CATHERINE,' Kath shouted out. Lucy was pushing her way through the crowd at the bar, taking off her scarf and hat as she got close. They hugged and kissed.

The barman was staring at them. 'Now I'm confused,' he said. They were regulars there. 'Which one's which?'

Kath ignored the question and turned to her friend. There was only one subject tonight - well, two, if her Latino ghost at the table was included - and as she paid for Lucy's Jack Daniels and Coke (always slightly pretentious, Kath secretly thought) she launched straight in.

'So - Dordogne. You're on?'

Lucy stretched her lips back, then took a sip from her drink. Her long blonde hair was in its usual birds' nest style. 'Umm.' She looked at Kath. 'Well, I was just beginning to have second thoughts.'

'Oh, come on. It'll be such fun.'

'Well ...'

'It'll be free. Almost. Apart from the flight.'

'Well ...'

'So why not?'

'Is Raúl coming?'

'I hope he is.'

'For definite?'

'He said he would.'

Lucy sipped from her drink again. 'That's the thing. You've got him. I'll be on my own.'

'No you won't. The whole team will be there.'

'I'm not sure it's my thing. Discussing Proust over fine wine.'

'I'll liven things up. Me and Raúl.'

'Promise?'

'Promise.' A smile from Lucy. 'Good. So - the others - do you think *they* will get on with each other?' said Kath.

'Do you think *they* will get *off* with each other?'

At which point Kath almost coughed up the contents of her bottle. When she had recovered, she said, 'So who'll end up in whose bed?'

'What about ...'

'Ben and Harriet?'

'Ben's gay.'

'Ben?

'Kath, are you blind?'

My sheltered upbringing, she thought. 'Art then?'

'Too old.' Lucy sipped again. '*Sorry Art*,' she trilled to no one in particular.

'Come on. Art and Virginia.' But the thought of the magnificent Virginia in her pearls and cashmere being swept off her feet seemed suddenly a bit much. 'Perhaps not.'

'Pete, on the other hand …'

'With Virginia?'

'No, no, no.'

'Anyway, he's a family man. He showed me the pictures of his two kids.'

''Scuse me. Men do that when they're bored with their wives.'

'What makes you say that?'

'Part of the guilt trip,' said Lucy, 'It's like, what I really want is home comforts and not just a blowjob. Yeah, right.'

'Language, girl. What would your mother say?'

'Ha. Not the best person to ask.'

'Lucy.'

'Joking.'

'But if Peter's on the prowl, that leaves Harriet - or …'

'Or '- and Lucy's voice lowered -' Shelley.'

'Now you're talking.

'That's the one.'

'In fact - now I think about it - I've seen a few sly glances.'

They stared at each other.

'That's settled then,' said Lucy. 'Another drink?'

The bar seemed to have livened up. Kath as well. 'So - you're coming?'

"Imagine you are trapped in the elevator with a senior publishing executive. Could you use this brief window of opportunity to sell your masterpiece …?"
Creative Writing course book

Peter's day ended with bad news.

Which was a shame, as it served to negate the effects of the good news he had received by email at 11 that morning.

The good news was that he had made it through the first round of the literary competition run by the *Writers Launchpad*, though even here his elation was tempered when, re-checking the rules during lunch, he realised that the bar at this early stage was low and he was in the company of a thousand others. Moreover the judging was done on the basis of pitch alone. It was only later that anyone would begin to read a single word of his uploaded manuscript.

Still, he consoled himself, he had demonstrated that he could write a pitch - a useful skill if he were forced to seek a new profession.

In fact, after entering the competition, he had decided to write a whole series of pitches, in lengths of ten, fifty, and a hundred words. He had then tried to memorise each of them - or at least the gist - the reason for this rote learning being the remote possibility of finding himself presented with the infamous elevator test.

Peter was not sure how he was supposed to engineer this hypothesised window of opportunity, short of stalking a few industry heavyweights around their offices. In addition he was uncertain whether the aim was that he would be serendipitously co-located with his victim for a mere two floors, ten, or fifty (the course notes had perhaps been written with Manhattan rather than Soho in mind). It made sense therefore to prepare for all eventualities.

The bad news, drip-fed separately to him during the afternoon, was contained in two further emails. These were the rejections of his manuscript from the last two agencies to which he had sent sample chapters. In each case there was a short, standard letter explaining in their different ways why they had rejected his work.

The tone of the first was brusque : '… *not the kind of fiction we seek to represent* …' It added, more caustically : '… *we advise* *checking an agency's existing authors <u>before submitting</u> to determine whether your work might be suitable for our lists …*' This was damning, but on the mark. For his first few submissions he had carefully selected agencies based on their tastes, and had even appended to his covering letters a few lines of crafted nonsense explaining why his fiction formed a perfect fit. But after a while he had tired of this and had instead adopted a scatter-gun approach. Clearly his aim had been skew with this one.

The second was more conciliatory: '*… while your work presents ideas which we found intriguing, indeed compelling, we felt at the same time that you had fallen rather short of the high objectives you set yourself …*'

This was more encouraging, but the net effect was the same.

The brush-offs were dismaying. He had dared to hope that the expression of interest from Quentin Booker might signal a change in his fortune, where rejection became the exception not the rule and where multiple agencies might compete for his work. He had imagined playing one off against the other, despite having read that agents regarded such behaviour as extremely bad form.

He did not mention the rejections to Janice at dinner. It remained out of their conversation until much later when they had gone to bed, so as to limit the time she might have to dwell on his failure.

'Well, what *are* your "high objectives"?' she said to him after he climbed into bed. Her voice was low, the lights were out. They lay, staring up at the ceiling, their bodies not touching at any point along their length. A part of him was aware of, and disturbed by, this fact, more so even than by the demand to re-examine his motives. 'What are you trying to write about?'

'I don't know. Life, love …'

'… The human condition?'

'Don't sneer.'

'I'm not.'

He sighed.

'What did that mean?' she said.

'What?'

She sighed herself and turned away from him in a slow, clumsy movement. There was silence for a few moments. He considered, and then decided against, the possibility of turning over and rubbing his fingers against her spine, softly, so softly, in the way she used to love.

'Well I wanted to write about people like me. Like us. Caught up in the maelstrom. I see friends in the City or on Wall Street, or working for multinationals which have abused their power. Colleagues and peers, caught up in the whole mess.'

There was a silence, and then, 'OK. Keep going.'

'Shady practices, stuff going on right at the edge of what's acceptable.'

'I'm sure there's a market …' Her voice faded. '…out there … with the recession and …' She did not complete the sentence.

He waited, and then said. 'But I wouldn't want it just to be about goings-on in the big city. I'd want some wider resonance … such as …'

Her breathing began to settle into a soft snore.

'… such as …'

He propped himself up on the pillow and put his hands behind his head. *Such as what?*

At least this time they had not argued.

He recalled a poisonous row just days before he started the Creative Writing course. She had mocked his literary aspirations. 'You'll never complete a book,' she said. It was one of those occasions where they had started quarrelling over some minor issue, its origin long forgotten, but where the argument had metastasised into a battle covering every aspect of their life together. They had refrained from a slanging match only because Katie and Emily were seated in their pyjamas on the floor in front of them watching television. As was so often the case, he lost his temper because Janice was right, not wrong.

She had pointed out that she never saw him with a book. Him, Peter, with his Upper Second in English Literature. And as soon as he attempted to deny her accusation, she said to him in a low voice, out of the blue, *Name the last thing you read.*

Purely by chance, he had for once a good answer to this cross-examination, although he said nothing. He had been sent for three days to Dubai to install some software at the UK embassy, and the thing that had caught his attention at the trashy bookstore in the Business Class lounge was the black and white photograph of an old university friend. His face fleshier, the hair thinner. But undoubtedly him. Peter knew he had become a journalist, but it came as shock to see him pictured on the back cover of each book in an identical stack of twenty.

An impressive debut, the blurb stated.

A superb thriller.

With consummate skill he uses his journalistic talents ... to skewer the venality and excess of his fictional Arab sheikhdom.

He read the first three chapters on the flight out, broke the novel's back on successive nights at his hotel, and burst through to the 'dazzling' finale on the flight home. The trouble was, it was not really that dazzling.

They had been in the same EngLit tutorial group at Edinburgh, and four years of Chaucer and Malory, of Conrad and Joyce, of Smith, Hume and Stevenson, had come to this. There was, Peter had to admit, a certain breathlessness in the prose, and a frisson of behind-the-scenes familiarity with the movers and shakers of a certain type of wealthy society. The portrait of a leading London-based hedge fund trader was, he learnt from friends in the City, wicked, shrewdly drawn and, as the blurb might have gushed, hilariously accurate.

But was this literature?

He remembered a group of them in a pub off Princes Street just after the ordeal of finals wondering whether they would ever read a page of serious fiction again.

It's comics for me from now on.

ITV sitcoms.

The ads before the sitcoms.

The jingles from the ads ...

But more important than any surfeit of the classics had been the intensity of his work as his career got going. Twelve hour days of programming, weekends on call. Specs to digest, reports to précis, arguments to rebut. He had energy only for the free-sheets on the tube home and a trashy DVD after supper.

Janice had always read. A lot. She still did. And she looked cute in those reading glasses.

Usually she read in bed. Here was the thing. He wished she didn't.

He never mentioned to his colleagues at work that he was writing a book. He wondered whether the other group members had done so. Kath, Ben, Lucy. The younger ones perhaps.

But many of his co-workers in the anti-hacking team - they preferred to call themselves the *hacking* team, and some were indeed poachers-turned-gamekeepers - would always, Peter guessed, value number over the written word. They were amongst the only ones at the department allowed to turn up at their Whitehall offices suitless and tieless, and this of itself created a certain camaraderie, a partners-in-crime collegiateness reinforced by late nights and cold pizza and warmish beer.

Peter sometimes wondered how he had been selected for their world, so different from the mainstream of big government data he had been involved in for most of his computing career. He had been taken aside by his boss one day to be led into a room whose door was locked behind him, where a man with thin, mobile fingers and an open-necked white shirt - a Mediterranean hue to his skin, some white in his black hair - sat on his own at a table. The intuition came to Peter that he was a twenty-a-day smoker. On the table, curiously, was a book with the title *Mossad - An Insider's Story*.

Peter was told that there was a vacancy in another department for which he might be suitable. The man seated opposite provided few details, and perhaps it was this air of cloak-and-dagger that intrigued him and persuaded him to accept the offer. Though it was a while before he found the right feel for his new duties. His first task had been to formulate a set of rules for assessing the suitability of passwords to online accounts. Peter spent some time considering these: minimum length, avoidance of consecutive characters, forced expiration dates. He presented this list to the man with the stained fingers, now his new boss, who read the suggestions twice over and then frowned.

'Peter,' he said, 'these are all very well. But where's the subtlety?'

'Subtlety?'

The man sighed again. 'Peter, do you have a girlfriend?'

He smiled awkwardly.

'Are you married? Imagine your partner has a separate bank account, but she won't allow you to access it. One day you're short, so you decide to hack her account. Now, think. What password would *she* use?'

'Are you asking me?'

'Suggest something.'

'Well ...'

'The name of her cat? The name of her mother? A former boyfriend?' His boss rubbed his hands together. 'Remember, this is an account she doesn't want you to get your filthy paws on.'

It came to him that he was being asked to think himself into the mind of the punter out there, whether this might be his wife, the user, or, more pertinently, the hacker.

'Peter,' his boss said, leaning back. 'We are like ... spies. Those deep cover agents, the ones who live and breathe their alter egos. Or the great actors, the Oliviers, the ... have you seen Rylance? Go. Experience it while you can.' And then he said, 'Or even the best novelists. The Hilary Mantels, the Jonathan Franzens. Like them, we must inhabit the skin of others.' He handed Peter's list back to him. 'We foil the hackers when we know what they're thinking. Preferably, before they do.'

He thought that over time he had gained some skill in the department's underhand trade. Perhaps his own writing had helped. But years later, when Peter told Shelley this story in the pub, she fastened her eyes on his and said, 'You know what I'm going to ask you of course?'

'What?'

'Guess the password for my bank account. Go on, then.'

For once he could not think where to start.

From: Arthur Redknapp <arthur1727@speedymail.com>
To: Shelley <shelley.banks@calbxer.co.uk>;
Virginia McCorquindale <virginia44@wazoo.com>
Cc: Peter Pindar <peter.pindar@thegateway.gov.uk>;
Harriet Spence <h.spence@collingwoodmorley.com>;
Ben Jacobs <ben.jacobs@centurydesign.com>;
Lucy Boland <lucy@miaow.com>;
Kathryn Kenton-Jones <Kath@miaow.com>;
Raul.Olivera@yahoo.es
Subject: Writing Competition

> Hey guess what
>
> You know that Writers Launchpad competition? 300 word pitch and the rest.
>
> I got through the first round.
>
> Yeeeeaaaaah

From: Kathryn Kenton-Jones <kath@miaow.com>
Subject: re: Writing Competition

> I thought you weren't entering.

From: Arthur Redknapp <arthur1727@speedymail.com>
Subject: re: re: Writing Competition

> I lied.

From: Harriet Spence <h.spence@collingwoodmorley.com>
Subject: re: re: Writing Competition

> I have a confession to make. I entered as well.
> And I'm through.

From: Virginia McCorquindale <virginia44@wazoo.com>
Subject: re: re: re: Writing Competition

Harriet, Art, this is so wonderful. Congratulations and hugs to you both. After all was said and done, I entered as well. And ... yes ... I KNOW I don't deserve it, but I also made it past the first round.

Oh, It's so exciting I can hardly bear it.

From: Harriet Spence <h.spence@collingwoodmorley.com>
Subject: re: re: re: Writing Competition

Anyone else?

From: Arthur Redknapp <arthur1727@speedymail.com>
Subject: re: re: re: Writing Competition

Anyone else?

From: Kathryn Kenton-Jones <kath@miaow.com>
Subject: re: re: re: re: Writing Competition

Not me. Perhaps I should have done.

From: Kathryn Kenton-Jones <kath@miaow.com>
Subject: re: re: re: re: Writing Competition

PS But well done to you all.

From: Ben Jacobs <ben.jacobs@centurydesign.com>

Subject: re: re: re: re: Writing Competition

> I DID, but haven't heard anything.
>
> Do you reckon that means I'm out?

From: Virginia McCorquindale <virginia44@wazoo.com>
Subject: re: re: re: re: re: Writing Competition

> *Oh Ben, Ben, I'm so so sorry ...*
> *V x*

From: Arthur Redknapp <arthur1727@speedymail.com>
Subject: re: re: re: re: re: Writing Competition

> Hey mate, don't let it get you.
> It was just a pitch. What do those f**kers know anyway?

From: Kathryn Kenton-Jones <kath@miaow.com>
Subject: re: re: re: re: re: Writing Competition

> At least you were brave enough to try ...

From: Peter Pindar <peter.pindar@thegateway.gov.uk>
Subject: re: re: re: re: re: Writing Competition

> I'm through

From: Lucy Boland <lucy@miaow.com>
Subject: re: re: re: re: re: Writing Competition

> So sorry Ben
> Hugs and kisses
> L

From: Shelley <shelley.banks@calbxer.co.uk>
Subject: re: re: re: re: re: Writing Competition

> Peter, you as well?

From: Virginia McCorquindale <virginia44@wazoo.com>
Subject: Writing Holiday

> *btw, Shelley, have you decided on France?*

From: Arthur Redknapp <arthur1727@speedymail.com>
Subject: re: re: re: re: Writing Competition

> Blimey that's four of us.
>
> 'Ere we go, 'ere we go, 'ere we go ....

"A writer is somebody for whom writing is more difficult than it is for other people."

Thomas Mann

Harriet finally put the phone down at ten o'clock. She had made - she looked down at the pad on the kitchen table in front her - nine calls, one after the other. Nine. And, it occurred to her, not one of them had been for pleasure.

She tsk'ed and shook her head. No. That was wrong. Of course a telephone call to her mother was a pleasure, even if it lasted too long and went over stuff that was really none of her business, like which DVDs Karl was watching. No. Wrong again. It was her business, although Harriet wished she would stop droning on about it.

She sat back in her chair and wondered whether she could indulge herself with a glass of wine. But Dieter was in Zurich for a few days and she did not want to drink alone. Besides, today was one of her no-drinking days.

She picked up her pad and looked at the list in front her. Nine items, with ticks by each. The child-minder, the mother of one of Karl's friends, the delivery people at John Lewis. Jackie at work, a journalist who wanted a quote on a resignation, her boss on that same resignation. Virginia. Jackie again. Mum. Right, so who else was there?

Dear old Virginia. It was Harriet's turn to host, that's what they had agreed, and that meant packing Karl off to a friend, and making sure the cleaner had tidied up and re-stocked the fridge. Hmm. She wondered whether it was too late to call Beata, just to check she would be in.

Christ, she could really do with that drink. But she just despised all those people on their routines - their diets, their yoga, their gym regimes - who caved in at the first temptation. Instead she wondered whether she might fit in an hour of writing before going to bed. She was whacked, but she needed to press on. Her laptop was there on the table in front of her. All she needed to do was …

At that moment the phone rang.

She had never considered the possibility of writing fiction as a young woman. This was not because she did not enjoy books. She did, especially at school, although she had rapidly grown out of the type of literature which was thought to be suitable for teenage girls. Its petticoats and rakish heroes seemed, even then, too insipid for the modern world. It was only later, well after her career in the City had got going and she bagged a contract to work at the FT, that its possibility became apparent.

In her twenties she had believed, perhaps unkindly, that writing books was the preserve of women on maternity leave. Many of her friends spoke of this ambition when the first child came. But when Harriet met them, haggard and sleep-deprived, immersed in toddlers' groups and school lists, it became clear that they would never get beyond the opening chapter, so confirming her view that too much time was as mind-sapping as too little.

At the paper, on the other hand, she learned quickly how to write copy. And many of the journalists she was working with themselves had books to their name, though usually non-fiction. But it was while researching a feature on the publishing industry, a time during which she interviewed agents, publishers, and even a couple of authors, that she began to reflect that it might be something she should try.

Much later it would come to her that the move into fiction writing reflected a change in her own personality. Or perhaps a mellowing, of which those mums might have approved. As if the rigidities and certainties of her education, in maths and physics, and then her formative years number-crunching at Barclays, had been replaced by a realisation that the nuances of emotion, and the plasticity of so much of human life, were best described by the imagination. By fiction.

Perhaps she had gone soft.

But she had been pleasantly surprised by the movers and shakers she had met in publishing, who seemed like people who knew what it meant to be at your desk at eight in the morning and to stick to a schedule. They were not all the hopeless dreamers one had imagined.

The decision to kick off the project had come when she rejoined her old bank and discovered that one of the most recent intake of trainees had himself already picked up agency interest from a synopsis he had submitted about high rollers on Wall Street. That discovery served as a challenge. She knew she had better get started, even before she had any clear idea what she would write about.

She remembered discussing it in bed with Dieter.

'Haven't you got enough on your plate as it is?' he had said.

'Oh, thanks for the encouragement.'

'No, what I mean is …' He twisted to face her in the dark. 'I know you. You won't do it unless' - his hand slid down the side of her body - 'you really go for it.'

She closed her eyes and sighed. He was right. At least on that score.

Later, he said, 'Well, go for it then. I'll read it. No bullshit.'

Harriet giggled, *No b-oo-llshit*, she whispered. Dieter had never quite lost his accent. 'I'm sure my mum will as well,' she said. 'That makes two.'

And at first it had all gone well. She bought the *How To* books, she signed on for an evening course, she learned about pleonasms, and adverbs, and how to kill your darlings. Her subject, well, it had to be High Finance. Plot and main characters soon came to her. And then, to her dismay, the whole enterprise began to slow down.

And she could not figure out why.

'What genre is it?' the tutor on the course had asked. Genre? It was true, it had started as a thriller, a tale of corruption in London and New York, but as time passed, something about the nature of fiction writing began to seep into her. Something about intrinsic value, about originality and insight, about the essence of human lives. It sounded self-important, and she felt uncomfortable discussing it, yet she was beginning to feel that, alone of the things she did, the value of her writing could not, should not, be gauged or measured by rules and process.

'It *is* a thriller,' she said to those who cared to listen. 'But I hope it's something more as well.'

'Like what?' said Dieter. He had not read a book since he left school. Too much Goethe and Schiller, he once told her.

She changed the subject. Yet something began to haunt her. Is it just drivel, she wondered. Is what I write tawdry, clichéd, derivative, shallow? Is it second-rate, stale, verbose? Does it miss its target? Does it have a target? Is it crap, is it just - bullshit?

Her parents were even less help. This was when the conversation got beyond the question of that biological clock and the possibility of a second child. They loved Karl to bits of course -

Karl, whose birth mother, Dieter's first wife, was now, it seemed, in permanent ashramic retreat in Tamil Nadu.

'Is there a nice bit of romance in your novel?' her own mother asked hopefully, although she might have been doubtful given how clear-sighted, even hard-nosed, her daughter was about most things.

'What? What's that?' her father asked, butting in. 'A book? Eh? A book, you say? Now why on earth would you want to do that?'

And Harriet wished she had never brought up the subject.

"Writing is therapy."

Graham Greene

Peter once heard a novelist explain that when he set out on his career he reckoned his first book would be semi-autobiographical, his second about a man of his class, his third about a woman of his class. Only gradually would his imagined world distance itself from his own. Only with his fourth might he have acquired the craft to create protagonists who were truly, well, fictional.

Whether this was generally the case, it was true that in Peter's book his hero was someone of the same age, culture and background, someone who faced many of the same urban problems as did Peter himself.

These thoughts came to him as he gazed at the fuzzy outline of his reflection in the screen of his laptop.

He was alone in the spare room. Twice he had shoo'ed out Katie and Emily, the second time with a touch of feigned irritation and a raised voice. The door was now closed.

His precise concern at this moment was that some of the problems his protagonist faced seemed to be escaping from the printed page and invading his own life. Like his hero, he had lately become preoccupied with the issues and the crises one associated with midlife. Not least of which were questions of marital fidelity, of the erosion of ambition and the blunting of passion. All were questions of ageing.

Peter was thirty-six. That was still young.

Surely.

He certainly did not see himself as old. His hair remained thick and retained its natural colour, the lines around his eyes were light and fine, muscle and bone were lithe, not yet shot through with the ache that had, in her final years, left his grandmother motionless in front of the TV all afternoon.

Had he wrestled with these insecurities before he started writing? Probably not. As he stared at the blurred outline on the grey screen, that thought troubled him as well. Moreover - returning to his initial worry - he wondered whether his novel suffered that his protagonist was so similar.

Peter clicked open the first page of Chapter Four. At the bottom, it said in small print on the right © *Peter Pindar*. This was a touch presumptuous. The idea that anyone might wish at this stage to infringe his copyright was - *let's face it*, he told himself - quite farfetched.

His finger hovered over the delete button, but his nerve failed and he scrolled back to the top of the manuscript.

He read.

> On a day when, for the first time that spring, the brightness of the sky did not betray itself in a wind so cutting that raw flesh seemed as exposed as it might have been in deep space, he looked out of his open window and knew that something had changed. He knew that a spirit had left him.
>
> He felt old.
>
> Or perhaps the spirit lingered still, but he saw through its tenuous promise for the first time.
>
> He thought of his Spanish lessons and his sax classes and the bargain he had struck with his South African trainer at the gym when he bet him he would lose his gut in six weeks. He thought of his career and he thought of the women he spied and lusted after on the train to work, women who no longer returned his glances but whose eyes increasingly followed the guy who stepped on to the train behind him, the fellow with the smoother skin, the slicker hair, the clothes cut in a style he could no longer bring himself to admire or wear.
>
> Once or twice he found himself surreptitiously examining these men, trying to find out what it was they had and he didn't, what quality it could be about them that those glossy and exciting women found so desirable. As if it were possible to break down and quantify this thing, and then, with this knowledge, rebuild himself, a touch here, a tweak there, a firmer stomach, a touch of hair gel, a new shine on his shoes. Refashioning. But this was predicated on time. On limitless time and opportunity. Time to try once, and then again. And if this failed, to try once more. But

the past and the future had flipped, and if once he had measured and staked out the past, and slotted the fragments of his personal history cleanly into each of his years, and if his future had the delicious uncertainty and open-endedness of a child's summer holiday, it was now his future which was roadmapped and timetabled, while his past had become increasingly opaque.

Where had the years gone?

He looked at the one-sentence paragraph that ended the section, and then opened up an old version of the text. It read :

Where had the years gone? <u>He knew he would never be fluent in a second language, he would never speak Spanish any better than when he left school. His fingers on the saxophone keys would remain forever a millisecond behind his thoughts. And the sound that emerged would remain that ragged set of notes which bore a merely apocryphal relationship with the melody that lay choreographed in his musical imagination.</u>

He decided he had been right to cut the bits with the underline before sending out to agencies. He re-read the rest of the text and marked up '<u>tenuous</u>', '<u>surreptitiously</u>' and '<u>delicious uncertainty and open-endedness of a child's summer holiday</u>'. *Should I have killed those darlings as well?* he thought.

But he hesitated again at the keyboard, and his mind turned instead to a woman who was non-fictional. A woman he lusted after. To Shelley, and then to the upcoming week in September, now only a couple of months away, when the group was due to decamp to France.

There were two major problems with the planned writing holiday. The first was that he had not discussed it at all with Janice, who was pressing him to make a decision on the family vacation in August. There were a couple of options, neither of which especially appealed: two weeks at the start of the month in the Scottish Highlands, his own clan basing itself in the holiday home that

Janice's mother had rented; or two weeks at the end of August traipsing around the churches and museums of Tuscany, the schedule arranged, once more, by Janice's mother.

'She's got a full summer lined up,' Peter had said when Janice laid out the possibilities.

'Mum needs our support now that Dad's -' a pause '- gone.'

I wonder where his new floozie's taking him, Peter did not quite say.

'Ibiza next year,' she said, and touched his arm. This was a running joke between them, a reference to their first holiday together. 'Besides, Mum can do the babysitting. Leaves loads of time for us to be alone.'

But that itself led to the second problem, or demonstrated rather how the first problem morphed into it. Which was that Shelley had not yet replied to say whether she was going to France with them. But if she did not come, would Peter himself wish to go?

And if Shelley decided against and he followed suit, would that make his feelings for her apparent to the others?

Yet even to entertain these thoughts was to bring in to the full light of consciousness the fact that he was considering an extra-marital liaison.

An affair.

For days after the Book Fair he had felt touched by a lightness of being, and also a sense that nothing the world could throw at him could pollute this mood. Perhaps it was, as had occurred to him that Saturday, a kind of *grace* such as the mediaeval saints described.

Had he ever felt this with Janice? Even when they were courting?

The screen faded. He pressed the touchpad to cancel sleep mode, and scrolled down. Of course it was the possibility of such feelings - or their absence - which served as an important theme in his novel.

> Old.
>
> 'I want to be young,' his grandfather had said once as Jack took him for a short drive away from the geriatric home, in one of whose top floor bedrooms he would die later that year. 'I want to be young and I want to be well.'

'How young?' Jack looked across at him. 'How young do you want to be?'

The old man frowned, and pressed against the cloud of dementia which had recently and relentlessly staked an invasive claim over his mind. 'Oh, thirty, I think.'

And Jack wondered why he had picked this particular year, this decade of his life. Not his distant black and white childhood, winters learning Latin declensions in grey stone Aberdeen schoolhouses, summers on Clydeside steamers, whose names and the names of whose captains he could still enumerate, one after the other. Or his twenties in the army, a posting in the Middle East, where a young man had been initiated, in quick and intoxicating succession, into the twin mysteries of violent death and sexual passion, the latter in the arms of an Italian diplomat's daughter possessed of a temperament so charged and alluring that, in a moment of unprecedented and Byronic fervour, he resolved not to leave his posting until he had her married and installed, with her own kitchen and coffee maker and in-laws, in a bungalow in the suburbs of Glasgow. Nor yet his forties when, seconded to Whitehall and with a career as a middling civil servant now stalled, he began to transfer his energies to an increasingly prickly daughter and the minutiae of the golf club's membership committee.

Stalled and *installed*. Soundalikes. He needed a synonym for one or the other.

And coffee makers. Did they have them in the nineteen-fifties?

And - adjectives, glorious, multiplying adjectives. Too many. But he loved them so.

He read the passage again, and thought about his own grandparents - his grandfather from Edinburgh not Glasgow, his grandmother Greek not Italian. Too similar? The connection too obvious?

In addition, like his hero's antecedents, his own grandparents, and indeed his parents, were all dead. None had lived to see his own children. And, with an insight he knew he might transfer to his fictional alter-ego, he realised that this, strangely, served as a point of friction with his wife.

He got on well, though separately, with both of her parents, whereas she had never been required to make the reciprocal effort with his. And the businesslike relationship he had with her mum and dad seemed, perversely, to sum up the temper of his marriage. Businesslike. Had he ever felt for her the low-intensity ecstasy that he felt with Shelley? Even when they first dated? He must have done, he had, surely, in their first few holidays together. And yet he had buried those memories. What he recalled instead from so much of their time together was the *busy-ness* of coupledom. This was especially true in the months before and after their wedding, when his whole life seemed to involve making sure things got organised. Engagement parties, legal issues, the stag do (his best man had been useless). Dealing with relatives, with honeymoon plans, the new flat. Appeasing Janice's friends when he got drunk and played the fool.

And then the kids.

No one had warned him, for instance, how much *gear* one needed for a toddler - prams, clothes, toys, bottles, blankets.

It was the simplicity of his feelings for Shelley that was seductive. And the fact that they had emerged as if by magic. From thin air. He found it impossible to pin down quite when his feelings had arisen. He could not recall particularly noticing her when the classes began over a year before, and yet something happened in the time between the end of the writing course and the start of the group meetings. He could not put his finger on when or how, and yet there was a Before and an After. And After, the group sessions became quite empty when she failed to attend because of illness or work.

He loved it when she argued. She had set views about the kind of books she liked - character based, plot irrelevant, she said she even forgot sometimes how they actually ended. When he listened to her advocating a view on something they had read, her blue eyes fastened on his, his counter-arguments would slowly unthread, become incoherent. He spoke nonsense. As if he had a crush. As if he were living the teenagerhood he had missed.

As a young man he had not had a lot of sexual experience. 'Don't you like girls?' his grandmother often said, these frequently her first words as he walked, alone, through the door of her house in Southend after the two hour journey out of London.

'What kind of a question is that?' he would reply.

'Why don't you ever bring one over?'

'It's not as easy as that.'

This was the essence of it. It was never as easy as that.

There had been, it was true, a few parties in his twenties where he had ended up, usually after too much wine, in the bed of someone he had not known twenty-four hours earlier. He never knew why it happened, why sometimes he was successful even if usually he was not. These young ladies were, in addition, people that he would often not meet again, despite the fact that the intimacy had been perfectly pleasant and the sex boisterous and fun. Where they did continue to meet, it was as if the sexual encounter had never occurred, and they slipped effortlessly back into Platonic friendship. He remembered Jane who told him, as they showered and dressed in the previous day's crumpled clothes, that she would not tell her boyfriend what had happened.

'Your boyfriend?' Peter had said, shocked.

'You met him last night. The blond guy who was dancing a lot.'

'What?'

'Don't worry, he'll never know.'

This kind of exchange convinced Peter there was a veiled dialogue between the sexes, a *pas de deux* of assumption and suggestion whose syntax and grammar he had once thought he might master but which remained beyond his abilities. Looking back, he wondered whether it was a language that one either acquired as second nature in one's youth, or did not pick up at all. Like skiing. He remembered the Spanish lessons his employers arranged for staff, abruptly terminated when their tutor was recalled to Bogota to defuse a family scandal which had erupted when a seventy-five year old uncle fathered a child with a woman half-a-century younger.

La vieja cabra, his tutor had told them under his breath with a smile and a shake of the head. 'But he was always the same, *siempre el mismo.*'

Shelley was so comfortable with intimacy. That's at least what he wanted to believe. Or had he misjudged even her? She seemed so tactile, quick to let her fingers brush an arm or a shoulder. And she was curious about his family, in a way that Janice was not.

'Pindar,' she once said in the pub. 'I'm thinking of using that name in my novel. Though with an 'e' - yours is with an 'a', isn't it?' She smiled when he nodded and took a sip from her half-pint of Guinness. 'Pinder,' she said. 'Not the Greek poet.'

And Peter remembered the ribbing he received as a schoolchild, first because of the alliteration of his first and last names, a source of malicious glee to his fellow pupils, and later from the unrealistic literary aspirations laid upon his shoulders because of the imagined connection, in the minds of world-weary masters, between him and this writer from the pre-Christian era. The independent school to which he gained an assisted place was not indifferent to tradition nor shy of its own. 'You should know this stuff, it's your namesake,' the head of Classics said. 'There must be some Greek in you?' In fact, there was, though it was on his grandmother's side, not his absent father's or late grandfather's. But her acquaintance with the ancient poet was weaker even than his own.

'Why my name?' Peter had said to Shelley, but she ignored his question and asked instead about his family.

'Where does the surname come from?'

For a while he tried to deflect the question, for reasons he could not quite pinpoint, but when she persisted - 'Come on, tell me about your folks?' - he gave what he considered to be the short version. He told her how his mother died while he was still young and how he had been brought up by his grandparents and how he never saw his father who, as far as he was aware, lived in Canada with a new family.

'How sad,' she told him, but he said simply that a child accepted whatever was given, and that what he had never known he had never missed. What he did not mention was that as a teenager he began to see the absence of conventional parents as a marker which set him apart, as did the presence of such additions to his lunchbox as felafel and tsatziki.

'You should write about it,' said Shelley.

'What?'

'Your background. It's unusual.'

In his room now he wondered when the occasion might arise when he could give her the long version, a version which, in coded form, shaped the backstory of his fictional hero; a version with which he became fully familiar only in the last year of his grandmother's life. In a half-dozen of his final visits, just before she died, alone, of a heart attack in her bed, he placed a microphone on the sitting room table at her Thames estuary house, switched on the recorder, and said, 'Talk.'

'About what?' she said as she grasped a mug of tea in both hands.

'Anything. Your childhood. Tell me about the Athens of your childhood.'

And she did talk. She did not stop until the tape ran out. Although there was little of Athens. 'I was never there,' she said, and she described a childhood in embassy compounds in Rome, Buenos Ares and Tokyo, before her father, a career diplomat, landed a position in Beirut. Peter would wonder later how Greece was able, so soon after the war, to project its influence into so many capitals, but that afternoon his grandmother spoke about the excitement of a teenage girl coming of age in a city with a promenade and beaches which was also an hour's drive from the ski slopes. 'We spoke Greek at home, French in polite society, and English at work.' Although, she added, she picked up enough Arabic to converse with the housemaids.

'You can't imagine what it was like,' she said, her tone for once faltering. 'It's a world gone forever.'

It was a period of privilege, of international schools and, later, of romance and beach parties and midnight drives to the mountains. It was also a period of rare stability in an uncertain region, although the ancient blood feuds of the Christians and the Muslims had been put aside and not buried. Her parents, never consciously acknowledging the fact of the family's good luck, appeared to accept that it was best enjoyed while it lasted, especially with an unpopular and authoritarian government back home. They were relaxed about their daughter's racy lifestyle, as long as she accepted her measure of the duties that came with the life of a diplomatic family. She enjoyed the embassy parties which she attended with her handsome father, slim, neat, with a dash of grey, and her elegant mother, especially as it allowed her to dress up and find her own way into glamorous society.

It was at one of these parties that a young man in uniform, with red hair and a permanently red face and an accented but precise grasp of French, asked her to dance. She refused. He persisted, and then later asked if he could meet her again. She eventually accepted, even if his dancing compared unfavourably with that of the lithe

Syrian boys who usually pestered her. They met, and met again, and her mother, sensing that her daughter was taking this friendship more seriously, learnt to cook carrots and brussels sprouts when he came later for lunch.

Peter found it hard to imagine his grandfather as a suitable catch, even when he looked at black-and-white photographs of the young man in uniform, his expression stern and composed, his eyes slightly raised as if towards some beckoning horizon. Yet the habit of self-deprecation, fundamental to the contemporary British psyche, was, it seemed, not then in vogue, especially as the decline and loss of empire was still a mere blueprint in the minds of a cadre of farsighted Foreign Office officials. Perhaps Great Britain still represented greatness to some, or at least stability in an unpredictable world; perhaps the young girl's parents, even the girl herself, recognised that the society they moved within was fragile and might shatter at any moment.

In addition, an air of mystery surrounded the young man. He would disappear from time to time for weeks on end, and say upon his return only that he had been on His Majesty's service in Yemen or Saudi Arabia. She never worried too much about these foreign adventures as she sensed that there was a certain exaggeration in their stated importance. She had seen his thin legs and narrow shoulders when they swam together at the beach, and she found it impossible to imagine this boy-man, barely older than herself, being able to twist the head off a chicken - the shopkeepers in the souks would do it right in front of your eyes - let alone engage in combat with another human being.

But something happened to change him, and a sense of desperate romance did flare up one day. He had been away on one of his jaunts. His mood was sombre, and as they drove to the corniche to have supper she found conversation strained. He usually spoke French with her, but this evening he stayed with English. They ate, he drank champagne and scotch, and then he drove her under the stars along the coast road out of town. They stopped at the edge of the desert and he told her that he had seen dreadful things, that good men had been lost in the line of duty.

He then asked her to marry him.

When she did not answer he put the car into gear and started the drive home. But he pulled off the road after fifteen minutes and begged her to say yes.

Alice and Harry Pindar were married six months later in a ceremony that took place in a Catholic church, although Harry's background was solid if indifferent Church of Scotland. The best man was another attaché at the British embassy, and it was at the embassy that the reception was held afterwards. They took a week's honeymoon in Malta, cadging a lift on a Royal Air Force plane, and yet even then the end of their respective worlds must have been very much in the minds of the couple. Alice's father was recalled soon afterwards to Athens. Harry, unnerved by what he had witnessed in the Omani desert, made plans for a sideways move into the civil service back home.

It occurred to Peter to wonder whether his grandmother actually understood the change that was about to take place in her life, this sudden shift from the exoticism and warmth of the Middle East to the austerity of late forties Britain. How much would she have known of Scotland, beyond the nineteenth century novels she had been forced to read in school, or the folksy images from Hollywood films? How much had her new husband told her? Or had the strength of their passion outweighed all other considerations?

'Your grandfather had so many big ideas when we first met,' his grandmother told him, and this seemed to Peter another puzzle, given the unambitious man that Harry became, the grandfather that Peter had known.

The following January the couple sailed to Southampton and took the train to Edinburgh. Would it have been the absence of colour that most struck the young woman, the sudden transformation of a life whose backdrop included bloodred sunsets, the blue of the Mediterranean, the sparkle of the gold souk, to a world of soot and grey and a countryside of leafless trees poking through the fog. Peter imagined a roll call of the northern cities through which the train might have passed - Sheffield, Leeds, Newcastle - was this, she might have asked, really the centre of the mighty British Empire?

At least the snow and the bleak clarity of the hills surrounding Edinburgh provided some escape from the grey, urban landscapes they had passed through. They settled, and survived, and in a way even prospered. Harry gave up his military pretensions. He acquired pinstripe and settled into his role at the Scottish Office. His wife used her languages to supplement his salary with secretarial jobs at firms of architects which maintained offices along Princes Street.

But cracks were appearing. Alice's mother visited after one year, and after a week of rain and damp and inedible food begged her daughter, in secret, and in tears, to come home. Alice refused, not because she necessarily disagreed with the assessment that this life was not for her, but because it was her mother who was pointing this out.

There were, anyway, some compensations. Alice found that despite everything she enjoyed the weekend walks in the hills with her husband, ending as these excursions always did with the search for a suitable inn, and half a pint of bitter and a plate of bacon and eggs. She loved the Festival, which had started up just five years earlier, and which, for a few weeks, left the city with the tiniest flavour of the cosmopolitan world which she feared had disappeared for ever. She loved her work, she loved the fact that a facility with languages, something so commonplace in Beirut that it was barely even taught, was in her new world a skill which made her unique. And also quite beguiling to the young men who, just out of university, laboured with pencils and slide rules at their designs.

The main problem lay with Harry's parents who regarded their son's marriage as something of a betrayal. Whether they had actively lined up a nice Scottish girl for their only son, the opportunity to arrange his future had been lost the moment National Service plucked him away from the confines of their homeland. They were at best cold with Alice, at worst rude and xenophobic.

There occurred a break in the story at this point, a break Peter would sense it was not wise to attempt to fill. What was clear was that his grandmother suddenly found herself in London on her own. There were hints in her narrative, clues provided by some of the events she described. A showdown with Harry's parents. A failure of nerve in Harry. An ultimatum. And a promise from her boss in Edinburgh that he would 'see her right' after discussing the matter with his partner in London.

There had been a separation of sorts, whose duration and whose resolution would never become clear. It surprised Peter that she did not take the opportunity to return to her family, and as his grandmother paused in front of the microphone he wondered what question he might ask, how he might probe for the answer. But as she began again he decided to let this secret lie, for it confirmed to him a truth which he knew and yet often chose to overlook, that the old once had their secrets, their moments of impetuosity, and the paths of their lives, now commonplace to a young and bored generation, once glittered with the excitement of the undiscovered.

'I had a lovely little flat in Chelsea - just a room with a kitchen really - with a charming landlady who looked after me,' she said. 'And friends. Friends. French, Swiss, Greek. London was wonderful then. I hear nowadays it's full of all those Russians.'

And Harry did follow her, eventually, though what shadowy nights of the soul he may have endured in the meantime were not recorded. He wooed her again, displaying for the second time in his life a capacity for romance that Peter found so hard to imagine in the slippered and cardiganed pensioner who loomed over his teenage years. A transfer to Whitehall followed, and then soon after a child and a move to the suburbs of Essex.

Kirsty, the girl who would become the woman who would be Peter's mother, became the glue that held the marriage together, at least until such time that the couple came to understand, with middle and old age, that they could no longer live without each other. Harry and Alice doted on her, Alice gave up her secretarial work in the City - she told her friends, with a pre-feminist sense of fatalism, that at thirty the bosses no longer wanted you - and settled down as a mother and housewife. She spent her days looking at curtains and local schools, while Harry's commutes became longer as they moved ever further into the country.

The young girl thrived. She was intelligent. And musical, which surprised her tone-deaf parents. She rode bicycles and horses and soon excelled in the local girls' grammar school. But the world of aspiration and career, which had shaped parents' expectations for generations, was again turning. The teenage girl listened to the Beatles and then to a host of other groups whose music struck her parents not merely as tuneless but as incomprehensible. Colour came to television, and then, it seemed, to the world it represented. Aristocrats flirted with villains. London's fashions, its nightclubs and celebrities were taken over by a strange alliance of the classes which excluded the drab middle.

And every teenager yearned to be part of it.

In nineteen hundred and seventy, as the era of the hippies began to topple and burn, its upheavals crashed into the world of the Pindars. Their daughter, preparing for her A-levels, was expelled from school as part of a gang caught with marijuana in their bags. Before her parents could even mount an appeal she had left home and found digs in a sprawling house in Camden without proper plumbing and which was shared, as far as her parents could tell, by a dozen other dropouts. She said she earned money as a model, and even presented her mother with a few pages torn from a fashion magazine whose name she did not recognise, with photographs of her daughter wearing clothes of almost unspeakable inelegance. And before even this state of affairs had settled she had joined a rock band due to start its first tour of New York in the new year.

Her mother wailed, her father retreated into work and, weekends, into the running of the local golf club, telling his wife that it was merely a phase. Alice was sceptical. Rightly so. The American tour was extended to include a mind-boggling number of states and campuses, and ended up on the beaches of Los Angeles, from where her parents received a postcard to say that their daughter had married a car salesman's son, in a ceremony presided over by an Iroquois Chief and whose guests seemed to be from the local chapter of Hell's Angels.

In Peter's grandmother's house there were pictures of her daughter, dozens of them. Pictures of a young child, of a girl in school uniform, climbing trees, on her father's shoulders. There were pictures of a studious fourteen year old, of a schoolgirl with prizes for her O-levels. There were one or two, cuttings from newspapers, of a girl-woman posing by the Golden Gate bridge, or in front of an old VW with rainbows painted on its side. And then there were one or two pictures - just a few - of an adult, more pensive, her hair cut short, now back in England and holding a child in her arms, her marriage burnt out before it had really started.

Peter knew that his grandmother sometimes turned these last photographs face down on the mantelpiece - he had seen her do this once or twice when she thought she was alone - and he knew that this final part of her daughter's life was simply too painful to recall. For Peter had no memory of his mother, who was dead before he reached his first birthday. It was as if she had packed so much into those first few years of her life that there was no room for more.

Her death was as sudden as it was shocking. She sat in the same deck chair in which Alice had left her, one warm Spring afternoon, while her mother went to the shops with the infant in his pram, except that her face, upon their return, was leaning slightly forward and her eyes were dull and her heart was still. And then Alice put her grandson down on the grass besides the chair and knelt and took her daughter in her arms and wailed and for the first time cursed this unutterably bleak and black-and-white Englishness which had boxed in her and her own desire for life for the last thirty years, until her neighbours, appalled and quite, quite unable to intervene, watched and finally called the police, and a young officer, just out of training and himself unable to figure out what to do next, picked up the baby and placed an arm around the grieving woman, now suddenly old, and waited with her until the afternoon light faded.

Peter always used to switch off the tape recorder as his grandmother reached this point. Now, fifteen years on, as he heard Janice calling the children for tea, he closed the Word file and switched off his laptop. He would not write anything that evening.

Once Shelley had said to him, 'You should write about your background.'
    Of course, he had done just that.

"Stand in the rain and catch the flu - just so you can describe what rain is like."

Zadie Eisenberg

I am sitting in McDonald's reading 'Unleashing the Writer Within' by Zadie Eisenberg. There are lots of screaming kids in screaming colours, there are excitable teenagers, shabby office-workers and - the odd one out - a man wearing a pinstripe suit and a gold hoop earring. I am trying to absorb the atmosphere of this place because I am going to use it as the setting for my story 'Dumped in McDonald's.' McDonald's is probably the most insalubrious place to get dumped in. But that's what happens to my heroine.

There is a man across the way from me who is trying to break the world record for eating the most fries in the shortest time. I examine my own burger - how to describe it? Like carpet? Cardboard? No, too clichéd. I must find the right words to sum up this brown patty. Perhaps the heroine's boyfriend dumps her just as she bites into her double whopper - her mouth is so full she can't respond? Perhaps as she then tries to swallow the stodge it gets jammed in her throat and nearly chokes her to death?

Back to me. Back to the book I am reading. I have been flicking through it for several weeks now - nibbling a page here, ingesting a chapter there; Zadie's encouraging words are sustaining me. Yes, it's true, Zadie - writers do have to be stupid. Even if it means getting the flu for your art.

Brilliant stuff. Right at the beginning Zadie says to set the clock and write to a deadline, not worrying about the quality. This isn't something that I'm in the habit of doing, but - having hit a block recently - my alarm has been set for an hour each morning and I'm giving it a go. It is really working. At the end of the hour is a cup of tea and a packet of M&Ms. All I have to do is write: even if it's crap. And that's what I did today. I started on the dot of 10 a.m., checking my watch every 5 minutes until I reached 11. Then I stopped. I had done my duty. I could hit the shops.

As I wandered round the shopping mall, I felt good. Today I had done some writing! Now, at McDonald's, I slurp my tea and flick through Zadie for another encouraging chapter. There is something interesting looking towards the end.

"Put all you've got into your writing," she says. "Don't treat it as a chore. Don't set aside an hour and then congratulate yourself for having done your duty. Writing is not about clock-watching. If you're not putting everything you've got into it, it won't be any good. If your working to order, then you need to take time off - perhaps for a year. Return only when you have something you are just bursting to say."

What? What?

My good feeling dissolves like the sugar in my tea. My whole strategy for beating writer's block - based, I might add, on advice from you, dear Zadie - is destroyed in an instant.

My brain feels like the hamburger between it's two baps: dull, lifeless and churned so often there is nothing left of the original stuff it was made from. I don't even want to look at Zadie Eisenberg. All those 'Dos' and 'Don'ts'. In fact, I don't want to read any more 'How to' books at all. But what do I do to get rid of the germs that have crept up from these pages, through my eyes, and into my brain? How do I stem the neuroticism before it takes over?

And suddenly I've got it. A daring idea, a bold plan. I get up from my table and walk through the restaurant. As I pass the bin - the bin for all those half-eaten burgers and greasy fries - I open it up and pop Zadie inside.

"Zadie Eisenberg," I say to myself. "You've been Dumped in McDonalds."

Lucy stopped reading and looked up at the others. There was silence. 'Well, that's it,' she said. 'That's all I've got so far.'

There was a sound of paper being shuffled. Ben's fingers scurried across his iPad.

'Well?'

Sniffing. Someone's summer cold.

'Say something. Was it rubbish?'

Virginia began to chuckle, and then Harriet and Kath and Shelley did as well. Art leaned back and let out a roar. Raúl, seated next to Kath, put his hands together in a silent clap. Virginia looked at Art, and her chuckle became a piercing bray which caused Peter to choke on his water.

'It's brilliant.'

'Lucy, it's delightful.'

'A scream.'

'Fucking brilliant.'

Harriet was beaming. 'Lucy, we've all been there.'

'Been where?'

'Hilarious.'

'Well done.'

Lucy stared at the carpet and raised her eyes to the others, her glance resting for a second on Virginia and Harriet, as if for assurance from the grown-ups. 'Well ... thanks ...' she said softly. 'Thanks.' She looked down again.

'Is this new?'

'What is it? Short story? Novel?'

'What's she called? Your heroine?'

'Is it autobiographical?'

'Have we come across her before?'

Ben coughed. 'Excuse me. Just one or two things I might change.'

'Go ahead.'

'Like ...' Ben cleared his throat. 'Sorry, am I the only one who doesn't quite, well, get it?'

'What's there to get?'

'Well, for a start, there are loads of technical things ...'

'Oh come on,' said Virginia. 'That's just editing.'

'No seriously. Look, Lucy, you need to get your apostrophes sorted out. I've just sent you an email with a list of things. You've got *it's* - with - where it should be *its* - without. And *your* - without - when it should be *you're* - with.

'And then you say <u>*nothing left of the original stuff it was made from*</u>. Well, if it's the original, you don't need the '*it was made from*'. And vice versa. It's one or the other.'

118

'Sure,' said Lucy. 'yes, you're right.'

'And later - this is a common mistake - you say *having hit a block lately - my alarm has been set...*'

'What's wrong with that?'

'*alarm* is the subject of the main clause. And I assume it's not the clock which has the writer's block.'

'Steady on, mate,' said Art. 'Not all of us have PhDs.'

'And *screaming kids, screaming colours*. Please.'

'Art, shh,' said Lucy. 'Ben, carry on.'

'And this "eating" metaphor. I know we're in McDonald's, but *nibbling a page here, ingesting a chapter there*. We get the message.

'Then, earlier on you say *I must find the right words to sum up this brown patty*. But *patty* - surely - is not the right word. It really feels like you've scanned the thesaurus for a word which is not *bap*.'

'Hang on, Ben,' said Shelley, 'I think you're in danger of throwing out the baby with the bath water ...'

'Cliché.'

'*Excusez-moi*. Look. Lucy's piece comes from the heart. And it's the language which has all the ... I don't know ...the pizzazz. The spontaneity. Lose that, and the whole thing falls flat.'

Ben flicked his finger across the surface of his tablet. Peter could see his Word app close down.

After a few seconds, Ben said, 'I don't see why you're having a go ...'

'I'm not having a go.'

'The whole point of this group is to support each other. To make suggestions to help improve what we've written.'

'Ben,' said Lucy. 'What you've said is very helpful.'

'Not everyone seems to think so,' said Ben.

'Hang on,' said Shelley. 'That's not what I'm suggesting.'

'What are you suggesting then?'

'Only that technique's not everything. Lucy's got the beginnings of something original here.'

'Yeah, well that's another thing,' said Ben. 'What is it? A confessional? A novel? Short story?'

'Lucy?'

'I don't really know yet,' she said. 'That's all there is. So far.'

'But you can't carry on like that for 70,000 words,' said Ben.

'Why not?' said Shelley. 'Her character will emerge, as time goes on. We know a fair bit about her already. She's a young woman, she's trying to write. Just like us. It's hard, she runs out of steam from time to time. Just like us. She lives in a city. Probably London. Like us.'

'But who wants to read about someone struggling with a second-rate Creative Writing course book?'

'Ben, you miss the point.'

'The point being?'

Shelley said nothing for a moment. She took a deep breath and said, 'What do the rest of you think?'

Peter's phone, set to silent, vibrated in his pocket. As he drew it out, he studied the flare of Shelley's nostrils and the colour coming to her cheeks. For a crazy instant he imagined himself standing outside a nightclub, perhaps some *boîte* in Marseilles, or Barcelona, and being slapped on the cheek by her in a moment of passion and anger - the thought gave him an erotic thrill.

He shook his head, as if to clear his thoughts. Shelley was absolutely right to make her point. Lucy's piece, while very much a first draft, had spark and charm, and it was important to focus on these aspects. In fact, as he thought about Shelley's spat with Ben, he found himself wondering what it really was that Ben was turned off by. And why his gripe got magnified when Shelley became involved.

He looked at his phone. The message was from Janice. He swore.

Janice had phoned earlier in the evening to say she was working late - the kids were on sleep-overs. Now she texted, *Finished early. Fancy meeting for drink?* He stared at the phone in his hand. How was he to play this one?

*

The meeting broke up soon after nine, and Ben and Shelley pleaded excuses - a previously arranged meeting elsewhere and an early start the next day respectively - to miss the post-literary discussion. Perhaps, Peter thought, they had had enough of each other.

It depressed him whenever Shelley left early. But her absence resolved a small dilemma. He texted Janice with the name and postcode of the pub they were going to.

In the two hundred yards from Virginia's house to *The Coach and Horses* he walked ten yards behind the others, silent and alone, and examined his conscience. The truth was he did not want Shelley to see him with his wife; and the reason for this, it came to him, was that to allow such a thing to happen would be to close a door which, until now, he had barely admitted to himself was even open.

A door. A gateway to a possibility. Was he mad to believe it existed?

If so, it was a delicious madness.

The subject of discussion in the pub remained Lucy's submission.

'It's a different piece from what you presented in class, isn't it?'

'I don't know why Ben said the things he did.'

'Did all that stuff *really* happen?'

'Don't tell me *you* got dumped in McDonald's?'

Lucy seemed surprised and delighted that they liked it. She rarely circulated her stuff to the others, despite their encouragement.

'You need to read more often,' said Art. 'I was getting bored with the usual suspects.' It was Harriet and Ben who submitted most frequently. 'That includes me,' he added.

'Bored?' said Harriet in a high-pitched tone. 'By *moi*? With my superlative, ground-breaking masterpiece?'

'Just joking, Hattie.'

Harriet for once took Art's shortening of her name with good grace.

'Raúl,' said Virginia. 'When are you going to honour us with a piece you've written?'

'Me?' Raúl sat next to Kath on a bench at the table. He had said little during the evening. Now he pointed to himself. 'Me?' he said again.

'Do you have anything? We'd love to hear it.'

Kath and Lucy looked at him. He looked down.

'Don't be shy, mate.'

'Well perhaps after one week I have something.'

'Two weeks. Next meeting.'

'Maybe three,' he said. 'Make it four.'

'Can't wait.'

Peter looked round at the others with a strange warmth. Despite Shelley's absence. The group usually worked pretty well, he thought. Despite the odd tiff. He knew, perversely, that he would rather be sitting in the pub with this band of oddballs than with his friends discussing the football. He corrected himself. No, they weren't oddballs. And then he had a curious intuition. Into his mind popped the scene in the refectory of the spaceship *Nostromo*, where the crew are chatting and bantering and enjoying their last communal breakfast before The Alien chews its way out of the chief engineer's stomach.

The others were staring up past Peter's right shoulder, as if the barman were about to reach down and collect glasses. Virginia presented a professional smile. 'Can I help you?' she said.

'Hi. I'm Janice.'

'Janice?'

Peter, lost in his thoughts, had not reacted. He looked up beyond his shoulder. His wife was standing there with a cheek-to-cheek grin, her finger pointing downwards. 'With him,' she mouthed. The scene remained frozen until Virginia, Harriet, even Raúl, all rose, a full second before Peter did.

'Janice, Janice. Of course. How are you? We've heard so much about you. I'm Virginia.' Hands were proffered, seats were rearranged. 'Here, sit down. Let me make room.'

Peter had finally stood up, and managed to pop a glancing kiss on his wife's cheek before she was pressed on to a stool between Virginia and Harriet.

'Where are the children? We want to see them. Too late I suppose. And not in this dingy pub. Peter. Manners. This lady needs a drink.'

'Er ...'

'Water. Sparkling,' said Janice. 'I'm driving.'

'Come on,' said Harriet. 'Have a drop of wine. Just a drop. The bottle's not empty yet.'

Peter waited for a second and then walked over to the bar. He bought a bottle of Highland Spring and another pint of beer for himself. There was a television perched on a high ledge showing Spanish football with the sound turned low.

'Who's winning?' he said to the barman.

A voice to his side. 'Barca. Two belters from Messi.' Raúl had joined him.

'Genius, that guy,' the barman said. An East European accent. 'Bloody Shakespeare and Mozart rolled into one.'

The universal language of football commentary, Peter thought. He said to Raúl, 'What can I get you?'

'Mmm.' Raúl stretched his neck. 'I'm good. Just catching the goals.'

The two men stood by the bar watching the game.

'Peter, at last,' said Virginia. 'Your wife's thirsty.'

Peter placed Janice's sparkling water in front of her, even though she held a half-glass of red wine in her right hand. He sat down. They all seemed to be getting on very well.

'So this is what you get up to every fortnight,' said Janice. 'It looks like too much fun. I can see why Pete never misses a meeting.'

'The hard work came earlier.'

'You should've seen us …'

'… fighting like cats and dogs we were.'

'About literature?' said Janice.

'Well,' said Harriet, 'There were strong views expressed about Lucy's piece.'

'Although most of us thought it was pretty damn good.'

'Who was for and who was against?' said Janice. 'Sorry, Lucy. If you don't mind my asking.'

'Ben and Shelley.'

'They've left.'

'To lick their wounds,' said Art.

'Talking of Shelley,' said Virginia, 'Does anyone know whether she's coming to France? The rest of us are decided, aren't we?'

'France?' said Janice.

'Our writing holiday.'

'Our writing *retreat*.'

'Our writing *bootcamp*. It'll be working and critiquing all day.'

'We're going September,' said Virginia. 'I can't wait.'

'I see. Is Peter coming?' said Janice.

'He's on for it. Aren't you, mate?'

'I see,' said Janice. 'And are spouses invited?'

Peter caught Raúl's eye. He found himself wondering whether Messi had completed his hat-trick.

*

'Why didn't you tell me?'

They were driving home. Fortunately Janice had stuck to one glass of wine. Peter was a pint or two over.

'I'm sorry. The whole project just kind of crept up on us.'

'I wouldn't have objected. If you had just told me.'

'I wasn't even sure we'd actually decided.'

'Sounded pretty definite to me.'

'I can always cancel. It's no big deal.'

'No. No. You must go. You must work on your book.'

'Why don't you come and …'

'And?'

'I'll work in the morning, we can sightsee in the afternoons.'

'And the kids? It's September. They'll be back at school. But … wait, let me see … we can always dump them somewhere. The council, Barnardo's, Battersea Dogs Home …'

They might actually like that idea, Peter thought.

He had a suspicion that nothing he might say would in any way fix something that could only heal itself over time, so he remained silent. He forced his mind onto other matters. *The first was a jinxing run from the corner flag, leaving three defenders trailing in his wake, then a one-two with Fabregas and a low shot. The second a cheeky chip as the goalkeeper came off his line …*

'Who's Shelley?'

'Who?'

'Your group. Who is Shelley?'

'Oh. She left early.'

'The others couldn't stop talking about her.'

'Is that right?'

'So mysterious, so captivating. Is she coming to France, Who's the ex-boyfriend, What exactly is her job ...'

'Yeah, she likes a bit of mystery. She's foreign. Or something.'

'Foreign?'

'Well. Australian.'

'You don't know?'

'I do know. She's Australian.'

'Bit of a *femme fatale*.'

'No. She's just like …'

'… Like?'

'Like all of us. Trying to get that first book off the ground.'

'Is she good looking?'

'I guess. Not bad.'

'Like Julie Christie?'

'Julie Christie?' Peter swivelled to face his wife. 'Who said that?' He had a sudden fear that he'd been babbling to the others.

'The old guy.'

'Art?'

'Art. He mentioned that film from the sixties, what's it called, *Billy Liar*.'

Peter remembered the film and the book, both of which he had enjoyed. Julie Christie, the star, the symbol of escape, the counterpoint to a grey, Yorkshire suburb. Yes, he thought, Art was right. That was Shelley.

'Art just fancies a younger woman.'

'Does he now? And what about you, Pete?'

He knew then that it might have been a mercy had he been dumped in the Coach and Horses.

'Do you?'

"Writing is not therapy."

Roland Denning

It was ten minutes past one, and Virginia, seated at a table by the window, was wondering whether it was late enough to ring Shelley to find out whether she was delayed or, worse, much much worse, had cancelled. She was just a tiny bit angry, and diverted her attention away from her irritation by forcing herself to examine the décor.

The restaurant, close to Covent Garden, was new-ish. Ceilings were high, the light came flooding in from tall windows. There were a lot of wooden surfaces. Waiters were young, polite, and hyper-active. It had been recommended by …

Dammit, she thought. It was surely immature to be late, whether because of carelessness, or, worse, much much worse, the desire to feign carelessness.

Then she saw her. Virginia did not wave. Instead she watched Shelley open the door and speak to the *Maitre d'*.

Just what was the girl wearing? Were those high heels yellow? But as she was directed over to the table, Virginia asked herself once more why Ben and Art weren't in love with her as well? Or perhaps they were. Perhaps they were too embarrassed to show it.

She rose as Shelley approached the table. They kissed. Virginia made a mental note to indicate early on that she would be paying.

'No trouble finding this place?'

'Looks lovely. No, none whatsoever.' Any note of sarcasm in Virginia's voice evidently washed over her.

They busied themselves with menus. Virginia, having watched various dishes being served at tables close by, was actually quite hungry, a condition of course not always in itself a necessary reason for meeting for lunch.

'So.'

'So.'

'How's the book?' said Virginia. 'You've not presented in a while.'

*

Jem was trying to figure out the best time to ask her Mum if she could go. At school she and her best friend Sandra had been discussing the dance in whispers all afternoon whenever the teacher's back was turned. The three of them - they would be joined by Sandra's cousin Cassie, who was just one year older than Jem - would be driven into town by Sandra's mother and picked up again when it was over at eight o'clock. Or later if, as she hoped, there were loads of encores, which, Sandra said, there always were. At least that's what Cassie said from last year.

Jem had already told Sandra she could go, and that she would cycle round to the farm on Saturday afternoon as soon as she had finished shopping with her Mum. The only problem, and she didn't dare tell Sand this, was *her Mum. Sometimes her Mum was a bit, well, difficult.*

"Who is this Sandra, then?"

"Mum, you've met her. Loads of times."

"What about her parents?"

"Oh, please, Mum."

All this had happened the last time, when she was invited to stay the weekend with her friend's family at their posh home upcountry. But after those two questions her mother had not come up with any more. Instead she sat back in the armchair with her fingers pressed against her temples, closed her eyes and pretended to sleep. Except that Jem knew she wasn't sleeping, because she kept on shivering whenever she, Jem, did something which made a noise. Like drop her knife when she was buttering a slice of bread.

Eventually, that weekend, she had stayed home. Her Mum was in one of those moods which might last an hour or three days. But however long it went on for, Jem knew that she had to do all those boring things, like pay Norm from the secret pot above the mantelpiece when he came round with eggs and milk and things. Or answer the phone when Mum's 'friends' called.

But it would be different this time. Mum hadn't had one of those moods for ages. In fact, at the moment she was quite chirpy. Jem suspected there was a reason for this, a reason not unrelated to the fact that she had come home late the last three evenings, and also the fact that she was wearing lots of that expensive oh-de-toilet she got last Christmas. Something was going on. Or someone. Jem wondered whether she might steal her Mum's handbag when she wasn't looking and check her diary.

She hoped she would not be back too late this evening, because she needed to ask her the big question about Saturday. But perhaps if Mum did arrive late she might be in one of her giggly moods - or her stupid moods, as Jem put it. Her mum just became so dippy whenever she had a glass of that sweet grock she liked to drink. Or, more likely, three or four. But the good thing was that you could ask her anything and she would say yes.

The only problem was, the next morning she forgot exactly what it was she had agreed to.

*

'Tell me,' said Virginia, 'Where did you get the idea for it?'

'The novel?'

The main courses had been cleared away and the two women were deliberating over which of the *dolci* they might share.

'Oh, books, articles, documentaries,' said Shelley. 'Also, my old Gran. She grew up in the Outback.'

Virginia narrowed her eyes and after a moment asked carefully, 'Is she - your Gran - still alive?'

Shelley looked down. She shook her head. 'But I've got all these family stories.'

'Like what?' Virginia was aware of the delicacy of the question, but she could not quite escape the prejudice shared by a few of her friends - and the curiosity that this engendered - that the whole of Australia, apart perhaps from the inner suburbs of Sydney, was a brutish mixture of Saharan heatwaves and the social attitudes of 1930s Tunbridge Wells.

'Oh. You know.'

Virginia waited.

'People were self-sufficient. You wouldn't see anyone new from one month to the next. Apart from the road-trains bringing in supplies. You had to look after yourself.'

'Those vast distances ...'

'If something happened, it remained in the community. No social services or anything.'

Virginia's senses were on alert. *If something happened ...* Hurriedly she called over the waiter and pointed at the *tiramisu*. 'Two spoons,' she whispered. She turned back to Shelley. 'So, Jem

- is she based on anyone? I mean, she seems such a spirited young thing … so much responsibility …such a young age …'

Shelley continued to stare at the extravagances on the dessert menu. She wound a few stray hairs around her right ear. 'It was a difficult time just after the war. A lot of men didn't come back. Some came back broken, if you see what I mean. But it was also empowering for women. I mean, someone had to run the farms. Fix the machinery. Do things.'

'I can imagine.' The waiter brought the sweet, two plates, and two coffees which he laid with precision on the table. Virginia waited for him to leave. 'The book seems, well, quite dark. I mean, her mum's lifestyle. And then, Jem's dad …?' She left the question hanging.

Shelley swallowed. She was still staring at the pudding. 'I'm still not sure about him yet,' she said. 'About whether he reappears or not.'

Virginia was for once lost for words. She had a sense that the boundary between fiction and Shelley's own history was being crossed, and the possibility of some indiscretion loomed. She wondered how she might steer the conversation. 'Your parents,' she said. 'Have they visited?'

Shelley chuckled. 'Dad's dead. Hated the poms anyway.' She shook her head. 'My mum - who knows - might be persuaded one day.' She picked up her fork, leaned across, and poked at the *tiramisu*.

'Tell me, Shelley, when did you arrive in London?'

'Ooh, God. Ages ago. Had my eighteenth birthday two days after landing at Heathrow. Six pints of Fosters in a basement bar in Notting Hill.' She looked up and smiled. 'Me all starry-eyed. Me and a hundred other antipodeans. All young. And dumb.'

And most of them seemed to work as trainers at her gym, Virginia thought. Or were they South African? She could never tell the accents apart.

'You've not seen your mother since?'

'Well, there's not much to tempt me back, I'm afraid.' She continued to pick at the cake. 'And she's not been here …'

'Oh Shelley.' Virginia reached across and laid her hand on Shelley's wrist. She could not stop herself. 'That's so sad.'

'Here, you have some.' Shelley spoke as she ate. 'I'm going to finish it.'

*

Curiouser and curiouser, Virginia thought. She was wandering in and out of the boutiques in Covent Garden thinking about lunch.

It had ended suddenly when Shelley's phone rang. Virginia sometimes felt mildly irritated at people's mobile phone etiquette at the dining table, but she felt minded this time to indulge her guest, especially when Shelley, after a few curt words into the mouthpiece, excused herself and took the rest of the call outside. Virginia took the opportunity to settle the bill.

When Shelley came back in, it was clear that something had changed. 'It was lovely,' she said. 'But I must rush.' She grabbed her bag. 'How much do I owe you?'

Virginia had feared an argument about splitting the cost, but Shelley's obvious sense of urgency ensured that her protestations were short-lived.

'Well, thank you so much,' she said as she kissed Virginia on the cheek. Seconds later she was out the door, sunglasses on, hurrying towards the tube station.

The thought came to Virginia that she might engineer a discreet meeting with Peter some time. But, then again, that might be taking her duties, such as they were, a bit far. That was plain poking her nose in, though she found the possibility hard to resist.

But she had learned a few things. Shelley had talked about her time a decade before at the LSE and the two years she had spent in Johannesburg. About Siseko, a campaigning journalist she had been with out there. Virginia had the impression that the relationship and its untangling had been complicated, and that he was not completely out of the picture even now.

She had the sense - she was not sure why the analogy came to her - that since then Shelley had rather *dipped in* to relationships, in the same way that she, Virginia, dipped in to well-thumbed Austen or Waugh. But as she reflected she realised that the metaphor was not quite apt. She picked up those old favourites for reassurance and for the pleasure of the familiar, whereas she suspected Shelley used this partial immersion to ensure that what she - how might Virginia put it - *picked up* could be *put down* with the minimum fuss. And before any emotional pull had really taken hold. Or was that over-egging it?

She feared further that some of these *wash-and-go* affairs had been with married men, and this was something of which she rather disapproved in her old-fashioned way. Yet such men, she knew, were ripe fruit from an overhanging branch. It was the case - and here she feared her views would not meet with the approval of the sisterhood - that wives transferred their love from their men to their children as soon as the first was born.

She had said to Shelley at one point, 'We all think you're a bit mysterious.'

'We?'

'The group. Us.' And Virginia wondered whether she had been a bit unwise to say this. 'But we do love a bit of mystery.'

Shelley laughed. 'So who's the real Shelley?' she said softly. Virginia waited. 'Well,' Shelley had said, 'You'll just have to read my book.'

And then Virginia stopped in her tracks. A shopper behind brushed by her. *Damn*, she whispered. She had forgotten to ask Shelley the all-important question. Indeed, this had been the reason for asking her to lunch.

Was she coming to France with them?

"Have mainstream publishers embraced the digital world? Do turkeys vote for Christmas?"
The Literator

Ben had recently acquired an addiction. And he had been introduced to it by his friend Marcus.

Half-a-dozen times a day, sometimes more, even when he was at work, he found himself compelled to check his position on the rankings at **www.the-literator.com**.

It seemed to him odd that the others, in both Writing Groups, shunned the use of the digital world, and especially the online communities which had sprung up to support wannabe writers with advice and feedback, tips from the pros, or FAQs for self publishing. Perhaps it was an age thing. Even in the other group, Marcus's group, most were half a generation older than he was.

These people valued a world of books with spines, of double-spaced hardcopy print-outs, of basements and dust and damp. Of the romance of those cathedrals to literature, the bookshops.

But this world was on life-support. Soon it would be history.

'Will that be true of writing groups as well?' asked Henry, the oldest in the *other* group. Loveable old Henry, who always turned up in jacket and tie. Henry, whose elegant prose described in fictional form the experiences of his diplomatic postings in seventies' Latin America. 'Will we be history as well?'

Pinochet, Galtieri, he once told them, *I met them all*.

'Screw all that,' Mary, the other American who from day one they called *feisty Mary*, pitched in. 'You'll always need the human touch.'

The thing was, it seemed to Ben and Marcus, there was quite enough of the human touch on *The Literator*. Those who signed up could upload their work-in-progress - and hundreds did - and then, better, have it read and critiqued by other members. The number of positive reviews, minus the negative, determined your rank. And Ben was currently equal eleventh out of two hundred and thirty-four.

It was the Wisdom of the Cloud.

His cause had been considerably helped by someone who signed herself (she?) as *LaraCroft*. 'Five Star,' Lara C gushed.

'Tarantino will be knocking at your door.' Other reviewers had been attracted by her endorsement, as was evidenced by the thirty-three *Likes* and just 2 *Dislikes*. The effect snowballed, and while other judgments were not quite as ringing, they were pretty positive.

Apart from one *HaroldBloom*. 'This just stinks. How could anyone read this sub-Carver crap? And how could anyone write it?' Ben had checked the user profile, which was mysteriously sparse, and considered making a complaint to the site moderator.

'Fuck him,' said Marcus, who was stuck at position one hundred and thirty-seven. 'Anyway, you'll experience a lot worse in the real world out there.'

But one of the problems of these reviews, all bylined with user aliases, was that they placed you under obligation, even if only moral rather than legal, to read their writers' uploaded entries. And then comment on them. And some were pretty ropey. Many presented themselves as cross-genre - *Fifty Shades* meets *LOTR* (Galadriel with whips?) - or mix-and-match from the standard canon - *Proust* meets *Irvine Welsh* (Ben had struggled to catch a glimpse of either literary giant). But he had forced himself to grapple with half-a-dozen the previous night between midnight and three, or at least the opening chapters. He added a few comments, positive where possible, to all of them. He had clicked the 'Thumbs Up' sign on the first five, but not the sixth, which was hot on his tail at position thirteen. Ben certainly did not wish to be responsible for his own novel being leapfrogged.

The trouble was that this morning he had discovered that in his sleep-deprived state he had muddled up a few of the reviews. The ChickLit entry was *Terrifyingly Violent*, the Sci-Fi was *heartwarming and sweet*, while the entry described as 'Christian' was - well, best not to go there.

Many of the contributors listed websites or Facebook pages on their profiles, which in turn often listed earlier books which had been self-published, and this was something he had discussed frequently with Marcus. The whole process had become so simple, it could all be done online, and you could get even get your books set up on Waterstones or, better, AnyBookAnyWhere.com - Ben was on an anti-Amazon thing at present. Print-On-Demand ensured costs were minimal. Marcus, who had an eye for visual design, had already knocked up a few sample graphics for front covers.

'You know,' he said, 'I'm thinking of just putting my book out there ...'

'Even if it's not ready?' said Ben.

'... well, you know, you can just modify the text as-and-when. If you need to tidy it up, if you do a re-write, then just re-upload.'

But, as a couple of the discussion-threads to which they subscribed suggested, even the necessity of hardcopy print-on-demand was falling away. People talked of producing their stuff in e-format only.

'But that's crap,' feisty Mary said when the *other* group discussed this, six of them clustered round a table at their usual spot on the mezzanine at the RFH. 'If you're constantly changing, uploading, changing, uploading, when do you ever finish the goddam thing?'

'Do you know, that's a good point,' said Moira, a classicist who was working on a dense piece of historical fiction - "The Prof", as Marcus called her. 'This commoditisation of the novel could lead to a fundamental change in the way we view books as finished works of art.'

'And also,' said her partner Carol, in life a psychotherapist who had guiltily let slip she was fictionalising a few of her more bizarre case histories, 'it could lead to the end of that archetype - beloved of Hollywood - and Stalin I should add - of artist-as-hero. If there is no *finished work*' - her hand actions left the others in no doubt about the implied emphasis - 'if it is always in flux, on demand, a group never a solo effort, then where's the catharsis, that sense of triumph when the creator once-and-for-all lays down her tools and the thing-of-beauty is finally hewn from the original marble block?'

There was a pause, until Henry said, 'Quite.'

'More beers?' said Ben getting up.

Marcus accompanied him to the bar. 'Hey what do you say,' he said as they waited, 'we make our excuses and head off?'

'Wha, now? We can't just leave.'

Marcus sighed. Ben guessed what was on his mind. Marcus had become disaffected with the scene at The Literator, and had been looking at writers' communities with more of an world-literature slant. 'You know,' he said, 'when I look at all those guys with their hobbits and vampires I don't see many Black faces.' [*Ha. Except for the orcs*, Ben said once when they were pissed and he felt like pushing out the boundaries. *Ha Ha*, said Marcus, *is that what you call Black Humor?*] Ben knew he was right, but he was reluctant to follow this line of thought too far in case Marcus began to have doubts about the group itself. He had a fear this friendship would drift apart before it got started.

'You still with the other mob?' said Marcus.

'You mean the *other* writing group?' Or, as Ben thought to himself, the other *other* writing group.

'Yeah. Them.'

'I am. But …'

'Perhaps we should think about striking out. Starting our own. We know enough people out there who are into our thing. Online. And some of them are a bit more, well, hip. You ever thought about it?'

'But they're in the States or India or Japan or somewhere.'

'So? We just Skype it.'

As Ben ordered the round he thought about the *other mob*, of Peter and Virginia and especially Shelley who was becoming just a bit too *prima donna-ish* for him. It would kind of neat, but also a bit sad, to declare that he no longer had any need for them as they were being replaced by a conference call.

'What's so funny?' said Marcus.

Ben said nothing. One thing he had not told Marcus about, one thing which he realised he was quite looking forward to, was the up and coming writing holiday.

'Nothing,' said Ben. 'Perhaps you're right.'

Perhaps Marcus was right. Perhaps they needed to find people closer, not necessarily in age, but in outlook. He, Ben, would need to think about this.

But not until after France.

"Good writers borrow, great writers steal."
Aaron Sorkin

'*M*iss, you all right? Miss? Miss?'

Jane felt the torchlight against her eyelids. Instantly she was awake, though her eyes remained closed.

'You all right?' A male voice. High-pitched, a cockney inflection. But apart from that, silence.

The silence of death.

'Miss?'

She opened her eyes. No, not death. She was alive. She looked around her. The people of London slept: women, the elderly, a few children not yet evacuated. The people who were her charges and whom she had betrayed by allowing her tiredness to overcome her. It was her duty to watch over them, here amongst the rats and the ads for luxuries of a previous age and the posters proscribing careless talk.

'I'm fine,' she said. She whispered, 'And I'm alive.'

'What's that, Miss?' She said nothing. How could she have allowed herself to doze? Even for a moment. 'Be daylight soon,' he said. 'All-clear'll be sounding, I'll warrant.'

She'd got his accent wrong. Yorkshireman. 'It was a long night,' she said.

'Aye. That it was.'

A long night. She wondered how many more of them she could take.

Soon, she would get up on her feet and wander amongst the sleepers around her, a gentle word here, a caress or a cuddle there, and prod them back to wakefulness. Later she would lead them up stairs and out the gates and into the morning - the jolt of daylight, the shock of a city which in the space of a few hours had seen its skyline once again transformed. Buildings gone, new craters in the road. Spiky remains of roofless houses.

Women wailing, men staring in silence. The bodies still not covered.

Jane would return to her digs, sleep for a few hours, and then prepare tea, toast and margarine. Later she would write to Henry, now swallowed up by the Navy, Henry, whose face dimmed in her memory by the month and the smell of whose pipe and cologne had long since faded.

Later still she would walk to the London Library and catch a few hours where she might relax with some reading before she signed in for duty at seven in the evening. And where, if she were lucky, if she were so, so lucky, Frank might also steal an hour or two and they would elope - just for the afternoon - to Soho for tea. Or, blessed good fortune if his room-mate was away, to his attic, tiptoeing up the stairs past frightful neighbours, where he would undress her - shoes, jacket, blouse, skirt - and then, gently, gently, let his fingers and his lips roam over her shoulders, her back, her stomach, and over other places which were never explored or named even in all her years of marriage. And it seemed as if these unknown ridges and contours of her body had been thrown up by this hateful war as it razed the contours of this, her city. And later the rhythm of her breathing might gently accelerate and she would shudder and turn her face into the pillow.

Afterwards they smoked and he watched her as she talked of the previous night and the screams of the children as the blasts came and went and masonry fell and Clapham station itself trembled. And the worst of it, when a sequence of bombs fell, one after the other, ten seconds apart, each one louder and closer than the last. Then everyone was quiet, and she looked into their eyes, the children and their mothers, and she saw each and every one mouthing the countdown of the seconds. And when the blast came, time itself froze and there was also wonder that the end had not arrived. But when the noise subsided they started counting once more - ten, nine, eight - in expectation of the next which would be yet nearer, and which might, just, be the last thing they would ever hear.

She stopped as the tears wound their way down her cheeks.

'You poor dear,' Frank said as he took her in his arms, and for a moment it seemed worth it. And she knew she would look back on these years as the only time she had ever been truly, truly alive.

Virginia said, 'I think ... I'll end it there.'

'Ouff.' Harriet mimicked the waving of a fan.

'Bit steamy.'

Peter and Shelley were silent.

'So. What do we think of Kath's piece?' said Virginia.

'You read very well,' said Harriet.

'Shame Kath wasn't around to hear it,' said Art.

She had rung half-an-hour before the meeting to say she couldn't attend. This was just after Ben had also phoned in his own excuses. A few moments later Kath texted to add that Raúl and Lucy would be absent as well. *So ignr my old crp#*, she said of her submission, emailed the previous week.

Of course we won't ignore it, my dear. We WILL read, and we WILL email our ... Virginia's reply required two texts, each spelt out in full. *... thoughts. And it's most assuredly NOT cr*p. Vxx.*

But Virginia had not read out Kath's final message to the group: *PS I cheated! Grannie helped wth ww2 details*

'Does that mean we can be really bitchy?' said Art.

'Well, Kath's certainly going for my crown,' said Harriet.

'Your crown?'

'The steamy stuff.'

'Do we assume this fling with our friend Raúl is going great guns?'

'Art!'

'Well, I mean. All you women seem to write about is sex.'

Shelley and Harriet and Virginia looked wide-eyed at each other.

'And we men,' said Peter, 'just write about what sad plonkers we are?'

'Don't know about that.' Art sniffed. 'But ... whatever, whatever. It's great. The piece is great. I'm just not too sure about this *contours* thing. Are those heaving breasts meant to remind us of St Paul's?'

'She's got just one? Ha ha.'

'What's up with you men this evening?'

'Sorry. Sorry.' Peter held up his hands. 'To be serious for a moment ... in fact, I thought it was a pretty assured piece of work. Somehow it seemed ... I don't know ... older ...'

'Older?'

'I mean, more mature. Written by someone not as young as she is.'

'Hmm.' Virginia breathed in, as if deliberating, and then picked up her phone. 'I should tell you. I received another text from Kath.' She squinted at the display. 'Here it is. Apparently she had help.'

'From who?'

'Her grandmother.' She read the text.

'Aha. Plagiarism.'

'Come off it,' said Virginia. 'It's research.'

'It's not just the details,' said Peter. 'When I said *older*, I was thinking of tone. And also, some of the insights. Like that last sentence.'

'Tone?'

'It's the kind of intuition someone gets who's reflecting on their past life. I bet her grandmother said that. About being truly alive. I bet she said exactly those words.'

'That's unfair.'

'Just guessing.'

'We can ask her,' said Art. 'Next time.'

'Might put her off,' said Shelley. 'She might think we think she's a fraud.'

'I agree,' said Harriet. 'We shouldn't be discouraging.'

Discouraging? Peter thought.

He observed Harriet discussing the point with Shelley, and then wondered why Ben had failed to show this evening. He sometimes seemed so antagonistic to the things Shelley said. Perhaps that was the reason for his absence of course. He let his gaze rest on Shelley's profile. Her hair, pulled back in a loose ponytail. Her blonde eyebrows. And in her blue-grey eyes and the directness of her stare a quality that he could only describe as translucent. He turned his gaze away. Virginia caught his eye.

'What do you think, Peter?' she said.

He forced his attention back to the conversation. He said, softly, 'I still think …' But the words did not emerge.

Instead he realised why it was that Kath's prose lacked authenticity. It was the young, it came to him, who experienced life in its raw state. It was for them that every experience felt burnished by the excitement of the new. It was a feature of middle age that the immediacy of everyday life began to fade. He had read somewhere that the colour cones on the retina of the eye returned a more muted palette to the brain as one aged. You could actually see this effect in the evolution of Monet's water lily sketches, in a sequence painted over a span of thirty years.

And war was one of the few things - perhaps the only thing - that wrung, out of the very stuff of life, that same rawness.

Kath could not know that. But her grandmother could.

He looked back down at the text, at the descriptions of Frank and Jane, and he imagined Shelley's back, her bare shoulder blades, her spine, and his own lips brushing against the smooth skin. And Shelley turning her face into the pillow ...

Perhaps war was not the only thing after all.

'Peter?'

*

They moved on to the pub where they discussed the use of *would* versus *was* -

>'Don't like it.'
>'Stick with the simple perfect, I say.'
>'I suppose she's trying to suggest a routine. Repetition.'
>'But it slips back into the past definite...'
>'... just as she orgasms.'
>'Ha ha.'
>'Boys!'

- they discussed whether the public had had enough of wartime romance -

>'The English Patient. Faulks, McEwan. They've all done it.'
>'So?'
>'It's a tired formula.'
>'A successful formula.'

- they discussed the use of slang -

>'So is that warden cockney or northerner?'
>'Accents - best to avoid.'
>'Unless it's spot on.'
>'Er - was this?'

- and, most of all, they discussed Frank -

>'Do you think Kath's grandmother has a secret tale to tell?'
>'Perhaps this is it.'

'Kath's book?'
'We'll ask her.'
'Next time.'
'Pete, what do you think?'

- and Peter found himself wondering whether a generation that was dying had experienced things beyond the comprehension of most ordinary people. Including those at the table.

And what struck him as the others talked was that these stories so often lay buried in the memories of the generation who had lived them, and that it required another's act of will to bring them into the public eye. This is what Kath was doing, what he had done, what all of them were doing. Providing that act of will. Giving voice and permanence to these histories -

'A penny ...'

- before they were lost. Forever. For a moment the weight of these innumerable backstories, the histories of every man and woman, left him with a feeling of piercing sadness.

'A penny for your thoughts.'

Shelley was staring at him. Peter had to take a moment to collect himself.

He shrugged.

'You were engrossed in something.'

'Who won Wimbledon in nineteen fifty-seven?'

'Come on.'

Peter leaned back. 'The function of literature' - he carefully articulated every syllable - 'how the old desire to see the world through the eyes of the young.'

'That's a bit serious for the pub.'

'Do I sound like a bore?'

'Like a literary critic.'

'Ha. I was thinking of Kath's piece.'

'Isn't it the opposite? The young wishing to see through the eyes of the old?'

'Not if it's her Gran speaking.'

'Do you think we were more critical with Kath absent?'

'More honest perhaps.'

'Are you going to email her that?'

'Email?'

'We are commanded -' Shelley's voice acquired in counterpoint a nasal tone, 'Virginia's orders - to email Kath our thoughts and opinions.'

'Head girl?'

'Air stewardess?'

He laughed again. 'The voice needs practice,' he said. 'Well, Virginia's right. That's the purpose of the group.'

'Is it?'

'What do you think it is?'

Shelley smiled. 'Don't know. Talking shop? Chance for a chinwag?'

'So you mean we're just playing …'

'A glass or two?'

'… at being writers …'

'Social club?'

'… and it's all just make-believe?'

Shelley wound her scarf round her neck. 'Dating agency?' She picked up her glass of wine and finished it, then stood up and put on her jacket. 'Gotta go,' she said, once to Peter and once more to everyone else.

Virginia and Harriet rose from their chairs and the women kissed. Virginia reminded her that Kath would be expecting comments the very next day. Shelley waved to Art and Peter. The group were silent as they watched her pick her way between the stools and over to the door. The silence lasted a few moments after it swung shut, until Art said, 'Where were we?'

Peter's eyes remained on the door.

*

Virginia was tired.

She never liked to be the last to leave at closing time. Indeed she was not overly fond of pubs, and, before the Group, rarely socialised in them. But there was a reason for staying late with Peter this time. She had noticed his gaze as Shelley departed.

The others had not stayed long. Art's daughter had appeared suddenly and left with Art at her side. She was dropping Harriet at the taxi rank.

'So.'

'So.'

Virginia had a glass of water in front of her, Peter an inch of beer.

'We like Janice,' she said.

'We?'

'The royal We. Us. The Group.'

'Good. She likes you.'

'When are you bringing the children?'

'Too young for an evening of literary deconstruction.'

'Give it a few years.'

'If we're still around.'

'How did you meet?'

'Us?'

'You and Janice.'

She watched Peter's eyes focus on a point over her shoulder. 'God,' he said. 'Years ago.' He smiled as if to himself. 'In fact, apparently I met her at Edinburgh.'

'*Apparently*? That doesn't sound very romantic.'

'She came up one weekend. One of the guys in my class knew her from home. He says - he told me years after - we met at a party. Neither of us can remember it.'

'How strange,' said Virginia. 'Surely when you ran into her later ...'

'It's weird.'

'So what happened?'

'We met again, in London. I was what, twenty-four. We just ... I don't know ... started going out. You know how it is when you're that age.'

'Peter, for me, it's almost pre-history. Things were very different.'

'Boy meets girl. I can't believe that's changed.'

'So was it love at first sight? Or second sight, should I say?'

He massaged his pint glass. 'I don't know. It all just seemed to move on tracks. We didn't get married straight away. It was only when we wanted to have children. But we might as well have been.'

'You make it sound ...' Virginia chose her words carefully '...all rather considered. Measured.'

He grinned, 'You know' - and changed the subject - 'this may sound a bit off in view of your ... but she admires ... you know she's a barrister ...'

'I do.'

143

'...she admires your ex-husband.'

Virginia sighed. 'Dear old Anthony. Yes. For all his faults, he was actually a good lawyer.'

'Apparently he's a legend in the profession.'

'I'm sure Janice will become one.'

'You may be right,' he said. 'She earns more than me. By a fair whack.'

'Does that worry you?'

'Why should it?'

'Girl power?'

'Virginia, you're not a fan of the Spice Girls?'

'Never heard of them.' She smiled. 'So. Tell me more.'

'Do you want a last one? Before they close?'

'I'm fine.'

'Yeah. Same here.'

'So.'

'You know, it might never have happened. Or at least, it might have been a bit different.'

She waited.

'Guess what? I will have another. A half. You sure?'

She watched him as he got his beer. They were the last in the pub. As he paid she wondered whether in twenty years he would be like Art with his Guinness. Whether the glass in the hand was the prop he needed.

Peter returned to the table and sat down.

Whether indeed it was the prop every Englishman needed. 'We flat-shared,' he said before he had taken a sip. 'Separately. Like Lucy and Kath. Then one summer, I can't remember how it came about, we had spare time on our hands. For what would be the last time in our lives, I sometimes think. She was ... what was it? ... she had just got pupillage. With a top-notch set. But she didn't start till October. Can't remember why. I had just done a course and was between jobs. We got cheap flights down to Ibiza. It was end of August, the crowds were thinning. Ever been there?'

'Peter -' Virginia shuddered. '- I think you're joking.'

'I tell you the island's beautiful. Honestly. Everyone should go. Just to ... *chill*. Even you must know what that means.'

'I think our Prime Minister does it.'

'Yeah. Right.'

'So.'

'So we went for a week and stayed for a month. We stepped off that tarmac into another world. There was no night or day, or perhaps the sun rose and fell but we didn't care and got up when we felt like it and slept when we passed out. We barbecued on the beach and got so tanned we binned the sunblock. We started in a hotel and traded down as the days went by till we were slumming it but we only needed a single bed. There was no pattern or timetable. We made and lost friends, we took a few days out on some rich guy's yacht, some German kid whose name was Krupp or Porsche or something. We ran out of money, but hey what the hell, it was paradise. We ate like kings, sneaked into clubs and chatted up the dj's, we worked the odd night at the bar and filched a few dollars to survive.

'Janice was into that book, you remember, they made a film of it ... the ... *The Beach*, that guy, who was it? Every backpacker had a copy ...'

Virginia shook her head.

'...same thing, but Thailand, a secret place to hang out and be with your friends, to own nothing but the t-shirt on your back, to get high and swim and fish and sunbathe. Until it all goes wrong but for us it never did and the last night we met our buddies and we hit the clubs and danced till four and then crashed on the sand and made love as the sun came up and we thought, let's phone home and tell them to stuff their jobs and just stay the rest of our lives, or better we wouldn't phone and we'd just let them get stuffed in their own time and what the hell whose lives were they anyway and we walked out to the edge of the sea and waded in till it was up to our chests and made love again and she looked so great and her hair was long and ...

'And then ...'

He paused for a second.

'And then we came out of the water and dried ourselves out. Twelve hours later we were back in London.'

Virginia watched him as he picked up his glass, drank and swallowed. He finished his drink, wiped his mouth and looked at her. 'The next day we put on our suits and went to work.'

She wanted to say something but could not think of the words.

'Hey. It's late,' he said. 'Do you want to share a cab? I've got an early meeting tomorrow.'

In the taxi back he said one more thing. 'You know, our bags got nicked at Heathrow. My camera as well. I haven't got a single shot of her from that holiday. Not one.'

"She who is tired of London is tired of lice."
www.missQuote.org.uk

The first half of August was, Peter would reflect in retrospect, a disaster.

Vivien, Janice's mother, who was reverting back to her maiden name of McPherson now that her husband of forty years had left her for Zen and sex (and other pursuits his bloodsucking floozie had introduced him to), decided that she needed to unearth her Highland roots, and that her daughter, son-in-law and granddaughters should join her in this exhumation.

'Do we have to?' Peter said to Janice when she outlined her mother's proposal. He had slowly been getting comfortable with, indeed enthusiastic about, the prospect of two weeks in Tuscany, the other option mooted for the family vacation.

'Mum's insisting,' said Janice. And as Peter's face scrunched in a frown she added, 'Peter, she needs our support.'

They would of course have to drive. The first setback, Peter hesitated yet to think of the d-word, was that he failed in his plan to get up to Scotland in a single day. The kids took too long to get ready and it was past midday before they left. This necessitated an overnight stop in an unspeakable motorway inn somewhere outside Newcastle, which, for some reason to do with a pony farm next door, Katie and Emily thought the most wonderful place they had ever visited.

'Can't we stay here for our holiday?' they trilled the next morning in rare harmony.

'Gran's waiting,' Janice reminded them.

The girls fell into a sulk-induced silence for the journey up to Pitlochry. Their natural exuberance returned about the same time Peter's satnav failed just as he was trying to unthread the final few twists and turns of the single-lane road to the Cairngorms cabin that Janice's mother had booked. 'Nearly there,' Janice said over her shoulder as warfare broke out in the back of the car.

The second upset occurred as they located the resort. Peter had forgotten that summer was a concept unknown north of certain latitudes, and the gathering rainclouds finally burst as they pulled up outside. Vivien was waiting for them with one umbrella in her hand which she used to shield the children. It was left to Peter to unload the car.

'Is there central heating?' he asked as he brought the last mud-spattered suitcase indoors. For reply Vivien pointed at the gate to the driveway fifty yards away which Peter had inexplicably left open.

But of course the countryside was beautiful, and the first part of the week idyllic.

There was sun enough to spend whole days walking the lower hills and exploring castles and strange granite formations. Katie and Emily were thrilled by the gory history of the clans and, gratifyingly for parents and grandparent, so exhausted after supper that intermittent broadband was not a problem.

But on the third evening, soon after midnight, Emily came into her parents' bedroom complaining of a tummy ache. After a cuddle and five minutes in bed next to Janice she was persuaded to return to her room. But Janice was woken by her crying half-an-hour later. The pain was worse, her daughter said, and Janice could feel she was developing a temperature. She sat by her bed and read to her and slowly began to panic until at four in the morning she decided they needed to do something.

Peter sighed, spent ten minutes using the fluctuating signal on his phone to locate nearby hospitals, then dressed and got the maps from the car. Janice woke Vivien who, remarkably, had slept through the fuss. 'You've got Katie, then,' she said anxiously to her mother as Peter bundled Emily into the car under the lightening sky.

They drove south to Perth, got lost in the centre, got a lucky break at an all-night taxi rank where a good samaritan riding shotgun in his cab guided them the final few miles to A&E at the Royal Infirmary. The queue of drunks and addicts took two hours to thin out, and it was coming up to nine in the morning when they were greeted by a smiling and whiskered man in a white coat who led adults and child into his consulting room. There was an uncomfortable moment when a prim lady in an old-fashioned suit joined them and even asked them to wait outside for a minute, but the doctor soon appeared again at the door - alone - and invited them back in.

Emily was sitting up on the bed in her pink tracksuit yawning.

'Fit as a butcher's dog,' he said to Peter and Janice. 'Isn't that right, lassie?' he added, turning to Emily. She smiled at him. She was enjoying the attention.

'Thank God,' said Janice collapsing briefly in a chair and then forcing herself up to embrace her daughter. It was left to Peter, as they were being shown out, to thank the doctor who assured him it was 'just one of those things'. Back in reception they took a moment to flop out on the plastic chairs and get their bearings.

'Hey little miss trouble,' Peter said to his daughter who leaned into him. 'What about some breakfast?' She grinned a toothy smile. He grinned back.

'Pete, are you sure we shouldn't wait awhile?' Janice's misgivings were not yet quite assuaged.

'For what? You heard the doctor.'

'Two hours ago she was so poorly.'

Peter shrugged. 'Kids.'

'These doctors. Can you trust them?'

'Let's go eat.'

'And that old witch who thought we were child molesters.'

But as father and daughter devoured scrambled egg and toast in a greasy spoon in the city centre, Janice's attention was distracted from her espresso by a headline in *The Times* which trumpeted lurid details on yet another NHS scandal involving misdiagnoses and needless deaths. It was clear from her silence on the drive back that doubts were fermenting. Five miles from home, with the folded paper still in her hands, she said, flat out, 'Second opinion.'

'What?'

'We need a second opinion.'

'But ...'

Back home, the argument continued for an hour around the kitchen table.

'Janice, Perth is not London.'

'So?'

'The doctors here have five hundred years of Presbyterian rectitude drilled into them.'

'What does that matter?'

'It's not as if our jolly wee man qualified in Karachi or Kampala ...'

'So you're a racist now?'

Some arguments Peter could not win. He spent the remainder of the day on the internet at the camp office, and the whole of the following day driving the family to a private clinic on the outskirts of Aberdeen where, after his credit card had been swiped for two hundred and fifty pounds, they were shown into the markedly better appointed office of an Indian gentleman whose string of letters, it appeared from the wall-mounted certificates, had been conferred on him by MIT. 'Drink lots of water', seemed, after two hours, to be his primary recommendation. He said he would email the full report later in the week.

The holiday took on a strangely subdued mood after that. The tummy aches, as twice predicted, did not return, but Emily nevertheless seemed to relish her new role as party invalid, and the other women in the group were happy to indulge her. That meant staying in bed all morning, and not exerting herself overly during the rest of the day. Which meant in turn less walking, no eating out, and certainly no pubs.

Peter escaped for a day to Edinburgh. He spent a morning locating and exploring old student haunts. The city's festival was in full swing, and for a while he was overwhelmed by the colour and the craziness of it all. But as the hours passed, as he walked the streets, caught a comedy act or two; as he observed the couples, the swarms of students, the tour groups parading on the Royal Mile; as he listened to the accents, the shrieks and the laughs; his alone-ness began to depress him. He found yet another single window seat in his *nth* Starbucks with his *nth* flat white and he thought, for the first time in Scotland, of the writers' group and then of Shelley. For five minutes he continued to stare through the café window at the crowds enjoying themselves. Then he got up, found his car, and drove back to his family.

Peter was glad that the girls had remembered the pony farm in Newcastle. It meant he had a compelling reason for suggesting they leave one day early. Less welcome was the news that Vivien had decided that attitudes in the Highlands were after all a touch parochial and that the search for her roots might wait another year.

'Of course you can,' said Janice, as her mother contemplated her early return to England. 'Of course you can come with us. There's room in the car. Isn't there Peter?' There was, although it was a squeeze with the luggage. But Katie and Emily were buoyed up by the prospect of re-acquaintance with their quadrupedal friends.

Fatally.

The poor creatures had been shunted off to another farm following Health and Safety concerns. Matters worsened when the receptionist quipped, with what he imagined would lighten the mood, 'Cheer up, girls. You'll probably be eating Black Beauty with your next burger.' This apocalyptic possibility, once implanted in their imaginations, led to floods of tears and vows of vegetarianism, promises adhered to for that evening at least as they foreswore their usual spicy beef pizzas.

The final grind down the M1, with its jams and roadworks, coupled with a detour to Maida Vale for Vivien, ensured that they were too late even for Match of the Day. And yet, as the holiday ended, one small victory emerged from the two week disaster.

The children were in bed, and Peter and Janice sat around their old oak kitchen table, with a fortnight's mail in front of them and two open bottles of Becks within reach.

As Janice took a sip of her beer, she took Peter's hand and said to him softly, 'You did well.'

'Well?'

'With Mum. With the driving. With Emily and her …'

Peter settled into a thousand-yard stare. 'Ibiza next year,' he said softly.

She still held his hand. 'What's that?' When he did not reply she picked up her reading glasses and returned to the pile of letters.

After five minutes she nudged him and handed him a card. 'Look.' Inside was a picture of a glamorous woman in a yellow dress, sunglasses perched on her head. She leant against an olive-skinned man in white shirt and slacks who, even Peter could tell, was better looking than any mortal man had a right to be.

'What a dreamboat,' said Janice.

'And who is she?'

'My school friend Antonia. She's getting married in Italy. Some time in October. She wants me to come.'

Peter's brain began to engage and his baser motives to click into gear. 'You've hardly had a holiday yourself, have you?' he heard himself saying. He turned to Janice and then to the card she was holding, and he was aware that her own mind was formulating its strategies as well.

'Hmm,' said Janice. 'Florence is so beautiful in Autumn.'

And as they gazed down at the card, a negotiation began to work itself out in the air between them.

'What do you say to …' Janice said tentatively.

The deal lay suspended in the ether for a further five seconds.

'A week in Bordeaux,' he barked. 'You baby-sit.'

'A long weekend in Tuscany,' she yelled. 'You baby-sit.'

Peter and his wife high-fived.

"Stripped down, Ulysses is a twit."
  Paulo Coelho commenting on the classic by James Joyce

"Clichéd", "Awful", "Tosh", "Puke-making"
  Comments on the work of Paolo Coelho
  (worldwide sales 150m)

The group had decided not to meet during the month of August because of the various holiday plans each of them had lined up for the month. However there was one issue of a literary nature which was vexing Peter, and that was the lack of any reaction from a certain Mr Quentin Booker. His agent.

He had disciplined himself not to be the first to call. For some half-understood reason he assumed that, as in teenage dating, the lack of such contact might make the other party, in this case himself the author, more alluring. Yet, as August passed, he wondered if he had simply been forgotten, or, worse, if his manuscript was, in the harsh glare of a professional's assessment, so awful as to be put aside without further comment. He realised he did not know what a suitable period was for an agent to reach a conclusion as to whether a submission was worth pursuing. He had sent in the book six weeks before. Surely that was enough? Or, alternatively, did the agent need more time to solicit the inevitably positive responses from colleagues, publishers, literary editors, Hollywood brokers?

Peter decided to wait until the end of the month.

In the meantime he booked his flight to Bordeaux and, after some negotiation, the time off work.

The group - or rather Virginia - had decided on the week of the 9th to the 16th of September. They would have one more meeting, on the 6th, the Thursday before, in which they could discuss such mundanities as a meeting point at the airport and the difficulties of left-hand drive hire-cars. In the circulating emails they could not quite pin down what they should call their time off. Working holiday? Retreat? Jolly? Janice had her own *let's-call-a-spade-a-spade* opinion. At work he hinted at an ailing aunt.

Of more interest to Peter, indeed the major concern which occupied his mind as he commuted in to a seasonally deserted

Whitehall, was whether Shelley had made the decision to come as well. He assumed from the *lack* of any email to the contrary that she had. But, as he thought about it, he realised he could not know for sure.

But if she did not come, how would he pass the time? Bootcamp would, after all, best describe the vacation. He remembered her final words at the last meeting with their suggestion of a purpose other than merely literary.

With a touch of slyness, he emailed Virginia to ask how many they would be, but when she replied *eight*, he found himself no wiser. V, H, A, B, K, L, he counted. Himself, that made seven. Was the eighth Raúl or Shelley? As he read the email on his smartphone at work, he found himself breaking out into laughter for no reason. 'Woman trouble?' his younger colleagues asked with a troubling insight.

On the last day of August, at five in the afternoon, he rang the agency and asked to speak to Mr Booker.

'Who is it for him?' a female voice answered.

'He has a manuscript of mine. I sent it in a couple of months back.'

'Name?'

'Pindar. Peter Pindar.'

A pause. Peter's bowels twisted and turned. 'He's away on holiday at the moment.'

That's fucking helpful, Peter thought. 'I see,' he said. 'Do you when he's back.'

'Let me see …'

Peter came close to ending the call at that moment.

'… Try phoning next Friday.'

'The seventh?'

'Is it? If you say so.'

'Friday the seventh. I'll phone then.'

*

But a call came to him a day earlier.

It was the Thursday of their meeting, soon after seven. Art and Ben were settling in at their usual chairs at Virginia's when his phone vibrated in his pocket.

'Anyone reading this evening?' Harriet was saying.

'We've got a special surprise this evening,' said Virginia. The doorbell rang, the others arrived.

'What's that, Virginia?'

Peter stared at the unfamiliar number on his phone and was about to let the call go to voicemail when curiosity overcame him. He stood up.

'Hello?'

'Mr Pindar?'

'Yes? Who's this?'

'Quentin Booker here.'

'Mr Booker,' Peter shouted. He mouthed *sorry* at the others and retreated to the kitchen. 'Mr Booker. How ...' he stumbled to find anything sensible to say. 'How was your holiday?'

'My holiday?'

'You were away?'

'In fact, I was in London the whole time.'

There followed a minute of conversation in which various bits of misinformation were clarified and crossed lines uncrossed and ...

I don't give a fuck, Peter thought. 'I see,' he said.

'So anyway,' said Mr Booker. 'Your manuscript. Let me get my glasses ... where are we ...'

Cut to the fucking chase.

'... Ah yes. Why don't you come in to the office and we can have a chat?'

'Tomorrow?'

'Can't do tomorrow. Monday?'

Peter sighed. *Shall I just cancel Bordeaux?* he thought.

At that moment Shelley walked in to the kitchen. 'Hi Peter,' she said. She filled a glass with tap water. 'Coming to France with us?'

*

The others were sitting around a table staring at pictures of Virginia's holiday home. They were at full strength. Even Raúl was present.

'It's big,' said Kath.

'It's beautiful,' said Harriet.

'Will we all fit in?' said Shelley.

'Three bedrooms upstairs, two down,' said Virginia. 'How many are we? Someone may have to rough it on the lounge sofa.'

Peter pulled up a chair and joined them. He wondered whether he had made the right decision on the phone. He wondered also whether he could tell anyone in the room what had happened or whether that might be tempting fate.

Quentin Booker liked his novel but had certain concerns about its commercial viability. He wanted to discuss these with Peter. Was Peter open to making changes? He remained hopeful that they could reach a conclusion satisfactory to both of them.

They would meet at the agent's offices at six PM on the Monday after Peter returned from Bordeaux.

Why didn't I suggest Skyping it from France? he thought now.

'I'll volunteer for the sofa.'

Should I ring him back?

'There's a river just next door.'

Why are agents so crap when it comes to technology?

'The Dordogne.'

I wonder what these 'concerns' are ...

'First day we need to get to Carrefour for a big shop.'

... these changes. And do I want to make them?

'It'll be a Sunday.'

I guess I'll have to.

'You're right. Well, we'll have to make do.'

Unless I can persuade him otherwise.

'Croissants and wine first day.'

The worst thing is ...

'Sounds like slumming. Ha ha.'

... the fucking waiting.

'Peter, can you see from there?'

*

At eight-thirty, Virginia shut her laptop.

'Enough. We can carry on the discussion in the pub later,' she said. 'Tonight we have a big treat. Raúl, are you quite sure you can't join us in France?'

Raúl shrugged his shoulders.

'But you can read to us this evening?' said Virginia.

Kath broke in. 'Look, I'm really sorry we didn't have time to email beforehand, so I've got printed copies here. Ben, Art, can you pass these round.'

'How exciting.'

'I hope it's not in Spanish.'

'Did you write it first in Spanish?' said Shelley.

Kath answered. 'He did. Even I haven't seen the English, so it's a first time for me as well.'

'Shall we sit on the sofas?' said Virginia. 'Slightly more comfortable.'

The members of the Writers' Group picked up their hardcopies and their glasses of mineral water and orange juice, and they moved over to the other side of the room. They set themselves down on sofas and cushions. Virginia switched on two side lamps. Kath and Lucy sat side by side on the floor. Ben sat directly opposite Shelley on a hardbacked chair. Virginia settled next to Art on one settee, Peter and Harriet on the other.

Raúl picked up a stool from the kitchen and placed it at the edge of the circle of readers. He cleared his throat.

GIANT

It was a cold evening in November. My children and myself were watching television. My wife was preparing an evening meal in the kitchen.

It was a three stories house. The landlady occupied the groundfloor and first floor was rented to two girls.

My family and myself used to live on the top floor.

Suddenly the front bell rang and one of the girls on the first floor went to answer.

The door was opened. The girl was running on the stairs and knocked down the grandfather's clock on landing.

Some one was knocking at our flat. My wife opened the door and I also went to see to find out what was happening.

It was Maria, one of the girls from first floor. She looked very frightened as she had seen a ghost and was shaking. She told my wife that there was a giant standing at the front door and asking for Mr Vargas.

I was wondering what that giant had got to do with me. I went downstairs and opened the door and saw my friend Mr Aguilar who came to visit first time since we moved into that house.

He was well built and seven feet tall and wearing black winter coat, Russian cap and gloves. He was really looking like a giant.

I brought him upstairs and introduced to my family. My children were frightened to see him.

My wife announced that the dinner was ready. We had our meal together. He stayed with us for an hour and left. Every one was relieved that the giant had gone back to his den.

Raúl looked up.

There was silence for ten seconds. Everyone's eyes remained on their copies of the text. Harriet frowned. Art suppressed a sneeze. Kath had gone crimson.

My God, Peter thought. *It's drivel.*

Part II

"And what should they know of England who only England know?"

Kipling

Shelley and The Good Australian.

Shelley Banks reckoned she must have been a pretty arrogant young woman when she first arrived in London on a March morning at the turn of the millennium. It was a week before her eighteenth birthday.

She had an extended-stay visa, a Lonely Planet, and two thousand dollars in an account, the money left to her by a dead uncle she had hated. And not much else.

To fill out the immigration form at Heathrow, she picked a posh hotel at random from the guide, but, once through, spent the hour-and-a-half it took to get into town searching for the cheapest place she could find in or around Earls Court.

The guest house she chose looked inexpensive - paint was flaking, the bins outside had not been emptied - but wasn't. She would learn in those first few days that an Oz dollar did not go very far. She discovered also that the old cliché about Earls Court, that it was a home-from-home for blokes from down-under, was also pretty worn. The hotel was run by Indians and the residents were Polish and Nigerian.

'You'll get a shock, my girl,' her father had said on one the few occasions when they had actually spoken in the days before she left.

'Go easy on her, Merv,' her mother had said.

'Just telling her like it is,' he said. 'Like it is. There ain't no fucking poms in London any more. It's all them darkies.'

Yet the thing that irked her about the area where she lived - for the first forty-eight hours she was intoxicated by the sheer *otherness* of the place - was not the prediction or its correctness but that her father had made it. After a couple of pints on her second evening - the beer, she knew, would take some getting used to - she wrote a postcard in jagged capitals to her parents.

'HEY DAD YOU WERE RIGHT. IT IS FULL OF DARKIES.'

Whether the card actually arrived or was censored for its offensive content she would never find out.

The first week she spent sleeping late, getting over the jetlag, doing a few of the sites - which all seemed shabby and a bit fake (she just didn't get Madame Tussaud's) - and carefully avoiding any bar which served as a refuge for her compatriots. There were many of these, some obvious, with names like *Outback*, or *The Digger*, others less so but where you could tell pretty quick from the accents and the absence of an English pallor. But after a week in which she had not spoken to a single person except to buy basics - food, tickets, booze, roll-your-own tobacco - she decided to bend her rule a fraction. And she quickly discovered the falsity of another cliché, that the Aussies in London were rough-edged backpackers who had ended up there after extended trawls through Nepal or Thailand. She found herself as likely to meet bankers and advertising executives, types she had imagined you saw only in the smart suburbs of Sydney.

And she was instantly popular. Tall, rangy - running and basketball had been among the only things she had excelled in at school, though she demonstrated an unAustralian indifference to sport - she had cut her hair Jean Seberg style a day after seeing Godard's *A Bout De Souffle* in a dive in Camden.

But if this popularity was contrary to an unspoken mission she entertained in crossing the world - a mission whose contours she still could not see clearly, though it did include some element of escape - it nevertheless put her in touch with networks and bulletin boards which were able to satisfy a few pressing needs. Her cash pile was running low, and she needed digs and a job. The first she found in a flatshare in Hackney, not yet fashionable, the second in a series of bars and coffee houses whose profusion was fortunate, since she got fired about as frequently as her shorter hair required trimming.

'Shell-eye, Shell-eye, please - the customer he always right,' one of her bosses told her, a lugubrious Greek who ran a café on Upper Street. 'Even when he wrong.'

'Not if he's an arse-hole,' she replied. She had sworn at one of these high-rollers who were apparently so invaluable to the enterprise.

'You tell him, girl,' the regulars at one of the tables chorused.

'And you lot can fuck off as well.'

This spikiness ensured a rapid turnover in men friends. But they were also put off by a certain reluctance in her when it came to sharing a bed, and this caginess came close to precipitating violence a couple of times, usually after an evening of drinking.

'Jeez, girl, don't you want to?' said one guy after they had been kissing for half-an-hour on his sofa when the TV had finished. And suddenly, and in a way she hadn't felt since that time she was a teenager, she felt hemmed in and needed to escape.

The man stood up, fists clenched, zipper down. 'OK, just piss off then.'

She walked home from Whitechapel, eye make-up smeared, dodging the unlicensed cabs and, on one or two dimly lit streets, the cruisers and the weirdos.

These were not necessarily bad men. If she met them in the days that followed they apologised. 'Sorry, babe, I was wasted. Too much booze.' But they never met again. She made sure of that.

It was after a full year that a different kind of opportunity presented itself.

She was working the late shift at a bar in a smart City hotel. Customers were few. One night a man showed up at midnight. He wore his overcoat over his suit - it was still close to freezing in April. She had been wiping glasses.

He ordered a double scotch, no ice. The accent was Australian.

'Hey, do you mind if I …' he fished out a big Mac from his coat pocket. She sniffed. 'Yeah, I know. Onions.' He looked around. The place was otherwise empty. She smiled at him. 'I'll be quick,' he said. And he was. He said between bites he hadn't eaten since lunchtime. Once she pointed to her lower lip and handed him a serviette. 'I'm still just a kid,' he said, wiping his mouth.

The man turned up the next night, and the night after. He ordered one drink. Just one, always the same. 'No ice,' he reminded her each time.

If it was quiet he talked about his job. 'I'm a fire-fighter,' he told her. 'Sort of. My company sends me wherever the corporate shit's hit the fan. London, San Fran, HK. It's fifteen hour days, seven days a week. Takes as long it takes, and then I'm out.'

'How's it going this time?'

'Tough one. But getting there.'

Once she offered him a second drink. 'On the house.'

He shook his head. 'Can't afford to. Can't afford the headache tomorrow.' He stayed his customary fifteen minutes and left.

She admired his self-discipline, especially as he never, never came up with that creepy move so many of the businessmen sprang when, she could tell, they were attracted to her - the snaps of the wife and kids.

'Where do you live in Sydney?' she said once. He had a ring.

He put a finger to his lips. 'That's my other life. And I'll be back there soon.' She realised then that she'd miss him. And the day he came when he ordered that second scotch and she knew it was over. And she knew he knew she had figured this out. 'Shelley, it's been a pleasure.' Her heart flipped. She wondered how he knew her name. But, of course, she was wearing one of those dopey nametags. 'Look this may seem cheap -' he extracted four fifties from his wallet '- but, hey, from tomorrow I don't need 'em any more.' He placed them in the leather folder containing the bill.

'It's not cheap,' she said, and her hand brushed his as she picked up the folder. 'And I still don't know your name.'

As she lay, naked and defenceless under the sheets, as he emerged from the shower, she felt an ancient hysteria swirling inside her. She squeezed her eyes shut. But she felt his fingers brush the hairs on her arm, her shoulder, her cheek. 'Shelley, Shelley.' His voice a whisper.

The next morning as he finished his packing in that precise way of his and she dressed in her uniform from the night before, he came and sat by her on the bed.

'Shelley, I have this feeling …' he kissed her on the forehead '… you're new to all this.'

'What, sleeping with a married man?'

'I meant … something else.' He looked her in the eyes. Then he said, 'It shouldn't have been me.'

She wrapped him in her arms and held him tight.

He got his taxi to drop her at her flat before it went on to Heathrow. Six months later she read that an Australian businessman with his name had been killed in 9/11.

*

Shelley Banks grew up.

It took some blagging and a fake letter from home but she was able to enrol at London University to do a course in Journalism and Social Science.

These were the days when the spandex shine on New Labour had yet to fade, though the mood on campus was too radical to support the government beyond welcoming its replacement of the last. Shelley, while attending the meetings and the demos, began to realise that a capacity for self-reliance made her uneasy with the party line. She had inherited a resilience from her parents - perhaps despite them - which left her outlook, though she hated to admit it, closer to her father's with its distrust of big-state intrusion. Moreover she was suspicious of an evangelical look in the eyes and the stretched smile of the prime minister. She had seen such men in the outback areas where her mother's people came from. Preachers, salesmen. They always meant trouble.

There were few English youngsters in the classes she attended, and she found herself drawn more to the single-issue politics which fellow students from Africa and South America brought with them. Apartheid and the exploitation in the Bolivian silver mines were just plain wrong. Whatever party you supported.

More important than any campus agitprop was the sense of purpose that her three-year course conferred. She had never seen the point of any of the stuff they taught her at school. Here, she was in control, and she worked hard to catch up on things she was assumed to know. These expectations came as often from other students as from the tutors. Her ignorance of Gramsci, Hobsbawm, Chomsky was a given. Yet she might also hear from one of her girlfriends, 'What? You've never read Germaine Greer? You? An Aussie?'

She stayed nights at the library, and picked up enough to bluff. For the first time in her life she found herself able to use learning as a tool, as a means of persuading, exerting power, even when she was not herself won over by the argument. She was dazzled by this, especially when it secured her an internship at The New Statesman in the summer break after her second year. How those phrases, so near to cliché from overuse, slipped off her tongue. What an effect they had. The magazine offered her an entry-level position when she graduated.

But these people weren't much fun. She had begun to grow her hair, and cultivated a vampish Kate Moss look. She was drawn to another of the interns. Siseko was from Johannesburg and was being sponsored by his government, though his accent was what even Shelley had come to know as Home Counties. Two years in a progressive public school in Sussex, he explained, though curiously his accent regressed when she overheard him once on the phone back home.

'Forget the class war for a change,' he said one evening. Siseko was the best-dressed man in the office, the only one to wear a suit and tie. 'Let's be decadent.' It was Nelson Mandela's birthday, and they toasted him in a champagne bar in Chelsea. 'Don't worry,' he told her. 'The ANC is paying.' None of their colleagues had been invited.

They were drunk the first few times they slept together, although, months later as she discerned in him a capacity for calculation, she wondered whether she had been the only one over-indulging. But perhaps, even then, that was the only way she could bridge the chasm between friendship and a physical intimacy she craved.

She followed him when he returned to South Africa to join the political team of a start-up newspaper. He secured her a job as a fundraiser. She began with a phonebook and a filofax, flattening her own vowels as best she could. 'We need sponsors,' they told her. What was unspoken was that she would act the foil to Siseko when they needed to tap the old white money.

She discovered she had a flair for it, and soon she was working on her own. At times it was a tough sell - 'You're going the wrong way, girl,' a few of the dowagers said as they told her they were waiting for their visas to Australia or New Zealand to come through. 'It's over for our kind.' It did not seem like that to her. There was still, a decade after the fall of apartheid, a buzz, a sense, once more after London, of the new, a newness tinged at times with a violence that made it, for reasons she was not mature enough to grasp, even more exciting. They became a minor celebrity couple, photographed at receptions and international rugby games.

But Siseko was ambitious, and part of that ambition involved the cultivating of links with a new and aggressive elite. Many of these were the sons of ex-freedom fighters, their parents now politicians, judges, academics, people who had pantheonic status in the society he was easing himself into.

Their sons. And their daughters. Soon Shelley was tired of seeing him on the gossip pages with yet another new-young-face-to-watch.

They lasted two years. More, she reflected later, than she had had a right to expect. It ended after a row in which he accused her of holding him back. And - unforgiveably in this, the new Jerusalem - of holding progress back.

'To create you have to destroy,' he shouted.

'So I'm just collateral damage?' she screamed. She moved out the next day.

Shelley had come to love the country. She loved her friends, she loved the experiment that South Africa was, an experiment that was ninety-nine percent successful, an experiment in whose shaping she had played a small part. But she knew she was a victim of the same rush to change she had relished a year or two before.

A month later he drove her to the airport. He carried her bags to the desk. Perhaps without thinking - perhaps, worse, after very careful thought - he handed her a business card.

'Siseko, I really don't need that,' she said, and she kissed him on the cheek. Then she walked through the departures gate.

Months later Peter Pindar would remember the writing holiday in France by the moments towards the end when things went both ecstatically right and catastrophically wrong.

And yet the first few days, from the Sunday when they flew in till the Thursday, were languorous and warmed by sun and good wine and better conversation in all the ways that his holiday with his family should have been and wasn't.

They flew into Bergerac on the afternoon of the ninth of September.

As the aircraft began its descent Peter reflected that there were strong reasons to be thankful he had a Kindle packed in his carry-all rather than books.

Janice had presented the e-reader to him a few days before. He had wondered at her motivation - perhaps a combination of *Thank You* for coping, with reasonable grace, with her mother during the family vacation, and good luck gift for the working holiday to come. She had pre-loaded the six shortlisted books for the Booker Prize. A nice touch, though he suspected she might be interrogating him on this reading list when he got back.

As he surveyed the packed body of the plane ahead of him - Ben, Kath and Lucy sat together two rows ahead - he knew that the reduced luggage had considerably simplified the process of negotiating the normal horrors of budget airline travel. He had his laptop, well, on his lap, his carry-all in the rack above. They would be out the arrivals hall and into the Bordeaux sunshine in minutes.

He shut down his computer, placed it under his seat, fastened his seatbelt and leaned back. A quick glance across two sniffy neighbours revealed the landscape of France, an aerial view inconceivable to their ancestors of just four generations back. Yet this wonder of the modern world occupied his thoughts less than the prospect of a week in the daily company of Shelley. The ten minutes in which the plane dropped out of the sky, landed with a two ungainly bumps on the tarmac, and taxied to a ramshackle arrivals lounge passed with a growing sense of election into a new world of dazzling opportunity.

And of danger.

They were indeed amongst the first to clear passport control, such as it was, and the first to be handed keys to one of a line of Renaults by green-uniformed car-hire staff. Peter drove, and he waited until he had successfully navigated a few kilometres on the wrong side of the road before he turned to Ben at his side. 'Right. Directions?'

He was mildly disappointed at the flat dullness of the countryside around Bergerac. But the greenery became lusher, more inviting as they began to follow the course of the river eastwards.

'*Etoile-sur-Dordogne*,' Lucy articulated in exaggerated accents from the back.

'Is that where we're heading?'

'How far?'

'Blink and you'll miss it.'

'Lots of GB number plates.'

'Don't worry. We'll be missing them as well.'

Peter felt a moment's urge to tell those in the back to quieten down, as he done so frequently to Katie and Emily a month before on the road to Scotland, but he resisted. All that was required of him, this time round, was to drive, listen, follow directions. After indeed blinking and missing it, they backtracked and located a hamlet of half-a-dozen houses clustered around a T-junction.

'It must be one of these.'

'Why don't you ring Virginia?'

'Got a signal?'

But Ben reminded them that the house would be empty as she had to pick up Art and Shelley who were arriving at a different airport.

'That's the one. Surely,' he said. A heavy green door, grey stone walls with a trellis of climbing plants. 'I remember the pics.' They parked off the road, walked through a gate across a small front yard. Peter rang the bell anyway. Lucy was the one who checked under the pot by the doormat.

'Got it,' she said, holding up a key.

'Hope we haven't guessed wrong.'

'They have shotguns here, don't they?'

Inside, the house was cool and dark. Off the hallway was a kitchen with a stone floor. They laid down their bags. There was a note on the large breakfast table.

Back at 6. Ben read aloud. *Make yourselves comfortable. V xx.*

'*Nous sommes arrivés.*'

'Shall we have a look around?'

'Let's wait till Virginia gets here.'

'I'll take a quick peek,' said Lucy.
'You sure?'

After fifteen minutes of poking around, Peter found ground coffee, a cafetiere, and a kettle. There were some iron-framed chairs in the grass yard in front of the house, and they took their mugs and sat outside as the heat began to wane.

'Will we all fit?' said Ben to Lucy.

'Big place,' she said. 'Three bedrooms upstairs. Two down.'

'Must have cost a packet,' said Kath.

'Virginia's ex is a QC. Fabulously successful.'

'Figures.'

They fell silent, and Peter dozed. The slanting rays of the sun felt glorious on his forehead. He woke to Art's shout.

'Oy. You lot. Working hard, I see.'

Virginia had pulled up outside in her Fiat. Shelley was sitting beside her waving.

'We all made it,' she said.

*

It was an hour before they had hauled in luggage, decided on rooms - Virginia and Art and Shelley upstairs, Ben and Peter downstairs, Lucy and Kath crashing in the living room - then freshened up and reconvened around the table in the kitchen.

'I can't believe it,' Virginia said, opening a bottle of champagne. 'We're all here.' She poured seven glasses.

'Almost all,' said Shelley. Harriet was due to arrive in midweek.

'Well, here's to Harriet.'

They drank, and Peter was aware at a semi-conscious level that the moment would be one to remember and savour. Ben and Lucy were taking pictures on their phones, but for Peter it seemed an instant of possibility which defied such framing, and he closed his eyes to imprint the scene in memory. *Here, now, this instant,* he thought, *this is it, this is where it happens ...*

'Don't you just hate budget airlines?' shrieked Lucy.

Peter opened his eyes.

'The queues,' said Kath, 'the cramped seats.'

'Wouldn't it be wonderful if we could just *skip* all that?' said Art. 'Just *arrive*. By teleportation.'

'But isn't all the hassle part of the fun?' said Shelley.

'Like scene setting?'

'Like backstory?'

'Like down payment,' said Shelley. 'The hard work we put in to get the prize.'

'I'd rather cut to the chase,' said Art. '*Beam me down Scotty.*'

'Well,' said Virginia, '*our* story begins *now*.'

Daylight faded. The kitchen lights were switched on. A pattern of moths soon lay fixed on the outer edge of the window panes. A three-quarters moon rose over dark outlines of the high trees outside.

Virginia rummaged around for ingredients for supper. There were eggs and ham, cheese and stale bread. A bowl of peaches and two bunches of grapes. A bottle of red wine. Ben helped her prepare, Kath and Lucy set the table.

Later, Kath said, 'We'll need a routine.' Empty dishes lay piled up at one end of the table.

'Routine?'

'This is a working holiday. After all.'

'What do you say we …'

'Bootcamp.'

'… we write in the morning, get a few hours in after breakfast …'

'Stop for lunch, I hope.'

'… stop for lunch. Read and discuss what we've done …'

'…a few more hours in the afternoon …'

'… review again at sundown …'

'… just in time for the first glass of wine …'

'Sounds perfect.'

'What about you, Peter?' said Shelley.

'What do you mean?'

'You've finished your book, haven't you? What are you going to work on?'

'Yes, Peter,' said Virginia. 'How's it going with the agents?'

He had not told the others about the developments with Mr Booker which had taken place just before they left. He had only told

Janice the day before. He was not sure he could bear to explain the disappointment if they knew he had come so close and was then to fail.

'No luck,' he said. 'All rejections, I'm afraid.'

'So what are you going to be working on this week?'

This was in fact a good question. He had a clean, 'release' copy of his novel, which was the one the agent had seen. There was another, a 'beta' version, which included a few revisions and amendments. Somehow, it was difficult to generate the enthusiasm to work on this.

'I might try a short story or two,' he said. 'Something completely different.'

'A diversion?' said Shelley.

'A peccadillo?' said Virginia.

Peter narrowed his eyes at her. He had to smile.

Virginia, then Shelley, Kath and Lucy, and, later, Ben, all rose from the table and retired to their rooms.

Peter opened another bottle of wine. Over half-an-hour, Art finished three-quarters of it. He talked, of his late wife, of his daughter and his grandchildren, and of a political thriller he had written in the nineties which he had never been able to publish …

'You never told us.'

'It was crap. I'd missed the *zeitgeist*. Or so someone said.'

… and then, moving back further in time, of his work in the eighties as a campaigning journalist covering the miners' strike. As he spoke, of battles between mounted police and miners, of his arrest for picketing, of the moment everything came to nothing and the strike collapsed, his voice became reduced to a low growl.

Peter had watched the recent funeral procession of Art's bête noire ('That bloody woman') from a second floor office window - she had left power before Peter could vote. His era's birth pangs reduced to pageantry and a sneering editorial in the left wing press. A struggle which, as Art told it, came close to tearing society in two. Peter asked him why he did not write about it.

Art's eyes were glassy. 'Why?' he said.

'Perhaps people would like to know the facts.'

'The facts?' Art finished his wine. 'The facts.' He poured the remains of the bottle into his glass and finished that as well. 'Trouble is, the facts always stand in the way of a good story.'

"I try to leave out the parts that readers skip."

Elmore Leonard

At nine the next morning Peter found Virginia alone at the breakfast table. She was in her dressing gown drinking coffee.

She did not move except to raise her cup. 'There's still some left.'

Peter walked over to the window and looked outside. Across the road there was a mass of bushes and a bank which led down to the river. Beyond was a line of cypress trees. After a minute he said without turning, 'It's quite beautiful.' As he watched, two swans swooped and then settled on the grey surface of the water, the stream's current carrying them backwards with hypnotic slowness. The clapping of their wings on the water as they began to preen echoed in the distance.

'It is.'

'How long have you owned this place?' He moved over to the stove and poured himself a coffee.

'Since the children were young.'

Peter had an odd sense of intrusion into a family history. He sat down. 'You sure -' he chuckled '- that inviting us was such a wise move?'

Virginia turned to him. 'Absolutely,' she said.

He nodded - 'Good' - then stretched and yawned. 'So. Where're the nearest shops?'

'One mile.' Virginia pointed. 'Eastwards.'

'I'll get some breakfast.'

It was such a pleasure, Peter reflected, to park precisely outside the place one wanted to visit. He was further gratified to find that his French remained sufficient to negotiate the purchase of a few basics.

After he left the shop, he took a minute to walk around the village. A simple stone church. A square and a war memorial. Flowers on every windowsill.

The streets were empty. A single jet fighter, crashing through the sound barrier, cut through a perfect blue sky.

Bizarrely, he had forgotten the turning into the town, and drove through flat country for five minutes before realising his error and backtracking. *My goldfish memory*, he thought. He drove fast, eager to get back.

The front door was open and the sound of conversation carried as he parked. He walked into the kitchen, found a plate from a high drawer, and laid the croissants on the table.

'Well done,' said Shelley. Everyone was up.

'Virginia,' said Ben. 'Is your wi-fi on?' He had his tablet in front of him on the table.

Art was rubbing his eyes.

'Late night?' said Kath.

'How do I make more coffee?' said Lucy.

'Ready for some writing?' said Peter.

'First one to a thousand words gets a prize.'

One by one they drifted away.

Peter, the last to go, returned to his room where there was a small and rather ancient wooden table. He cleared the surface and shifted it over to the window, laid his laptop down and powered up. He saw that Ben, seated precariously on a garden chair, was working outside. *Nice idea*, Peter thought, though he felt strangely inhibited about joining him. A private activity like writing, it seemed to Peter, needed to be carried out in a confined space.

He opened up the most recent version of his novel and looked at the first page. *Before and After*, it said at the top. He had never been entirely happy with the title. Too late. This was the version the agent had.

The decision to leave his novel untouched for the week and instead to complete at least two short stories, a plan he had discussed the previous day, firmed in his mind. He closed the file and opened another in which he kept material for future work: characters, plots, themes, ideas, first lines. He skimmed through.

- *A man drives his estranged brother across Europe to a clinic in Zurich. It will be the last journey for one of them. His illness is terminal. Can the two be reconciled?*
- *A respectable elderly man in blazer and club tie hurls a flour bomb at the prime minister's car. Hauled before a*

> *magistrate he pleads guilty and is fined. A day later he does the same again. Why?*
> - *A man wishes to meet his previous lovers one more time, but they rebuff him. He invents a story that he is dying. Does he rediscover an old flame? Or does his deception unravel [with hilarious consequences - ha ha]?*
> - *A gap year student is robbed in the jungles of Thailand. He decides to fake his own death.*
> - *A successful city trader is robbed in the backstreets of Hong Kong ...*
> - *A woman's marriage of twenty years is over. On a holiday in Central America she is robbed in the backstreets of ...*
> - *...*

He opened up a new document. 'Go on, pick one.' He spoke to himself in a low voice. 'Doesn't matter which. Just write.'

After half-an-hour he had not moved. The document on the screen in front of him remained pristine and unblemished.

In a corner of the table he noticed a tiny die which he had missed, a leftover perhaps from a Christmas cracker.

During the second year of his degree a brief craze had swept the university to let one's life, every decision, trivial or serious, be ruled by random processes such as the flip of a coin. There had been a wildly popular book on chance and freewill whose title now escaped him and which he recalled as depthless and hip. A friend of his spent six hours swearing by the philosophy until a coin toss over buying another beer went against him.

He threw the die. The number one fell face up. He typed, *The Last Journey*.

So.

So.

So.

What are the brothers' names? Why did they fall out? Is it cancer? Alzheimer's?

After another hour, he rose to get a coffee. In the breakfast room he met Art who was troubled, it seemed, by a similar writer's block.

'Hey.'

'How's it going with fictional Tony?' said Peter. 'Been redeemed yet?'

'Just had some news. Real news. Bad news.'

'Oh, I'm sorry.'

'Bloke I used to know. Heart attack. Three line obit in *The Guardian*.'

'Gosh, Art. Really sorry. Was he well known?'

'Lead guitarist with *The Crimson Rats*. Don't worry, you won't have heard of them.'

'Were you close?'

Art shook his head. 'Hadn't seen him since …' He counted on his fingers. ''78? '79? I just remember, me and him, in the 100 Club watching some vomiting punks on stage … who were they now?'

Peter waited as Art's memory slowly turned.

'Fans pogoing. Me and him. Damn, I was going to be his manager.'

Art picked up his mug and went outside. Peter watched him walk across the road to the river bank. He stood sipping his coffee and staring across the river.

After a while Peter followed and went outside. He drew up a chair and sat at the garden table. He nodded to Ben.

'Art OK?' said Ben. 'He was swearing like crazy.'

They both watched him. 'I think so,' said Peter.

And quite suddenly he had his way in.

The Last Journey.

They were close to the Swiss border. After a while Dick started to hum. It was a song the two of them knew by heart, though Harry had not heard it for thirty years. Not since they jammed together in a basement bar in London. As the song reached its chorus his brother began to sing the words. He waved his arms as he sang and his hand brushed Harry's as he shifted down a gear.

A sign ahead said Douane.

To-the-Eton-Ri-fles, E-ton Ri-fles … And then Harry's mouth opened as well, for once not to talk or to argue or to dissuade. But to sing. For the first time in three decades the brothers sang, together, and in a kind of harmony.

To-the-Eton-Ri-fles, E-ton Ri-fles.

*

Shelley was at her desk by the window in her room upstairs. She looked down at Peter and Ben who sat in garden chairs and chatted.

Ben's hair was thinning. Not Peter's though. Even though he was older. His was not even grey. Peter was lucky, she could tell, his was a head of hair which would remain thick into old age.

As he got up she thought of a man she had known briefly as a teenager, an Australian guy, a man who was now dead.

*

At one o'clock, Virginia called out that she was preparing lunch. Peter had written eight hundred words.

In the kitchen the table had been laid. There were cheeses, hard and soft. Ham and salami. *Flûtes*. A green salad and a vinaigrette. A bowl of peaches. Jugs of water and fruit juice.

'Yum.'

'Who reached a thousand words?'

They ate, and talked, and drank coffee and talked some more. At three Ben suggested they get back to work. 'Bootcamp? Remember?'

'Time for a siesta, I think,' said Kath.

Ben picked up his iPad. There was silence around the table as they watched him take up his place in the garden outside. Peter felt his own eyelids weighing down. For a few seconds he was lost in his own floating world.

'Hey.' A shout. 'Hey, you guys. Check this out.' Ben turned. He waved to them from outside. 'Hey, have a look at this.'

'What's up?' Shelley called out through the open windows.

'*The Writers Launchpad*. They've just announced the next round. That novel competition?'

Within seconds, they were out the door and crowding round Ben's tablet.

'Who got through the first round?'

'I know Harriet did,' said Virginia. 'And, er, me, of course.'

'And me,' said Art.

'And me,' said Peter.

'Let me see,' said Ben, leafing through the web pages. 'There's a link to the semi-finalists ... Somewhere.'

He scrolled down.

'Here we go.'

'Spence.' There was a list of names. 'Harriet.' A shriek. 'There's Harriet. She's through. She's through.'

Peter placed a hand on Ben's arm as he scrolled. 'P's,' Peter said. 'Just stop a sec at the P's.'

Osborne, Patel, Poulter, Ramakrishna ...

'Damn,' said Peter.

'What about Virginia?' said Kath.

'And Art,' said Lucy.

Ben's fingers moved up and down. 'Looks like ... Harriet's the only one.'

'No, wait,' said Virginia. 'Scroll back up.'

'Where to?'

'A's.'

'What are we looking for?'

'A's. Let me see. *Ambrose, Virginia.* Yes, yes. Yes. I can't believe it.'

'Who's that?' said Ben.

'It's me. It's me. I used my maiden name.' Virginia pulled up a chair. 'Oh my god. How exciting.' She sat down rather too heavily. 'Oof. How exciting. I must email Harriet.'

Peter edged away from the group. He watched them for a few seconds and then returned to his room. He pulled up the website on his own laptop, re-checked the list, and checked his email. Nothing.

The others were still clustered around Ben. *Gosh, how exciting.* Virginia's voice carried. No, not all the others. Art was once again standing on his own looking out over the river.

It was small-minded, Peter knew, to begrudge others their success. And yet .... *Gosh, how exciting.* Even though this competition was pretty minor in the scheme of things. Even though he was actually seeing a real agent as soon he got back. Even though the method of selection was totally arbitrary - staff at *The Writers Launchpad* plus the detestable Phyllida Fowst with her daytime TV bookclub. Despite all these things he felt ...

'Damn.'

... he felt outrage that someone had looked at a collection of words whose assembly he had sweated over, words whose sum presented a narrative which described something important to him and, surely, to humankind at large, and then concluded that its value was no greater than the discarded newspaper in which you wrapped a kebab.

Gosh, how exciting.

He whispered to himself, 'Jesus, Virginia, shut the fuck up.'

*

At six Peter closed his laptop and joined the others in the kitchen. The question of the moment was whether to eat out or not. Nobody felt much like cooking, and at Virginia's prompting, they decided on a cheap bistro in the nearest town.

'If we can somehow avoid the local youth,' she said.

'With their scooters …'

'… and their Gauloises …'

'I hardly think is this Beirut or Bogota,' said Kath. 'Or even Hackney.'

'Anyway,' said Lucy, 'I wanna meet them.'

They took two cars. Over crêpes, frites, croque-monsieurs and pichets of red wine, they argued over who had written the most during the day.

At some point, for no reason, Ben and Kath and Lucy started talking in the voices of their characters. The older members of the group watched in bemusement. Ben spoke Jimmy Cagney, Kath did *frightfully* and *awfully*, Lucy did Essex-girl. 'I am one anyway,' she said.

After a while Shelley joined in with a high-pitched Strine.

'What's that supposed to be?' said Ben.

'Character, Ben.' Lucy shrieked at him. 'You're Al Capone.'

And Kath collapsed in giggles.

'What are you strange people doing?' said Virginia.

'Come on,' said Kath. 'Join us.'

'OK,' said Ben. 'On my word, switch to the person to your right.'

'What's that?'

'Switch,' said Ben.

'Cor blimey,' said Kath. Art sat next to her. 'Who's yer bird mate?'

'That's pathetic,' said Art.

'OK,' said Ben. 'Switch. Switch again.'

And Lucy pitched in with a few *streuths* and *mates* and even a Fosters lager.

'Is that supposed to be me?' said Shelley sitting two places away.

'Switch.'

They were back by nine. They opened another bottle of wine, and crowded around Ben's tablet once more as he showed them round such wonders of the web as www.theliteraturevirus.org, www.proseworkshop.com, www.stylecounsel.com, and, most pertinently, www.plumb-your-novel.com.

'What on earth is that?' said Virginia.

'Writer's block? Geddit?'

'I'm always using these sites,' said Ben. 'For hints and … and … here we are.' He clicked on a section labelled Literary Games. He read out loud. *1. Write a story excluding words with the letter 'e'. 2. Use a random generator for every tenth word. 3. Write two texts and intersperse consecutive sentences. 4. …*

'Hmm. Looks like jolly hard work,' said Virginia.

'Here's one,' said Ben. 'Just the thing for us.' He opened up the page.

'Any more wine?' said Art.

'Under the sink,' said Virginia. 'There's a case of plonk.'

'Did you all remember the person sitting to your right?' said Ben. 'At the café?'

Art picked up the corkscrew from the table.

'I must say,' said Virginia, 'I still can't get over *The Writers Launchpad*. Getting through to the next round.'

They heard Art swear softly as he struggled with the cork.

'I must email Harriet and congratulate …'

'JESUS.' They turned to Art. The wrapping on the neck of the bottle was ripped away. There was a fleck of blood on the palm of his left hand. 'Jesus, Virginia,' - he sucked off the blood and clenched and unclenched his fist - 'will you stop going on about that fucking competition.'

The room was silent.

'Jesus.' He poured himself a glass of wine and went out the front door. After a moment they saw him in the dark outside. He sat at the garden table. They saw a match being struck, and then the red point of a lit cigarette.

'What did I say?'

'He had some bad news today,' said Peter. 'I think he's a bit down.'

'I think he's been drinking,' said Kath.

'Er, are we going to do this game?' said Ben.

*

After a quarter of an hour, Peter refilled his glass and went out into the darkness outside. He sat down on a garden chair and gazed up at the sky. He could discern a dull cover of white cloud sweeping across.

The door opened behind him. Shelley found a seat next to Art and put a hand on his shoulder.

'Hey Art,' she said. 'Got a spare ciggy?'

Peter saw him fumbling with a packet of Marlboros and then a box of matches. 'Didn't know you smoked,' he said.

'Oops.' She lit up and inhaled sharply. 'Don't tell.'

He snorted.

'Hey, don't worry about that stupid *Writers Launchpad* crap. You did better than me.' She gripped his arm. 'I got dumped at the first round.'

He snorted again. After a few seconds he said, 'I better apologise to Virginia.'

'Tomorrow'll be fine. She's gone to bed anyway.'

'If you fancy it,' Peter broke in, 'we're doing this game tomorrow. Only if you fancy it.'

A car passed along the road in front of the house. They waited for it to go by and for the sound of its engine to fade.

'What's the idea?'

'Remember the café? You write five hundred words of the novel of the person who was sitting to your right.' He tried to see the reaction on his face, but Art was turned away from the kitchen light. 'I've got Shelley.'

'I think Kath's got you,' she said.

'Should be fun,' said Peter.

Art took a puff. His cigarette was dead. 'Yeah. Should be fun.' He got up, ground it into the grass, and walked back to the house. 'See you tomorrow,' he said.

Shelley said, 'Take care, Art.'

Peter and Shelley walked for a while. They strolled past the six other houses that constituted the hamlet.

'Hmm,' she whispered. 'I'm a bit light-headed.'

It was a moment before he realised she was referring to the cigarette.

'It's a while since I had one of those.'

Apart from her voice there was silence. In the sky above, the edge of the moving cloud was punctured by the moonlight.

'Early to bed,' said Shelley. None of the other houses had lights on.

'Early risers.'

'Like where I grew up.'

'Melbourne?'

'Before that. Out in the Northern Territory.'

'Don't even know where that is.'

'Typical pom.'

'Tell me about the place.'

And she did. Just a little. Though the land she took him to was grim.

Closed communities scattered across the plains. Men absent for months as they followed the work. Women engaged in a low-intensity war against them when they returned.

'I knew men like Art,' she said. 'Out there the boozing ends in violence.'

'Art's not like that,' said Peter.

'No,' she said. 'But there is that same ... that sense of failure as guys get past middle-age. I saw it in my dad's mates.'

He longed to see her face at that moment, but she stood in shadow.

'Art's wife is dead, isn't she?' she said.

'Have you met his daughter?'

Shelley chuckled. '*The devil wears ...*'

'It's not *Prada*.'

'...body armour.'

'I hope he finishes his book,' said Peter. 'I really do.'

She seemed to consider this for a while. 'You know, I'm glad he blew up this evening.'

'Glad?'

She had stopped walking, and Peter paused as well. By the outline of her hair he was aware that she had turned to face him. 'It was just getting a bit ... cosy.' She started to walk again. 'I mean, writing can't be cosy.' She touched him on the arm. 'Can it?'

The Game.

Kath was pretty good about getting up in the morning. Certainly, on the basis of the holiday so far, better than Lucy who struggled, especially if she had had a few glasses of wine.

Perhaps it was Kath's upbringing, the drilling into her by her mother and her brothers that an hour slept through was an hour wasted. So she made sure she was first to use the downstairs bathroom the next morning, before Ben and Peter had bagged it, though she did get caught by Ben in her bath towel as he emerged from his room. She wondered whether Lucy's instincts about him were right. She was usually spot on with men. Unlike Kath.

Back in her room she dressed and tidied up her sheet and duvet - spread out as they were on one of the sofas.

'Hey Luce -' she opened the curtains a fraction. There was a groan from the settee on the other side of the room '- it's a beautiful day.'

She left her friend to her slumbers, picked up her phone, and went into the breakfast room. There was no one there. She poured herself a glass of orange juice and checked her texts. She frowned. Nothing from Raúl.

He had decided not to come to France well before their last meeting, citing requirements of work. In fact, his work was all cash-in-hand and, it seemed to her, entirely outside any prescriptions of schedule. She had a fear that his change of heart was due to something different, a cooling in his attitude to the group. This was not helped by his reading the week before. The truth was, the occasion had been embarrassing. She knew the others well enough to know that their positive comments afterwards had been for reasons of politeness only.

'Hey.'

Ben walked in from the corridor.

'Hey.'

He immediately began to load up the espresso machine.

'Ben, are we playing your game today?'

'Yep. As far as I'm aware.'

'I've got Art.'

'Lucky you.'

'Don't be mean.'

In fact, the more Kath had thought about it, the more she thought the game was a pretty good idea. She would have to write something in the voice of a person of a different sex, from a different age group, and in a style which she sometimes did not enjoy.

They had laid down a few ground rules the previous evening. Each of them would have to provide an alternative title and five hundred words of prose. The segment would have to pick up from some episode that had been circulated to the group in previous emails. No new characters, though this rule could be bent. They would read out each other's offerings at the evening meal. (Virginia would be cooking.)

'So how do I imagine myself as an old curmudgeon?' she said.

'I don't know,' said Ben. 'That's the point. To find out.'

She wondered how her brothers would react if they could see her now - trying to picture herself as a loser - something she often wondered when she needed to measure herself up to a difficult task. She imagined the hint of a sneer on the lips of Herb, who managed x squadrillions of funds in the City; or Max, who at this moment was arse-wiping - as he put it - a bunch of squaddies as they learnt how to extract the pin from a grenade without blowing themselves up; or Ed, currently brainstorming in Silicon Somewhere in the American MidWest.

No. She corrected herself. They would never mock. They were too bloody well good-mannered.

'Any thoughts on a title?' she said. 'I suppose I need to come up with one.'

'What's Art's current title?' said Ben.

'Don't know. You know -' in her mind she went through all the members of the group '- none of us have one. None of us have figured out a title for our books.'

'What about Peter?'

'Apart from him. No one. Isn't that weird?'

'Titles are hard.'

'Wouldn't know. Never tried.'

'Well I've got one.'

'You kept that quiet. What is it?'

Ben turned to her. 'Promise you won't laugh?'

'Why should I?'
'*The Grift.*'
Kath said nothing.
'You are laughing,' said Ben.
'No I'm not. It's just …'
'What?'
'What's a grift?'
'Kath.'
'You'll hardly attract readers if they don't understand the title.'
'Well, you just have to read the damn thing then.'

*

Virginia had half-hoped that Ben's game would have been forgotten by the morning. But listening to the group over breakfast she knew her hopes were misplaced. At the table there was a certain excitement about the exercise, in the same way that there had been in the early days of the creative writing course on which they had first met.

Describe your hero's living room. Describe a happy memory; a painful memory; an accident observed by two people; why your worst enemy hates you.

It was the flexing of the muscles of the imagination. And - to extend the analogy - the hesitation she felt, setting aside any fear of the tedium, was that of the person contemplating a return to the gym after long absence. The sinews had gone soft.

Her doubts were compounded by the fact that, of the other writers in the group, she had drawn Ben, and there was a casual quality to the violence in his prose that she found a little distasteful.

After breakfast she was able to put off the hard work by spending an hour doing some weeding in the front yard, and, sunhatted, trowel in hand, this gentle and therapeutic physical labour gradually worked off her irresolution. She was touched, furthermore, when Art approached her - he had been absent from the breakfast table - and, with something of the same arthritic difficulty she had had, lowered himself onto one knee and then the other with, it seemed, the purpose of accounting for his behaviour.

'Look, last night. Really sorry.'

At least he was not proposing. She looked at him, breathed in, and said, 'Art. Please. Don't worry about it.'

'I was way out of order.'

'I understand you had some … distressing news.'

'Some old mate. Gone to the great gig in the sky. Hey. It happens. At our age.'

She touched him on the arm. 'I'm so sorry.'

He smiled briefly, and then attempted to rise. He placed a hand on the garden fence to stop himself toppling. 'Blimey. Can't get up.'

Virginia steadied him. 'Here, let me help you.'

At eleven, she put away her garden tools, prepared a cup of tea, and went up the stairs to her bedroom. She sat in front of her computer and looked through the various submissions that Ben had made to the group. As she skimmed through she wondered whether her further suspicion that his fiction had a trace of misogyny was justified. The women, if they were not ignored, were victims. She struggled even to find any trace of female love interest.

She had heard somewhere that the Jack Reacher thrillers - she had never read one - were popular amongst women readers. Something to do with the strong, silent type who would protect the girls from the bad guys, and who would never, absolutely never, ask them to iron his collars. She drummed her fingers on the table and found her attention caught by a book she had brought from London. *The Annotated Letters of T S Eliot*. She picked it up, glanced at the pages she had read the previous night, then put it down with a moment's irritation.

Jack Reacher. She had never read one. Perhaps she should.

She returned to one of Ben's submissions. A woman is tied down on a chair in the middle of the room. She is about to be murdered by two assassins. She has no backstory. She has not even been given a name. *My poor dear,* Virginia thought. *Who are you?*

She typed in a name, *Mary Lou*. Polish? Italian? Irish. *Mary Louise O'Connor*. Born New York. No, Ireland, but family emigrates when she is two. Harlem. Or is that suburb African American? Boston.

Father alcoholic. Mother worn out by childrearing. Education sketchy, nuns spiteful and cruel. Leaves home for LA. Waitresses, works as minor actress. Porn? No, she still has some dignity. And then falls absolutely head-over. He looks like Paul Newman, circa 1969. It's his beautiful blue eyes. But Brad's in trouble with the loansharks.

She'll do anything for the schmuck. After hours she empties the till where she works.

Why, Mary Lou? And Virginia felt moved to tears for her Everywoman. *What led you to this, my poor dear?*

She began to write.

*

'Hiya,' said Shelley. 'What's for lunch?'

'Smelly cheese, Savoie ham, fresh bread …' said Virginia.

'The regular prison diet,' said Art.

'Poor us,' said Peter.

Shelley caught his eye and felt for a moment an almost painful desire to find out how he was getting on with her story, but decided, for now, to let him just get on with it. She had been a bit wary the previous evening about the whole exercise, and was relieved it was Peter doing her book. She might have been less keen if one or two of the others were peering behind the mask of her Jem.

She sat down next to Lucy. 'How's it going with The Game?'

'Like - slowly. Who've you got?'

Shelley looked across the table. 'Kath, I've got you.'

'Poor you.'

'I'm enjoying it.' She reached across the table, picked up a bowl of green salad, and ladled a portion on to her plate. 'Try the vinaigrette,' said Ben, blowing out through his mouth. She spooned a single drop over the lettuce leaves. 'Kath, I heard your Gran helped you with the historical stuff.'

Kath did not reply. She looked back at Shelley and said instead, 'You ever been to Balham tube station?'

Shelley shrugged. 'May have done. Why?'

'I used to work down there. If you look very, very carefully, there's a plaque on the wall. I bet not one commuter in a hundred sees it.'

'What's it for?'

'It's …' But Kath decided to leave it at that. 'Check it out on Wiki. You'll see what I mean.'

'You're being very mysterious,' said Lucy.

'I know what it is,' said Virginia.

'Check it out,' said Kath. 'Seriously. You'll see. It's ...' she reached across and grabbed the cheese platter '... like there's so much there under our noses.'

When Shelley returned to her room and googled, she had it straight away.

On October 14th 1940 an armour-piercing bomb fell on the road by the station. The rail tunnel collapsed. Other sections were flooded. Sixty-four people sheltering from the raid were killed. Sixty-four. One bomb.

She re-read Kath's piece. Women and children counting the seconds till oblivion.

The trouble was, basing one's fiction too closely on historical events made it sometimes seem contrived. As their course tutor once said, the truth makes bad fiction.

And there was another problem, especially if it was your own history. Sometimes it gave too much of the game away. But that was a question for another time.

She returned to Kath's story and wondered what her take might be.

At least a few titles came to mind. She toyed with a date.

'*October 13th, 1940.*'

*

Ben had suggested The Game in the first place and persuaded everyone that it would be fun.

But by bad luck he had drawn Lucy, whose work he could not stand.

He looked at the pieces she had circulated and wondered what, if anything, he could say about the dreary Zadie Eisenberg and Lucy's drearier heroine. The thing was he liked Lucy. He and Lucy and Kath had met one evening in the queue for Fabric. They were with their own crowds but the three of them had sneaked off for a quick one at a pub nearby. The craic was good, the girls were fun, Raúl looked moody and magnificent. They would do a repeat one day.

He just hated her prose.

And Shelley. It had been a bit uncool arguing with her when they discussed Lucy's piece a month or two back. But sometimes Shelley played up a bit too much to that old antipodean riff. The old cultural chip on the shoulder. And that sixties hairstyle was just …

He stared at his screen. *Boring, boring*, he muttered. He began to type, 'All work and no play makes Jack a dull boy.'

It had grown cooler. The afternoon shadow was shifting across the garden table where he worked. And he needed five hundred words … He typed.

All work and no play makes Jack a dull boy.
All work and no play makes Jack a dull boy.
All work and no play makes Jack a dull boy.
All work and no play makes Jack a dull boy.
All work and no play makes Jack a dull boy.
All work and no play makes Jack a dull boy.
All work and no play makes Jack a dull boy.
…

*

Lucy thought, *Why am I here?*

She skimmed through the chapters of Peter's book which she had on her laptop, and knew that the trouble she was having went right to the root of why she had been uneasy about coming on this holiday.

'I'm just an Essex girl', she whispered to herself.

'What's that?' said Art. He had come into the kitchen, where Lucy liked to work, for his afternoon tea.

'Just muttering.'

This stuff that Pete was into, based apparently on his own family history, was just a bit too highfalutin for her. Some girl had arrived from somewhere hot to get married in somewhere cold. And it was all impressions and emotions, tensions and guilt trips.

AND NOTHING HAPPENS.

She wondered what Aunt Christina would say to her now. 'Kid, you gotta stick at it.' No doubt. She pulled up her aunt's Facebook page. Christina Bungay. There she was, in your face, bleached blonde hair cut short. In one picture she smoked a cigarillo. Lucy wondered whether to send a message. 'Please help …'

Aunt Christina - in reality a neighbour and family friend since before Lucy was born - was actually the person who had inspired Lucy to try her hand at this writing game. Her website said she had sold 25 million books in eleven languages. Lucy tried to imagine it. If she made just fifty pence per book, that was ... well, still a fair bit of dosh. Most were about Charlotte 'Charlie' Beretta who, despite the male chauvinist bozos in the force, was still in charge of an elite murder squad at the Yard. You don't pick up one of her books, they grab *you*, by the throat, and don't let go until the scumbag who crossed our Charlie has been spat out and strung up by the goolies, usually on the very last page.

Even Lucy's Dad played her audiobooks in the car. Her Dad, who left school at fourteen and said not knowing how to read never stopped him making his fortune in the building trade.

Even Lucy's Mum, who said Christina was the only *nice lesbian* she had ever met.

Why can't I write like her? she thought, *Why do keep on getting stuck on the girlie stuff?*

'Help me Christina.'

'What's that?'

'Nothing, Art.'

She took a section of Peter's prose and copied it to a new file. It read :

Once or twice he found himself surreptitiously examining these men, trying to find out what it was they had and he didn't, what quality it could be about them that those glossy and exciting women found so desirable. As if it were possible to break down and quantify this thing, and then, with this knowledge, rebuild himself, a touch here, a tweak there, a firmer stomach, a touch of hair gel, a new shine on his shoes. Refashioning. But this was predicated on time. On limitless time and opportunity. Time to try once, and then again. And if this failed, once more. But the past and the future had flipped, and if once he had measured and staked out the past, and slotted the fragments of his personal history cleanly into each of his years, and if his future had the delicious uncertainty and open-endedness of a child's summer holiday, it was now his future which was roadmapped and timetabled, while his past had become increasingly opaque.

She wondered how Christina would handle this, and it came to her that of course she wouldn't. She'd junk it straight away. Lucy could almost hear her voice, 'Jeez, here's someone who'll never use one syllable when four will do.'

She began to write.

Sometimes he checked out these other guys. Did the chicks really go for them? If so, was it the pecs? The number one crewcut? The winkle-pickers?

Truth was, he didn't give a fuck.

There was a word that some of her mother's friends whispered to each other as they lunched together after the gym - what was it?

'Liposuction,' Lucy said out loud.

'What's that?'

*

Art felt he owed it to Virginia to treat her work with respect, even if the world it depicted was very different from his own and from any other he could imagine. He had been rude to her enough times, usually when he had a hangover and felt rotten. He wanted to make clear that it was not her writing. And yet as he looked at the stuff of hers which he had on his computer he knew he'd been given a tough call.

He re-read a story, *Friends of the Royal Opera*, in which an older woman running a charity takes on an intern from a sponsoring bank. The woman finds out that her young assistant is dating an older man. Gradually she begins to suspect it's her ex-husband.

There was a section where a group of women at a wine bar list the reasons they like the male sex.

Men were witty.

Men were good-mannered. They were bad-mannered. They had influence and power. (Yes, the girls had to admit, the exercise of power was alluring.) Men were practical. It was not that they could fix cars, it was that they knew someone who could. They made decisions in different ways. They thought the unimportant was essential, the important trivial. ...

If you asked blokes in a pub why they liked women they'd probably answer in two words. One of which might be 'Big'.

He speculated that it was impossible for a man to write from a woman's point of view. He had been watching *Question Time* on TV at his daughter's.

'She's wearing the same outfit,' Rosa remarked about a politician on the show.

'What?'

'She was wearing exactly the same thing at PMQs the other day.'

'So?

'So.'

What was amazing was that she had noticed. As if it mattered whether Ed Miliband wore the same suit two days in a row.

Art sighed. He did not want to seem rude. He'd be damned if he did not produce something that afternoon. He decided he needed a role model. More than that, someone from whom he could, well, filch. Old enough so that they were out of copyright. Not so old that the style was out of date. He began to google. Muriel Spark, Virginia Woolf, Katherine Mansfield …

Katherine Mansfield.

He located a website with her short stories, copied the text from three of these into three word files. He then opened a new document.

Brilliant things these computers, he thought. *Whoever came up with cut-and-paste? Genius.*

*

'Supper ready at seven.'

Virginia called out again. 'Everyone?'

It was getting late, and Peter had to wrap up the piece he had sketched out.

He would not have described himself as a believer in fate, but the fact that the previous evening he had drawn Shelley suggested that any hypothesised gods were smiling on him. He was fascinated by her writing. It gave clues to the enigma of her background either through similarity or contrast. And it was a particular quality of her spiky heroine Jem, which someone in the group characterised as *damaged*, that intrigued him most.

He was charmed by the faux-naïf style of the prose, something which some professional writers tried and failed to achieve. This was what he sought to emulate in his five hundred words.

He had focused on one particular aspect of the girl's household, the *men* that her mother entertained. That she was borderline on-the-game - could one be borderline? or was it, like being pregnant, a case of 'you are or are not'? - added a sinister element. Peter had written a section in which a procession of beery and unshaven men, in town for the seasonal farmwork, are received during the course of an afternoon.

But reading the piece back he felt faintly disturbed by it. Shelley brought a calming influence to the group. Yet that surface of serenity - he suspected, he feared - covered a brittle core which was yet to be tested, at least when he had been around. That it might be one day evoked a protectiveness in him. He wanted to be there when it happened. A worry began to take shape that anyone reading his piece might infer less about what he thought of Shelley's writing and more about what he thought of her.

A further problem was that he had no idea whether Shelley actually wanted to take her story in this direction. That he had forced it there left it - and him - looking slightly soiled.

'Damn.' Peter often spoke quietly to himself as he wrote. He swore once more, and let his finger brush the delete key.

But to erase the file, to turn up with nothing, would be equally insulting. To the Group and to her. It would be saying he could not be bothered.

'What should I do?' he whispered.

'How's it going?' A female voice behind him. He slammed the lid of his laptop shut. 'Oops,' she said. 'Not that bad I hope.'

He had not turned round but he knew it was her.

'Am I interrupting?'

He twisted and faced her. 'You surprised me.'

'You weren't checking your favourite porn site?' She giggled.

He did not know quite how to respond. Eventually he said, 'Just finishing up. You know I drew you yesterday?'

'I do. Of course.' She walked over to his side. 'Can I have a peek?'

He stared at her, mouth open. 'Well, ...'

There was no escape.

*

They only got as far as the titles.

They had dined on Virginia's roast chicken, which, though excellent, had taken two hours longer to cook than planned, and they were all fairly drunk by the time they ate.

'So,' said Ben as they cleared the plates. 'The Game?'

Kath: '*La Vieja Cabra*', by Arthur Redknapp.
    ['What does it mean?'
       'Oh Art, you old goat …']
Virginia: '*We need to talk about Mary Lou*,' by Ben Jacobs.
    ['Second choice,' said Virginia. '*Worth Dying For.*'
      'Why?'
      'Google it.']
Shelley: '*The Last Day,*' by Kath Kenton-Jones
    ['The last day of what?'
      'Just … *The Very Last Day.*'   ]
Ben: '*Here's Johnny*,' by Lucy Boland
    ['Sorry, Lucy, it's a bit cruel.']
Lucy: '*How to do Lipo*' by Peter Pindar
    ['Sorry, Peter, this is crueller.']
Art: '*Men are from Pluto, Women are from the planet Earth (probably),*'
        by Virginia McCorquindale
Peter: '*A Profound Work of Staggering and Extraordinary Complexity and Beauty*,' by Shelley Banks.

'Hmm,' said Ben. 'We're not very original.'

"I can always tell the ones who are doing it for real. It's that quality of single-mindedness."
Creative Writing tutor.

Harriet was already exhausted when she cleared arrivals in Bergerac at two in the afternoon the next day. She had done three hours at the office in London, arriving at six to clear up loose ends, and had then caught the train, travelling for once against the tide of commuters to get to Stansted airport for her flight.

She was mildly elated, perhaps because of the light-headedness brought on by her lack of sleep, but also a touch miffed that the fun and frolics had been going on without her. Ben had sent an email describing The Game. They could have waited until today.

'Hey.'

Still. She had got through to the next round of *The Writers' Launchpad* competition - more than could be said for most of the others.

'Hey. Harriet.'

She looked up. It was Peter. Right in front of her. She stared at him for a few moments. 'Sorry. I'm in a dream.' He had of course arranged to meet her.

'No problem. Here, I'll take that.' He led her to the car and loaded up her bags. 'How was the flight?'

But as they drove out of the airport and headed eastward she was more interested in prodding Peter to explain how everyone was getting on. She needed to know that the location was as idyllic as she had hoped, that their days were as productive as the seclusion should have guaranteed, and that the regime was not quite as monastic as had been initially threatened. Peter's replies were to the point. 'Yes.', 'Well...' and 'No.'

'I'm targeting ten thousand words by the time I return,' she said.

'That's ambitious.'

Harriet was not going to bother justifying her aim. It seemed to her there was little point in the break unless she came home with something. But as they moved on to a side road which followed the meandering route of the river, as the conversation slowed and Harriet began to take in the density of the greens on the riverbank, the languid flight of the ducks over the surface of the water, she felt her resolve loosening.

They pulled up to find Ben working outside on his tablet, Virginia weeding by the stone wall, and Kath and Lucy in sunglasses stretched out on the grass.

'A hive of activity,' Peter remarked. He touched the horn lightly. There was a chorus of greetings.

It was decided, while Harriet sat at the kitchen table with a mug of tea, that there would be some swapping of rooms. She would have Ben's, Ben insisting he could comfortably make do in the living room. Art swapped with Peter as he had sprained a muscle and getting upstairs was becoming difficult.

True to her word she disappeared straight away to get started on the writing.

'Head out for supper at eight?' Virginia suggested. 'There's a *gargote* I think we should try.'

'Gargote?'

'Greasy spoon,' said Harriet who once set herself to read Zola in French.

'The place is actually considerably better than that,' said Virginia. 'But still easy on the budget.'

'As long as there's wine,' said Art.

Le Bistro du Coin was indeed more than a greasy spoon, and there was wine. Harriet and Virginia discussed the next phase of *The Writers' Launchpad* competition. It seemed that it was being thrown open to the public in the next round. The entries would be available on the website, and readers would be invited to comment online. Their postings would contribute to the judges' selection of the finallists.

'I'm so nervous,' said Virginia. 'Just imagine. The general public reading my material.'

'The hoi polloi.'

'I'm relishing it,' said Harriet. 'It'll be great to get outside our little glass bubble.'

'So. Glad you came?' Shelley asked her.

'Hmm.' Harriet stretched and leaned back. 'Ask me Sunday.'

"... man wants two things: danger and play. For that reason he wants woman ..."

Nietzsche

There had been some discussion at the bistro about taking a day out to do some sightseeing.

'Not me,' said Harriet. 'I've just arrived.'

'I'm happy to stay home …' said Virginia. '… and *cultiver mon jardin* …'

'Ha ha.'

' … but I can suggest a few places for the rest of you.'

At breakfast the following morning two camps began to emerge. Peter favoured the prehistoric cave paintings at Lascaux. Ben, Kath and Lucy wanted to look round the town of Bordeaux. Art was still in bed.

'Caves sound good to me,' said Shelley.

'Lascaux's closed,' said Virginia. 'But there are others. Here, I have a local guide book somewhere.'

The five of them left soon after ten. Peter drove to the nearest station where he dropped off Ben and Kath and Lucy.

'Any of you know any French?' he shouted as they climbed the steps to the ticket office.

'We'll manage,' Kath shouted back.

'Just take the train heading west.'

'Doh.'

Shelley climbed into the front passenger seat as Peter started up the ignition. 'Well, it's just the two of us now,' he said as he eased into gear.

'I'll map read.'

The weather had clouded over in the morning. For the first time since they had arrived in France there were a few drops of rain. But if he understood the French brochure correctly they would be underground most of the time. Of more interest to him was his company for the day.

'Warm enough?' he said looking across to Shelley. She had a chunky cream jumper, black scarf double wrapped at her neck, black jeans. And lime green plimsolls.

'Watch where you're going,' she said, catching his glance. He did not tell her he found it a constant delight to check out her clothes.

'So is my novel a work of staggering genius?' she said.

'Perhaps I was referring to the bit that I wrote.'

'I see.'

'Joking. Anyway, I couldn't have written it without your bits as inspiration.'

'My *bits*? Hmm. Not sure how to take that.'

Peter frowned. His language had been clunky. After a minute he said, 'That was silly. Truth is …' he glanced at her once more. She had put on her sunglasses and was staring at the road ahead. '…I almost deleted everything I had written. I didn't much like it. My *bit*, that is.' She said nothing. He tried to explain. To row back. 'The thing is, I felt a bit uneasy about treading on your toes. I wasn't sure whether it was a direction you wanted your story to take.' He wondered how far he should go with this. Whether he should touch upon what had troubled him earlier, the suspicion that the story inadvertently, or even deliberately, revealed something about her. 'I guess what I'm trying to say is, for those in the group - for every first novelist - there's a lot of *us* in the stuff we write. In your case a lot of *you*. And that's what I was trying to pin down.'

Traffic slowed as the rain increased in strength. 'There's a right turn coming up,' she said. 'Next roundabout.'

He tried to see round the line of cars ahead. He had read, depressingly, that the French were becoming as obsessed with speed cameras as the British. Perhaps that was why the traffic was moving so slowly. He wondered whether it was possible to overtake the vehicle in front.

'Do we ever get beyond it?' said Shelley.

'Beyond what?'

'What you said. Writing about ourselves.'

'Well …' he decided against any heroics on the road '… I remember at university when we talked of the great writers we used phrases like *rendering the specific into the general, unearthing the universal in the routine of the ordinary. Assimilation. Sublimation.* That kind of stuff.'

'The great writers? Like who?'

'Well - if you fancy them - in the modern era - Updike. Roth. They work on a small canvas, New England sexual mores or Jewish Manhattan streetsmart. They construct a ... a ...'

'A what?'

'Well, to use the bullshit, an allegory of modern life. That is, of course, if you're persuaded by those two writers. Which I'm not specially, by the way.'

'You sure as hell won't get a job on the *New York Times*,' she said. 'So why not?'

'Roth - oh - misogynist and repetitive. Updike - early work, too purple. Later work, too obsessed with sex.' *And just why did I say all that?* he wondered. *And what was all this nit-picking?* The 'purple' jibe was a criticism they made of his own prose. 'How to make sex boring - read Updike.' He swallowed, and swallowed again. He just couldn't keep his mouth shut.

'I see. That's two literary giants out the window then. So who are you persuaded by?'

'Who?' There was a defensiveness in his chuckle. 'Do you know, some of us who did that EngLit course didn't pick up a book for ages afterwards. We all had a bad reaction against serious literature.'

'Is that why you went into IT?'

He paused before answering. 'That was why I took the creative writing course last year. To try and rediscover my passion for it. Trouble is, I've missed the boat. The book as an art form will be dead in ten years' time.'

'You didn't answer me.'

'Answer what?'

'Who are you persuaded by?'

Peter slowed as they approached the roundabout. 'This is the one,' Shelley whispered. 'There's a sign.'

Peter said, 'Anyone who can tell a good story in under three hundred pages.'

Shelley laughed. 'That settles it for Proust and the rest of the French greats, I suppose. And just about all the Russians.'

'And most nineteenth century authors. People don't have the attention span these days.'

'I saw those Hilary Mantel doorstoppers Harriet had in her case.'

'Historical fiction. Different ballgame. Dan Brown with pretensions.'

'So that's her out the way as well, then.'

Peter was silent. He tightened his grip on the wheel. The affected flippancy of his tone was becoming just slightly nauseating.

'Well I'm tempted by her,' said Shelley. 'But then I never had the luxury of your kind of education.'

'What kind was yours?'

'Encouraging kids to read was not high on the priority list.'

Again he said nothing. He suspected - he knew, she had said so - he sometimes came over as just another pom. There was a patrician arrogance in his effortless assumption - and then the casual junking - of something as precious as literary sophistication.

'Don't worry,' said Shelley, answering an earlier question. 'I'm not Jem.' Then she corrected herself. 'Except insofar as we all are. Every teenage girl.'

'Ha ha. The universal from the quotidian.' He thought, *Did I really say that?*

'Is that a famous quote?'

The compliment, intended to repair his blundering tactlessness, had just compounded it. 'Perhaps it means, Shelley, you're the real thing. A genuine writer.' *Perhaps it means, Shelley, I should turn back now.*

They saw a sign for a place called *Les Combarelles*. 'That's us,' said Shelley.

As they got closer there were further signposts for *Les Grottes* which eventually directed them off the road onto a stone track leading up a rocky hillside covered in thick vegetation. The grey of the trail and boulders above them was reflected in the thickening cloud cover. Peter pulled up outside a small wooden office. The door was locked. There was a notice indicating that the next tour started at two-thirty. They had forty-five minutes to get some lunch. Retracing their route back into the nearest town they found a roadstop where they had soup and bread, mineral water and coffee. They were five minutes late buying their tickets. '*Vite. L'entrée est sur la colline,*' the woman at the hut said. '*Aie. J'aime les chaussures,*' she shouted after them.

'What's that?' said Shelley.

'Your shoes. She's a fan.'

They trotted up the slope and met a party of a half-a-dozen tourists, three elderly couples in sensible waterproofs, waiting by a cave in the rock face. Their guide, a studious looking man with straggly hair and beard, led them through an iron gate and inside. '*On verra ici …*' he began, but Peter's French was not sufficiently fluent to allow him to follow without concentrating. He let his attention lapse and breathed in the dank atmosphere. The others in the group, apparently knowledgeable about the caves' history, conversed with the guide in low voices. Peter and Shelley followed at a slight distance.

The entrance was wide and high, but began to narrow as they walked further in. There was a trail of low-power lightbulbs strung up on cables attached to the rock at shoulder height. The guide had a torch but he warned them that they could not use their own or take pictures.

'Where're the paintings?' Shelley whispered.

'Hang on. We're not there yet.'

They walked for five minutes and the group became single file as the walls and the ceiling closed in. The air cooled and from time to time they had to duck. The guide waited with his flashlight, warning them where they might bang their heads against the overhanging rock.

'Peter.'

The group pressed on.

A hiss. 'Peter. Wait.' He turned and walked back. Shelley was breathing heavily. 'Sometimes I …' She touched his arm. '…closed spaces ... claustro …' She swallowed. The flashlight ahead flickered back over them. '*Y a-t-il un problème?*' She clutched at him and gulped air. Her eyes were closed. Slowly her breathing steadied. After a while he saw her open her eyes and nod. '*Nous venons*,' he called out. They turned and edged forward. The guide waited until they had caught up. '*OK?*' Shelley still had his arm. '*Oui*,' Peter said. The guide studied them for a moment and then turned. The passage twisted to the left and to the right. Conversation ceased. The silence became absolute, broken only by their footsteps and the rustle of their clothing as they pushed further into the hillside.

The guide stopped. He waited as the eight of them pressed around him. He shone his light against the wall of rock at the side. There was nothing to see. In his other hand he had a short pointing stick such as Peter's colleagues might have used in a PowerPoint presentation, and he used it to trace an outline, taking extreme care to avoid even brushing the surface of the rock. '*Ici,*' he said softly. '*Le bison. La tête et ... le corps.*' There were murmurs of recognition amongst their French companions, but Peter still saw nothing. And then as with the random shapes of clouds or inkblots, or those Rorschach tests which had once been fashionable, it came to him. There it was, the shape of a solitary animal. Why had he not seen it before? He looked briefly at Shelley. She stared open-mouthed, childlike. Her panic forgotten, Peter thought, as a child's nightmare is forgotten with the morning. After a while the guide led them forward a few yards. Once again his flashlight and then his pointing stick danced against the shadowed surface of the rock, and once again Peter's imagination required their prompting before the shapes emerged from the stone. '*Le manmouth en face ... deux chevaux.*'

The guide began to talk at length, to explain the background of the people who created these things, and this time Peter focused on the story he told, one of hunter-gatherers spreading into Europe, living a precarious life on the edge of a retreating ice age, retreating themselves into caves like this for ... what? For safety, the guide said. And Peter wondered whether it was as a refuge from the harshness of the earth and the rain and snow, though it was hard to imagine that this cold, fearful place could be more congenial than the world outside. Or from the hostility of the land's predators, which, he saw now, included cave lions, bears, mammoths. Or was it the solitude they sought, the chance to free the imagination from the tyranny of the senses and let it wander. '*Figures féminines.*' Arms, thighs, breasts, Picassoesque in their intimation of the sensuous in two or three curves. Who did they envisage might see these images, this staccato narrative of their lives? Others like them? Or their gods? Or men like Peter, godlike in the capabilities, though not in their frailties. Perhaps it did not matter. Perhaps it mattered only that they recorded what they saw and felt and could know that this record might, just might, transcend the impermanence of the flesh which circumscribed their fragile lives.

Shelley had released his arm, and he saw that she was standing up close to one of the French couples and talking softly with them. In their accented English he made out a few phrases. *Pre-history. Dawn of time.* But the details seemed to him of less interest than the record itself. As if a record of humanity deposited in some time capsule in deep space would be any the less important were it never deciphered by hypothetical starmen. Its significance would be simply that it existed.

The transition back to daylight was jarring, even though it was gradual and the sunlight outside was still weak under the cloud. They stood blinking and rubbing their eyes. As he adjusted to the glare Peter sought out the guide and thanked him. For a moment he wondered whether to offer a tip but he imagined the curt refusal - *Monsieur, ce n'est pas Disneyland.*

Shelley stood with the French couple either side of her. They had claimed her for their own. She called him over.

'Peter, I want you to meet Bart .. Bart ...'

'Bartolomé.'

'And Francoise.'

The quick movement of her eyes still hinted at the earlier panic. 'Excuse me,' she said rather too obviously. 'I need to find the ... '

'*Toilettes?*' the woman suggested. Shelley gave her her broadest smile, turned and headed down the hill to the office. Peter watched her as she reached into her bag and put on her sunglasses.

'You are artists yourselves?' the man said.

'Artists?' said Peter.

'Writers.' His wife corrected him.

'Shelley exaggerates,' said Peter. She had an unEnglish lack of self-deprecation. And, it came to him, an easy empathy for strangers which his own countrymen often lacked.

'Such a charming young lady,' the woman said. 'Australian? I hope she is feeling better.'

'Did you enjoy the caves?' the man said. 'Thirteen thousand years old. Before the pyramids.'

'And all this history, here, in our own dear France.'

'The first pornography,' the man said.

'Oh, *tu es ridicule*,' his wife scolded.

The man winked at Peter. He said nothing. He rather agreed with the man's wife.

In the car he studied the map. He looked up as Shelley climbed in. 'Feeling better?' She ignored his question.

'That couple recommended a historical town not far from here. If I can remember the name ...' She leaned across to look at the map. 'Starts with an S ... Here. Sarlat.'

They got back on the road and headed further east. For five minutes the rain picked up but then lessened. Peter talked. 'Mammoths. I thought they only existed in Siberia.' 'Did you hear what that French couple were saying?' 'I never knew the difference between Neanderthal and Cro Magnon.' But after a while, her silence prevailing, he focused his attention on the road. Half-an-hour later they entered the drab outer suburbs. They slowed as modern brick gave way to older grey stone. They parked as soon as they passed through the perimeter wall which was marked out by the twin towers of a rampart. They found themselves walking a street lined with shops selling local artefacts and expensive chocolates. To the side were stepped and winding alleyways too narrow for cars. They left the road and climbed slowly, stopping as they pleased to examine a church entrance or a memorial, and came eventually into a wide square with a cathedral. Lighter, beige stonework. Turreted buildings tight packed. Either side of the church were cafés with outside tables and uniformed waiters ghosting between them. They sat under an umbrella and ordered coffee and cakes. A film of rain lay over their clothes. From the absence of English at the tables he guessed the customers were local. Overtaken by an image from a *Nouvelle Vague* film fashionable when he was a student - its name escaped him - Peter found himself thinking how he and Shelley might be seen by the other patrons. Sophisticates escaping their Parisian lives? Unfaithful husband - or wife - on a tryst? A stillness settled over him as he allowed himself to wallow in the fantasy. He tried to preserve the silence, to maintain the pretence before their Anglo accents gave the game away.

The illusion dissolved.

'Thank you,' Shelley said as her coffee was laid in front of her.

Peter looked away and smiled.

Shelley took off her glasses. 'What's the joke?' she said.

'Alain Delon and Catherine Deneuve.'

She seemed to pick up on it. 'Jean Seberg. I used to have my hair like her.'

Peter tried to visualize the look. The image was subtly intoxicating. 'So we'll discuss Sartre and I'll whisk you off in my open-top into the sunset.'

'To our deaths?'

'Not that bit.'

She cut off a piece of cake and placed it in her mouth. She watched him as she chewed. His gaze flickered down to her lips. He had noticed some of the men at the other tables staring quite openly as Shelley sat down. The smugness he felt at this was something he enjoyed with a guilt that was quite exquisite. He pointed at his own lower lip and handed her a serviette. 'I'm just a kid,' she said softly as she dabbed her mouth.

They finished and paid up, and as they moved away he felt compelled, in some show of ownership to the leering men at their backs, to retain a close proximity to Shelley as they walked, to demonstrate a physical contact, however slight, whether by the brushing of his hand against hers, or the rustling of their coats as their jackets rubbed together, and as they came up to the cathedral and stared up he let an arm drape over her shoulder and she did not tense nor did she ease herself out of his grip but instead turned her face towards his and he looked into her eyes and they kissed briefly and as they entered the cathedral and walked up the aisle towards the altar she took his hand in hers and Peter looked at the carved image above the pulpit, this man with his message of a deferred salvation in which he had never quite believed, and he had instead the sense, dizzying and quite overpowering, of interloping into this house of God with his own alternative and finer vision of paradise. And as they turned to face the empty pews and walked back past the bowls of incense and out through the heavy wooden doors and down the stone steps he thought for a moment to explain this but instead turned to face her and they kissed again.

Back in the car he looked at her before he started the ignition.

'Jean Seberg?' he said.

'Alain Delon?'

'*Les flics* at our back.'

'The world on our tail.'

'We could just drive. Head east.'

'Where to?'

'Nowhere. Just keep going.'

They sat in silence for a few moments, and then Shelley said, 'Virginia's cooking. We said we'd be back at eight.'

Peter nodded. He started the car, eased into the traffic and followed the *périphérique* until they came back to the western entrance. He turned on the wipers as the rain started again.

'Looks like we missed it,' said Shelley.

Later, as they got caught up in rush-hour traffic, she began to talk.

'Do you know, once when I was a kid we went to see some Aboriginal cave paintings. Out near Kimberley. That's way up north, right out in the middle of nowhere. I can't remember why, I think we must have been visiting Dad's relos. Can't remember much about it. Except one day being shown a gun, an old rifle. They lived right out of town. Desert somewhere, some old shack with bits of rusting car in the yard. Someone, my uncle maybe, he sets up these cans on a fence twenty yards away. And he tries to shoot 'em down. Misses every time.

'Crack. Bang. I was covering my ears and crying. They thought that was fucking hilarious.

'One day we all get in the pickup and drive out to see these caves. Those days there were no fences or tickets or anything. You just turned up and had a look. And I saw those pictures in the rock and just kind of got it. I *got* those pictures. Red I think they were. And people not just animals. And not just outlines. All painted in they were.

'Any kid would love 'em. Any kid would want to touch 'em. I tried to trace a finger round the edges.

'"Don't do that," Mum said. "Leave 'em be."

'I started to cry again. I didn't understand.

'"Just imagine a million fingers like yours." Mum was trying her best. "They'll fade away, love. We don't want that do we?"

'And my Dad said, "Let the kid do what she likes. They're only fuckin' abos."'

Shelley was silent. She pulled on her sunglasses once more. Peter reached across and took her hand.

'Twenty thousand years old,' she said. 'They're only fuckin' abos.'

*

Ben and Kath and Lucy were already at the house when Peter and Shelley got back. It seemed they had not got very far from the station at Bordeaux but instead found a place for lunch nearby and stayed over a couple of bottles of wine for most of the afternoon. The major incident of the day had been on the way back when they attempted to direct the taxi driver from the local station to Virginia's village. The three of them realised then that they did not in fact have the faintest clue what her address was. The journey necessitated three calls on Ben's mobile, handed by him to the taxi driver for the duration of the ride, in which Virginia tried to guide him country lane by country lane.

'Just imagine if there were no mobile phones,' said Shelley. 'Lost forever.' They were all seated around the kitchen table. Virginia was waiting anxiously for her duck cassoulet to brown. Harriet was preparing a salad.

'Wasn't so long ago,' said Art.

'How did you survive without them?' said Kath.

'It's like not having cars ...' said Lucy.

'... or anaesthetics,' said Kath.

'... or Youtube,' said Lucy.

'... or Shazam,' said Ben.

'Shazam?' said Art.

'Here, I'll show you.'

Peter's eyes followed Shelley who seemed totally immersed in the flow of the conversation around the table, and at a level which he could not quite understand he was happy to watch and say little, as if in describing the magic of the caves she in some way represented the views of the two of them. As if what they thought and felt was a unity and did not require addition or amplification from him. And with that intuition came the very first inkling of risk, of an emotional depth from which he might be unable to extricate himself.

But he also realised - quite suddenly, when Virginia checked the oven door and the aroma filled the room - that he was starving. Virginia judged that the cassoulet was ready and carried the dish to the table. Kath and Lucy and Ben, who had protested earlier that they had eaten enough to keep them going all week, appeared to acquire second wind and they made space amongst the wine glasses and the bowls of salad and olives.

Virginia, as she was about to serve, had a sudden flap and wondered whether she should get out the candles and switch off the lights, but after a minute's discussion it was decided they were too hungry and everything seemed so perfect anyway, and they ate and talked, about mediaeval Bordeaux and prehistoric art and modern French cuisine, and very little about literature although Harriet insisted her fingers had not left the keyboard all day, even if it was too soon to judge whether the four thousand words she had strung together in fact constituted literature.

Later, as they passed the plates of cheese and the bowls of fruit amongst each other, Virginia raised the question of a repeat the following year if people were willing.

'We'll all be published by then.'

'We'll all be famous.'

At that moment a call came through on Kath's mobile. 'Excuse me,' she said.

'We'll be on book signing tours in America or Japan.'

'We won't have time next year.'

'For France?' said Virginia. 'For me?'

'Who will have the biggest advance?'

'The sleaziest agent?'

'Me please.'

And then one by one they stopped talking and there was silence and they looked across at Kath at the end of the table. Her eyes were fixed on a point in mid-air a few feet away from her and as Peter watched it seemed as if her face changed colour and became dull and was instead lit by a low inner gleam and there was an uneven sheen of sweat, not over her forehead, but over her lower face as if she had dipped into a bath of oil. No one sought to move or to speak. She might have been in another room enclosed by soundproofed glass.

Peter saw then it was not sweat. It was tears.

Lucy was the first to react.

She got up and walked round the table and knelt at Kath's side and put an arm around her shoulder and then took the phone. She whispered into it, 'This is Lucy, Kath's friend.' She listened for a minute or two. Twice she said, 'Yes', and then she ended the call, put the phone down on the table, and pulled Kath up as gently as she could by the shoulders and led her into the next room. After a few seconds Virginia got up and followed her.

There was a period of hysteria, of a shrieking from next door which was not quite recognisable as human. After two minutes Virginia came back into the kitchen. Harriet asked if they should call the doctor.

'What is it?' said Ben.

'Who is it?' said Shelley, and something seemed to clear in Peter's head and he cursed himself for his slowness.

Virginia looked at Shelley and said, 'There's a bottle of brandy in the cupboard. Yes, just there. Can you … just a small measure.' She sighed. 'Shelley, it's her brother. He's in Afghanistan. There's been an incident. It'll be in the papers tomorrow.' Virginia returned to the other room. Shelley followed with a glass tumbler in her hand.

The screaming subsided. After a while Harriet and then Peter collected the dishes and cleared the table. The others, perhaps sensing a need for the reassurance of physical routine, helped as they could. When they had finished they sat round the table in silence. Peter and Art poured themselves shots of the brandy.

After half an hour Virginia came back into the kitchen. She whispered to Peter, 'Can I ask a favour? Kath'll want to go home tomorrow. Can you check the flights? Perhaps Lucy as well.'

'Sure.'

'Tell me how much it costs and …'

'Don't worry. We can sort it out back home.'

'You're a dear.'

Peter left the others and went upstairs to his room. He opened up his laptop and as the wi-fi connected he stared out the window at the night sky. He laid his credit card on the table, and got up and switched off the main lamp. He worked by the light of his screen. Outside, there were a few stars visible. The cloud had cleared and he could make out the contour of the trees across the river.

After a few minutes he heard the door open behind him.

'Two seats tomorrow,' he said. 'Twelve thirty, Bergerac airport. Shall I book?'

Virginia came up behind and placed a hand on his shoulder. He pressed the *Purchase* button. As the hourglass span he looked out the window again.

'I said it once before, didn't I,' he said. 'It's beautiful.'

'You did. It is.'

Later he saw Kath and Lucy and Shelley in fleeces and sweat shirts sitting outside on a wooden bench facing away from the house. They sat quite still and said nothing. They sat with their arms around each other and stared at the sky.

He went downstairs to the kitchen, said goodnight to everyone, and returned to his room. He washed, undressed, and lay on the bed. As his eyes closed he remembered his grandmother once telling him that his grandfather had killed men in action. He had found this implausible then, and yet an image of a young man in the desert suffused his drifting thoughts. He switched off the light and soon dreamt, of himself crouched into a ball, pinned down in a shallow trench, of tracer shooting by on either side.

He awoke suddenly.

His eyes adjusted to the darkness and he raised his head. The door was open and there was a figure standing just inside. She wore a long t-shirt loose to the knees. 'What ...?' She put a finger to her lips. She closed the door with meticulous care, stood for a few seconds, listening, and then moved on tip toe towards him. He stayed still under the duvet on his back watching her. She lowered herself onto the end of the bed.

She placed a hand under the duvet and he felt a single fingernail brushing against his shin, and she curled her knees up on the bed and raised the duvet a fraction, and then a bit more, as if gently unpeeling. She shifted her body over his left leg, and sat with her ankles folded underneath her and raised the finger of her other hand to her lips once more. She stayed that way for a few seconds, head tilted. In the low light which penetrated through the thin curtains he made out the merest suggestion of her eyes and lips. She straightened up, leant back and trailed both hands, fingers splayed, under the arches of his outstretched feet. And from there slowly up between his toes and over his ankles and his legs. His breathing became measured, deep, rhythmic. Once she leaned forward and rolled a finger around the hollow of his belly button.

She leaned back and lowered her hands flat against his thighs and glided them forwards in a slow rotating motion until her fingers touched and interleaved. He saw her tongue dart once between her lips. He stared at her mouth and raised his hands towards her, but she did not lean to meet him but instead drew her grip close and swayed, silently, slowly, left to right and to left again.

She shook her hair and he thought of the cypress trees in the night sky as their leaves rippled in the wind.

His breath became ragged.

After a couple of minutes she reached to the side and he guided her fingers with his own to the dark shape of a box of tissues. She pulled a sheaf and rubbed her hands and his stomach and then took off her t-shirt and laid her body alongside his with her back to him. He turned onto his left side and kissed her shoulder and his right hand explored her hip and the crevice between the cheeks of her bottom but she took his hand in her right and felt underneath for his left and guided them both to her breasts and she whispered, 'Just hold me.' He placed his face against her hair, suddenly matted and stringy, and lay still. After a while he released one hand, pulled the duvet over the two of them, reached his hand forward again and moved his face down towards the rounded hollow between her shoulder blades.

He tried to preserve the moment, this moment, in his waking consciousness, but he could not do so and he dozed. As daylight began to filter through he imagined she slept face forward in his arms. But in the morning she had gone.

"Freedom is the recognition of necessity."

Hegel

Kath and Lucy did not emerge from their room until a quarter to ten. They wore scarves and jackets even though the day was fine, and dragged their wheelie-bags behind them.

The others sat around in the kitchen, Peter with car keys, wallet and phone on the table in front of him. Ben was unshaven, his hair spiked up. He had slept on Art's floor.

'Do you have everything?' Virginia said. The young women nodded. Peter picked up their bags and carried them to the car outside. The rest of the group followed. In the small garden out front Kath went round everyone in turn and hugged them. Peter watched Shelley, taller by four inches, hold her tight for ten seconds and whisper in her ear. Kath and Lucy got into the back of the car. Peter closed the door and the boot, climbed in himself and started the engine. As he moved off, the five figures on the lawn, each of them silent, with one arm raised in farewell, seemed to him in their stillness and in the uniformity of their gesture to be witness to the adventure's end.

Months later, at an exhibition of Edward Hopper prints, amongst the diners and the lovers, small figures pinned like butterflies on a downtown American landscape, he caught that same sense of inertia and finality.

On the drive to the airport he kept the conversation to the technicalities of air travel - had they packed everything? Passports? Cash for the train at the other end? At check-in, as he completed the purchase of the tickets, he was thankful for the short queues and the controlled informality of provincial French airports.

'I've got you seats together,' he said to them.

'I owe you,' said Kath.

'We'll sort it out back home,' he said.

He waited until their flight was called. He gave one final wave as they went through passport control but they did not look back.

He did not return straight away but picked a city at random from the signposts at the first junction outside the airport and headed for that and then headed for the next one afterwards. He thought as he drove of those he had loved and lost. A friend at school who died in a freak skiing accident. His grandfather, whose death occurred just before his university years. His grandmother, her death just after. With his blood relatives, the grief had been the greater because they raised him, and yet bearable because of a sense of lives well lived. He thought of his mother, of whom he had no conscious memory. It was impossible for him to mourn her except in the abstract, and this incapacity in itself caused him some considerable pain.

He recalled the story of the moment his grandmother found her in the back garden, a story revealed to him with glacial stoicism only a year before her own death. He knew that that stoicism masked a grief which would have overwhelmed her had she allowed it free expression.

The death of a daughter. And his mind went down a path he feared to tread.

He stopped for petrol. After he had paid he parked in a far corner of the forecourt and took out his phone. He flicked through the pictures of his children, and he remembered the first time he had visited Janice in hospital after the birth of Katie, younger of the two by eighteen months. It had been difficult. Janice lay in bed exhausted and in pain, back from a place where men could not go. Just a hair's breadth from defeat, it seemed to him.

He calculated the time in England. One twenty-five PM.

He dialled her mobile number.

'Peter. Hi, how's it … ' He heard her swallowing 'Scuse me, I've got a sandwich … that's better. How's it going?'

'Fine.' There was a pause.

'So what's up?'

'How are Katie? Emily?'

'Good. Great.'

'At school?'

'Yep.'

'When are they back?'

'Normal time. Oh wait, I think they're going straight to … yeah, you remember Timothy, Mark and Judy's boy. Party or something. The girls are staying over tonight.'

'Damn.' Another pause. 'Do you have their number?'

'Judy's? Somewhere. Why?'

'Can you get it?'

'What's up?'

'I need to ... Look, can you pick them up yourself?'

'Pete, I've got a client meeting this afternoon. It's all arranged.'

'I want to speak to them.'

'What?'

'I need to speak to them.'

Janice was silent for a few seconds. 'Pete, what's up?' When he did not answer, she said again, 'Tell me, what's up?'

'When are they back tomorrow?'

'Midday. I don't know. Pete, I'm getting worried now.'

'Janice, I ... ' He leaned his forehead against the steering wheel and closed his eyes. At Sarlat they could have driven east. But they didn't. They didn't. 'I love you Janice.'

He heard her breathing. 'What's happened Pete?' Her voice was low. 'What's going on out there?'

'I love you Janice.'

'I love you too. Pete? Pete?'

'I'll ring tomorrow. I'm OK. I'll ring tomorrow. At midday.'

He arrived back at five. The garden was empty. He parked the car and walked along the road in front of the house and found a grass area where he could see the river. He sat and watched the debris from the previous day's rain, loose branches, leaves, flotsam, all drifting with the slow current.

After ten minutes he heard someone coming up behind him. Shelley sat down three feet to his right.

'Kath and Lucy get off OK?' she said.

'Yeah. They'll be back by now.'

'It was good what you did for them. The tickets and everything.'

Two swans flapped as if preparing for take off and then settled back on the water. Peter studied their movements.

'Shelley,' he said. 'I've been a fool.'

The swans tried a second time. The first twenty yards of their flight were precariously close to the surface.

'I love my wife. I love my children.'

At that moment the image came into his mind of Bill Clinton protesting his innocence on TV. *I did not have sexual relations with that woman* ... The finger wagging, the expression of affront. He looked across at Shelley at his side, and he knew he was in a bind from which there was no painless escape.

'I used you. And that was quite unforgiveable.'

She continued to stare ahead.

He tried to recall whether he had ever shown Shelley the pictures of Janice and the children when they had been alone. At the Book Fair. Or in the pub afterwards. Quite suddenly he was sweating. The possibility that he might have done, the hypocrisy of the gesture, cut right through him. Its hypocrisy and its creepiness. When what was on his mind was simple betrayal.

'Yesterday was wonderful,' he said. 'The caves. I will never forget them. I will never forget being there with you.'

He wondered then whether she would just get up and go. He wanted to look across at her face once more but did not have the courage. Or, he knew, the moral right. He knew also that if her voice broke it would break him as well.

She said, 'Alain Delon? Jean Seberg?' Her tone was steady. 'The *flics* at our back?' She picked at a blade of grass and twirled it around her finger. 'Perhaps I used you as well. Perhaps we needed each other.'

He looked at her, and realised that in fact he knew nothing. He knew nothing about the very people who were closest to him. And if he knew nothing about them, how could he ever write about anybody else, whether real of fictional?

'You know, Pete, when I was a teenager I thought sex was only about power. The power men have over women because they are stronger. Later I found out women had power as well, the power to withhold, to manipulate.

'Fucking. It was all about fucking people over.

'It's taken a long time to work out it's also a good power. A power to give pleasure. To share. It's been a long, long road. But you know what? I'm getting there.'

She stared at the river and told him a story about a man she once met when she worked in a bar, and with whom she had shared a grey anonymous bedroom six floors above for a single night. Nothing asked, expected or exchanged beyond the warmth of the moment together. A man whose name she had not known twenty-four hours earlier and whom she would never see again.

Peter asked her if she ever tried to contact the man. She said no, she said she knew nothing else about him. Except that he was dead. He waited for her to explain but she did not, and he wondered why she was telling him the story, and it came to him that it was its transitory nature that she was trying to recapture, and that its beauty lay in this. And he understood also the kindness of the gesture, that she sought to soften a pill he did not deserve to have sweetened.

And then she said something which threw him once more. 'Here, give me your phone, let me see them.'

'Who?' And as he realised what she was asking he tried to stall. 'You've seen her already. You met Janice. At the pub.'

She sniffed. 'I left early that night. You remember? I had a row with Ben.'

He stared at her and then handed her his phone. He watched as she paged through the pictures. Janice, Emily, Katie. She lingered over the children before she handed the phone back. She said to him, 'You don't need to apologise to me, Peter. There aren't that many decent blokes around. But I think you're one of them.'

Shelley and The Bad Australian

After Johannesburg Shelley found her skills were actually in demand on the charity circuit.

She had an ability her English colleagues lacked: the capacity to say to a man in a thousand-pound suit on the fortieth floor of a Canary Wharf skyscraper, *I Want Money*. To say it to his face, and have him open a cheque book and take her for lunch rather than throw her out. In one case, a Swiss tennis pro turned tech entrepreneur, they partied later and then slept together. The next day he doubled the amount of the cheque. They dated once or twice until he returned to Zurich.

It was not the only time. Occasionally, back at her flat, alone, it sometimes disturbed her that both sides, both she and they, could treat the transaction so casually as just another barter.

After seeing a documentary about Anna Wintour, she cut her hair once more, the ferocious Wintour bob Shelley judging to be more effective in persuading likely targets.

''Scuse me, do we know you?' her colleagues said the first day she arrived in with the new look. The office was in a rundown part of Clerkenwell.

She took a part-time MA in International Relations at City University, and even found herself being sounded out by the government of Gordon Brown - oddly, amusingly, she thought - to join a steering committee on Foreign Aid.

'You sure I'm your kind of person?' she said to the civil servants who approached her, an old political scepticism reasserting itself. Came the banal reply, 'This is a government of all the talents.'

She also found herself being contacted by girls she had known at school. This surprised her. She had always regarded the place as a sink from which the only successful exit was early escape. Yet here she was getting feelers through the new social media from these same girls, now women being posted by multinationals to London. And for the first time the possibility arose in her mind of visiting a country she had long ceased to call home.

It was from one of these high-achievers that she received a hand-written note from her mother. Poppy had arranged to meet her at the bar of a boutique hotel in Shepherd's Bush, near where Shelley lived, and the two women sat two tables apart for fifteen minutes before they recognised each other. 'My God,' shrieked one. 'I don't believe it,' brayed the other. And like Siseko all those years before, Shelley found her accent slipping back to its earthier roots as they reminisced about playing truant and smoking dope in the yard.

'Here,' said her new friend as she handed over a letter. 'My mum's still in contact with yours. She asked me to give you this.'

'Not sure I want to read it,' said Shelley, but Poppy said, 'I think she's a bit desperate.' Shelley delayed opening the envelope until Poppy went to the Ladies.

Her father was dying of cancer. He might even be gone by the time Shelley received this letter. 'Anything wrong?' Poppy said when she returned. Shelley forced a smile. 'Where were we?' she said. But she spent the next week in an agony of indecision. Eventually she told her boss that she needed to take a week off, and booked a flight to Australia that day.

It had been spring when she left, and she found she had forgotten the strength of the autumn sun when she stepped off the plane in Melbourne. She was equally disoriented when the man at passport control said to her, 'Welcome home.' She spent an afternoon locked in the hotel room with her head in her hands, before she decided to ring Poppy in London, get Poppy's mother's number, and contact her first.

'Shel, Shel. Is that really you?' It took a minute of flapping, of shouts to her husband Howie, before the woman mastered her shock and remembered her manners. 'I'm so sorry for your loss,' she said. Shelley found it hard to conceal her relief at the implication of this, that the waiting was over. 'You'll be going to St Patrick's for the funeral of course?'

Shelley managed to persuade her not to call her own mother, to save the surprise for herself, as she put it. She then went out, bought a black dress, black shoes, and a pair of sunglasses. Two days later she turned up with no warning at a Catholic church near her old home. The service had already started, and she sat on her own at the back. It was more crowded than she had expected, and she feared she could not face a public confrontation on the steps outside.

The order of service listed the address of the reception. She left before the end and took a taxi waiting outside to the working men's club where it was being held. She suppressed a shudder as she walked through the doors and saw the lines of poker machines on one side. That the reception was being held in a 'pokie' did not surprise her. She asked at reception and was directed to a members' area. On the door outside was a note, 'Reserved for Aileene Banks and Family. RIP Mervyn'.

There was a bar. She ordered a scotch, sat and waited. 'Sorry to see him go,' the barman said. 'Good bloke, he was.' Forty-five minutes later the mourners began to show. Shelley scanned the arrivals as they walked through the swing doors in the mirror behind the bar. Soon she spotted her. Her mother. In black, wearing a hat, her two sisters at her side. Shelley did not move.

It was Poppy's mother who guessed right about the woman alone on the stool at the bar, and for a minute Shelley thought the ensuing panic might precipitate the death of a second parent.

A scream. 'My baby.' The room was silent, until Shelley's mother began to wail. She was helped into a chair. 'My baby. My baby.' Shelley was dragged over by a posse of aunts and unknown cousins and made to sit at her mother's side. Her mother grabbed her head and pulled it into her lap.

The afternoon was the hell she had imagined.

It was eight in the evening before the crowds had gone and Shelley was able to find a car to take her and her mother home. She arrived to find her mother's sisters there already. It seemed Gillian and Nora were staying over, though the three older women were so tired they went to bed early. Shelley watched TV for a couple of hours and then spread a few blankets over the settee.

The next morning her aunts decided that mother and daughter needed time alone and left early to go shopping. Shelley, uneasy, almost panicky in her old home, kept herself busy preparing breakfast and tidying the living room. Her mother sat on a chair in the middle of the room and watched, her body swivelling as Shelley dusted and cleared.

'I couldn't believe it yesterday. I just couldn't believe it. So tall. I thought you were a film star.'

Shelley had not brought a change of clothes. She wore the same dress and heels.

'Cate Blunket or someone.'

Later her mother took her upstairs to her old room where Gillian had been sleeping. The walls were bare, but her mother brought out an old box. 'We still have all your things.' She corrected herself. '*I* still have them.' And her mother began to weep silently.

Shelley took the box. Old posters, of goth rockers, concert promos, Bogey and Bacall in black-and-white. Polaroids of friends. None of her parents.

'What'll you do?' Shelley said when her mother had recovered. 'Now?'

Shelley shrugged. 'With all this. The house.'

They sat a foot apart on the bed. Her mother stared ahead. 'I don't yet. Nora said to come live with her in Queensland.'

'Will you?'

'Perhaps. Not just yet.'

They sat in silence for a while.

'He was a good man,' her mother said. 'In his own way.'

And then Shelley froze inside. She closed her eyes and clenched her fists and told herself to say nothing. To say nothing. But she could not stop herself. She opened her eyes. 'He beat you. Mum,' she said. 'He beat you.'

And then her mother began to whisper. 'Shelley, I know what he did to you. I know.' Shelley gasped. Her eyes widened. She got up. 'Stay, stay.' Her mother gripped her arm and began to weep again. 'I just knew if I said anything to anyone, they ... they would take you away from me.' Her mother leaned into her, but she freed herself from her mother's grasp, ran out the room and down the stairs.

She called a taxi and went to see the priest who had conducted the service. Shelley asked him if there was anything practical she could do.

'I'm flying back to London next week, but if it's a question of money ...'

The priest shook his head. He prepared tea for both of them. 'You caused quite a stir yesterday.'

'I almost didn't come.'

The priest looked at her, cut a corner off a slice of cake, raised it to his mouth and then put it down. 'Look, Shelley. I know things were difficult at home. The Lord's ways can be mysterious. But we need to move forward. Merv was a man of his time.' Shelley's self-control did not waver this time. 'A man of his time.' She said nothing.

Back at the hotel she rang the airline and brought her flight forward. She called her mother just before she left for the airport the next day.

'So soon?' She heard her mother start to cry again. 'Oh Shelley. When does your flight leave?'

'Four hours from now.'

'Don't go. Don't go. Oh, wait. I'll meet you at the airport.'

Shelley did wait at check-in until the final call. She saw her just as she was heading towards passport control, her mother's face red with exertion.

'Sit down,' Shelley said to her. 'You'll have a heart attack.'

They found two plastic chairs. Her mother recovered her breath and gave her a small pink carry-all. 'I prepared some things. Cakes. Biscuits.'

'Well, thank you,' said Shelley. 'That's sweet.'

'And photos and stuff. Of all of us.'

They looked at each other in silence. There was a call for stragglers. 'Oh, I can't bear it,' her mother said. 'That's you, isn't it.'

Shelley got up. And then they hugged. Once. But when Shelley walked through the gate, she did not look back. On the other side of the barrier she found a waste bin and threw the carry-all into it.

*

Shelley did not escape so easily. A few weeks later she received - again, with Poppy as intermediary - a package from her mother. Inside was a diary. There was an unsigned note which said simply, 'You should have this.'

The diary covered the years of nineteen forty-seven and forty-eight, and it was quickly apparent that the entries were written by a teenage girl. On the inside front cover was a name, Charlene O'Rourke, but it was a few pages before Shelley realised it was her mother's mother. She knew little about her grandmother except that she had died in a car accident before Shelley was born.

She read every page and every entry that night, and, in tears, did the same the following. She saw too much of herself in those pages. In the handwriting, in the rawness of the prose. And in the fear of and the disgust at the world of adults around her.

She started a course of counselling. The therapist, an ancient, birdlike woman with thick glasses who had a practice in Golders Green, listened, hunched and observant, and said little. But at the end of the third session, Shelley looked up at her and said, 'This is bullshit. I'm sorry. It's me, not you.'

The woman was quick to mollify. 'It's never *you*.' Perhaps unwisely she used the p-word. 'It's never the patient.' Shelley cringed. The therapist's eyes narrowed. She put her hands together. 'May I suggest -' she had a slight European accent '- you might try other ways of exploring these issues of yours.'

'Like ... like what?'

'There are many different forms of therapy. Some even encourage people to express themselves through the arts. Dance. Or music. Or life writing ...'

'*Life* writing?'

'Let's just call it - *writing*.'

Shelley never returned, though one day after work, meeting friends at her old college, she picked up a directory of evening classes starting the following term.

That summer she changed her hairstyle one more time.

Her friend Vince made films. Camp, tipsy after cocktails in a Soho bar, he showed her the designs for his next production.

'The Swinging Sixties,' he explained as he presented sketches and story boards. On the bar he laid out pictures of the stars of the era. Terence Stamp, Brian Jones, Mary Quant, Jean Shrimpton. Shelley studied the period ephemera in silence.

''Ere, Shel, you all right?' Vince saw himself as something of a cockney sparrow. Cockney wanker, as his friends put it. But he did have the odd moment of acuity. 'You look a bit down, girl.'

'I'm fine.'

He looked at her. ''Ere, do you wanna be in the film?'

'Vince, I can't act.'

'As an extra. For a couple of scenes.'

'What do I have to do?'

'Dress up, turn up, then chin up while the camera rolls. Easy as piss.'

Shelley riffled through the news cuttings. Photos of Mick Jagger. Julie Christie. 'She's beautiful,' she said.

'’Ere. Go to Carlo's. He does all our films and ads. He's got a salon just round the corner.'

Shelley looked doubtful.

'Take this snap,' said Vince. He handed her the picture of Julie Christie. 'Tell Carlo I sent you. Say you want a barnet like this. Get you a new you. A new Shel. Give them blues the finger. You'll look just great.'

And Shelley went to the salon, and she re-styled her hair, and she sat in on the scene. And she secretly agreed with Vince that she did indeed look just great.

The next day she enrolled in a creative writing course.

Part III

"There is no thief like a bad book."

Italian Proverb

Janice and the girls were at home when Peter returned from Stansted on Sunday.

As promised, he had called Saturday afternoon to speak to the children. When the phone was handed back to their mother he related the details of Kath's bad news.

'Oh. Poor, poor girl.'

'We were all a bit spooked,' he said, aware that his behaviour the day before might need some justification.

'Poor you.'

Despite the explanatory call, Peter was still gratified to see his family waiting for him when he opened the door of his house. After he had caught up with kids news - Katie and Emily soon lost interest in his pictures of France - he sat alone with his wife in the kitchen. They had mugs of tea in front of them.

'Still, you have your meeting with that agent tomorrow,' she reminded him. 'That's something to look forward to.'

She was right. It was business as usual. The world had turned on its axis, the angel of death had not visited this household.

His meeting had in fact dropped out of his thoughts over the previous few days, but as the evening wore on he began to think how it might go, about what he should say and how he should say it.

The following day he took with him to work hardcopies of the email exchanges, the covering letter he had first sent, and various unrelated scraps of prose he had written over the past few months: essays, short stories, sketches. At lunch he went to a nearby square with a patch of grass, found an empty bench, read through his papers and rehearsed his pitch. He left work at five fifteen. He used the kids as an excuse for his early departure - as he always did.

The agency was located near Charlotte Street just north of Soho. He was there at five minutes before six. 'I'm Zoe,' a young assistant told him. The name sounded familiar from the website. 'Just wait here a moment.'

The premises were spread out over three floors, of which the two he passed through were cluttered with books and manuscripts filling every available space. He had assumed, for no reason, that agents would be divided into two types: fearsome and minimalist and surrounded by technology and paperless offices; or charming with reading glasses poking out of frayed waistcoat pockets. Cool/thirty or bumbling/fifty. Paul Smith or corduroy. LA tan or

English pallor. The grin of a wolf or the grin of a labrador. The office suggested in each case the latter.

But Quentin Booker was difficult to typecast. 'Mr Pindar. Peter. Hi, I'm Quentin.' The handshake was firm. He appeared to be a trim forty, and was dressed in a crisp grey jacket with an open-necked white shirt over jeans and black shoes. 'Shall we go?' he said straight away. And yet twice at the door he turned back to collect first his papers and then his glasses. With a final shrug to the heavens he led Peter out of the office and towards Tottenham Court Road.

Peter had read about fabled literary lunches that lasted all day and in which the bottles of wine outnumbered the participants. In times of frugality it was clear, however, that the keynote was sobriety. They entered a Starbucks.

'The usual for you Mr Booker?' The staff were on familiar terms.

'And for my friend ...?' He looked at Peter who asked for an extra strength cappuccino. And then, 'Dammit. I've left my card back at the ...'

'No problem, Mr Booker.' The staff were accommodating. 'Next time.'

But Peter sensed an opportunity. 'Here, I'll pay.' He brought out his wallet and smiled at Quentin. 'I'm not Franz Kafka.'

'Franz ...?'

'... starving in a garret.' After a second he added, 'Joke.'

'Ha ha. Yes.'

They carried their coffees to a table and laid down their files and folders.

'So. Peter. Peter Pindar. I've read your manuscript. My assistant has glanced at it. Some good stuff there. Some ....' He made a twisting gesture with his hand. 'Hmmm. But, tell me. Tell me first about you. Why do you write? Have you published before? Won any prizes? Any magazine articles? Tell me everything.'

Peter talked briefly of his background, his job, his family. There was not much to say about connections to the industry. In fact he had none. Of course that was why he sought an agent.

He spoke instead of the creative writing course and the writers' group.

'Good. Good,' said Quentin. 'Any plans for your next project?'

Can we get this one off the ground first?, Peter thought. *Please?*

'We do like to build long term relationships with our authors,' said Quentin.

'A few seed ideas. Not sure yet where they're headed but ...'

Quentin interrupted. 'So how much do you know the modern world of books? It's changing fast. Ebooks, free downloads. Do you have a Facebook page? Do you tweet? Do your *protagonists* tweet?'

'Er ...'

'Immersion in character. Try it. Well worthwhile.'

'I'll give it a ...'

'You see, what I'm saying is ... what I find most young writers fail to realise is - I use 'young' with a touch of licence here - is this. They think that, with their masterpiece, the world of literature will come running to them. And the grateful paying public will follow. In fact - unless you're Hilary Mantel - God, I wish she was one of ours - it's the other way round. We go to them. We cajole, we tempt, we beg. And if they demand a better product, we give it to them - well - at least we think very seriously about it. Are you prepared for that?'

Peter was unsure how to take this. Was he suggesting books were like baked beans? But more than that, Peter was slightly unsettled by the direction of the conversation. He had hoped, unreasonably, that Quentin's contribution might be limited to just one word. Which could take one of two binary and mutually exclusive values. But of course, if that were to have been the case, the business could have been transacted by email.

'I accept,' Peter said carefully, 'that one needs to, how shall I put, present one's work in the best possible light.'

'Well put. Well put. Let me ...'

'After all, Kafka and Dan Brown need not necessarily be polar opposites.'

'I'm sorry?'

Shut up, you're wittering, Peter thought. 'I just meant ...'

'Quite. Let me ... where was I? ... let me make it clear I'm not saying it's like X-factor - God, how the BBC's dumbed down these days - but there is ... or is that the other mob? ... there is a creative tension between what the writer wants to say and what the public wants to read. We can't have it all our way.' He waited for Peter to nod his understanding. 'Have you ever had an independent critique? *The Writers Launchpad,* for example.'

'No. I ...'

'Do you think you should?'

'Do I …?'

'Most writers,' Quentin explained, 'even the most accomplished, even, might I suggest, the saintly Ms Mantel, usually try to do too much. Their books are twice as long as they need be. It's rare that a manuscript is not improved by the judicious use of the red pen.'

'Was there anything specific in my book?' said Peter. 'Any particular chapter? Or …'

'The central section meanders a touch. My assistant got a bit bogged down. She's not finished it yet. Rather inundated at the moment. Might require a bit of further tweaking.'

There was silence for a moment. They drank their coffees.

'How many re-writes have you done?' said Quentin.

'Two. Major.' Peter reflected. 'No, three. And a fair number of minor chapter re-writes.'

'Who else has seen it?'

'My wife. My writers' group.'

'Have you read it out loud?'

'Er …' Peter wondered where this was going. 'Some of it.'

'All of it?'

'No.'

'You should.'

'I should?'

'The spoken text,' he intoned. 'Helps spot the flaws.'

'Are there any?'

Quentin looked at him. 'Another coffee? No? I might just …' He got up. 'Damn. My wallet.'

'It's OK,' Peter said. He opened his own and handed him a five pound note. As he waited while Quentin went over to the counter, he pulled the correspondence from his case and glanced through it. The initial letter, the synopsis, the replies, the …

'Do you know I'm inclined to …' Quentin sat down with his refill. He had trousered the change. Peter put away his papers. 'I'm inclined to wait until Zoe has a break in her schedule. Get her point of view as well. That'll give you a chance to finish it.'

'But I have finished it.'

Quentin looked at him. 'So you're not interested in making changes?'

Peter barked, 'I didn't say that.'

'It *is* your book of course.'

'I'm sorry, I meant to say, that's not quite what I meant.' He sighed. 'Sorry. What I meant by *meant* was, that I *could* make some changes if ...'

'Let's discuss titles,' said Quentin, and Peter began to feel that the whole thing was running away from him. *Before and After* was, they agreed, a little vague as a pointer to material and style - 'You can sell a bad book with a good title.' *Does that mean my book is bad?* Peter thought. They discussed genre segmentation and where in the market he would like to position himself. Peter heard himself say that his day job gave him a good sense of the real world and that he understood business and marketeering.

'I thought you worked for the government?'

'Yes, but ...'

He felt like cringeing. It was precisely to get away from this balance-sheet mindset that he had started writing. Discreetly he checked his watch. He had a curious sense of being in the away stand at Old Trafford where the fans wait against hope for an injury time equaliser. But the ball never gets outside their own penalty area.

Quite suddenly the staff were tidying up around them.

'Well, Peter, it's been lovely to meet you. I so love meeting new talent.'

Quentin raised a finger for silence, reached into his pocket and extracted some loose change which he spread over the table. 'I always like to leave something for the real workers,' he said. He communicated his intention with a brief smile to a waiter holding a broom at the next table.

He got up from his chair. 'And next time -' he pointed at Peter's chest for emphasis '- the drinks are on me.'

Peter gathered his things but said nothing. Quentin led him to the door, and then, outside, proffered a hand.

Peter said, 'Mr Booker, can I speak honestly for a moment.'

'Of course. That's why we're here.'

'Can I ... cut to the chase. Is it a Yes or a No?'

"It is understood that the soldier killed last week in Afghanistan, named yesterday as Captain Max Kenton-Jones, was involved in support operations for special forces ...

... The battalion's CO said he was 'regarded by all who had the privilege of serving with him as the one of the very, very finest of his generation ...'"

The Daily Telegraph

'We seem sadly diminished after our interlude in France,' said Virginia. Five members of the group sat in the living room of Harriet's house in Clapham, husband Dieter and son Karl having been dispatched to Karl's room to play their recently acquired copy of Black Ops IV. It was eleven days after the group had flown back. 'I assume you all had last week's message from Kath?' The email had been brief and touching and had thanked everyone for their fantastic support in her moment of darkness. 'I received another over the weekend.'

Virginia explained that Kath had informed her she was taking a break from her engagements in this difficult time, and for that reason would not be attending future group meetings. She also indicated in a postscript that the family would be holding a private service and that those wishing to send flowers were asked instead to contribute to a named charity.

'Why the emails all come to me I'm not sure,' said Virginia. 'I'll forward you the details of course. However -' she looked at everyone in turn '- I've since had two more, one from Lucy saying she is taking a break as well. Perhaps not so surprising. But also, more mysteriously -' she looked sharply at Peter '- from Shelley, who says that for personal reasons she is withdrawing from the group also.'

'Mysterious,' said Art.

'I think we should still send a card to the family,' said Harriet.

'With that I most certainly agree,' said Virginia. 'Anyone wish to add anything?' Again she looked at Peter.

He had known that one of them, either he or Shelley, would have to leave the group. It was like an affair at the office - one of the two had to go when it fell apart. It compounded his guilt that she had pre-empted the difficult decision.

Peter had in fact received messages from both Kath and Shelley, but he did not reveal the receipt of either. The two respective replies, however, were amongst the most difficult he had ever had to make.

The message from Kath thanked him for organising the plane tickets and asked how she might reimburse him. He eventually crafted an email in which he stated how he was so sorry for her loss, and also that there was absolutely *no necessity* - he added the italics on a third re-read - for her even to think about the money until she was ready.

The message from Shelley was a letter - an old fashioned pen-and-paper letter. She began by saying she was not sure whether Peter shared his usual email address with Janice, so she had written by hand instead. It went to three pages.

Peter had an old satchel which he kept locked in the attic. That Janice had never asked about its contents led him to suspect she kept something similar, somewhere, perhaps at her mother's. He knew that this satchel was where he would hide Shelley's letter. He sent a reply from a secret gmail account, a reply which, though short, took him two days to compose. Somewhere in it he used the phrase 'in another life, in another universe'. He knew the moment he pressed *Send* that the tone was mawkish and wrong.

And yet - it was truly, deeply, madly what he felt.

'Well, if no one wishes to say anything, shall we start?' said Virginia.

But there was a third communication of note that he had recently received.

'Before we do,' said Peter. He opened up his laptop. 'Let me read you something. This will make you laugh.'

> Dear Peter Pindar,
>
> Thank you for letting us read your manuscript.
>
> Now that I and my assistant have had a chance to read it, I regret to tell you that we don't think we can take this further.
>
> To my mind the combination of leisurely, semi-literary family saga and contemporary love story does

not quite work, although there are good things along the way. By the end I felt you had taken too long to get there, and interest flagged.

However we think sufficiently highly of your writing to suggest we would be happy to read anything else you write in future, should you wish to send it to us.

Yours Sincerely
Quentin Booker.

PS My assistant Zoe adds the following :

If I may make some personal comments ...
a) The France section. Cut by a third. And ditch the 'Deus ex machina'.
b) Sex and literature. They just don't mix. (Except when they do of course.)
c) I much prefer the funny bits.

My own views of course - other agents may think very differently.
Best, Zoe

Peter looked up. 'Da-Da. So there we have it. Two years work down the pan.'

'You kept that quiet,' said Virginia.

'Cunts,' said Art.

'What was he like?' said Harriet. 'This Booker character?'

Peter chuckled. 'Bark of a labrador,' he said softly, 'bite of a wolf.'

'What's that?'

'Publish online,' said Ben. 'I'll help.'

'Oh Peter,' said Virginia. 'We might all just give up now.'

'Come on, all of you,' said Harriet. 'Come on, us. We knew it was never going to be easy. We're in it for the long haul.'

It was not clear that Harriet's attempts to rouse the team were successful. They met next at Art's in Shepherds Bush, but by quarter past seven Ben had still not shown and Harriet suggested they start without him. He had neither emailed nor phoned, and Peter had an intuition that Ben would be dropping out as well.

'Art, you're reading today?' said Harriet. He had circulated material a few days before.

Virginia appeared out of sorts. She had not said much since arriving. She interrupted now.

'Harriet, before we proceed, can I ask, have you been checking the website for *The Writers' Launchpad*?'

'Have they announced?'

'I don't know. But there have been a few comments posted.'

Peter had avoided the site since his failure to get through the previous round of the competition. He opened up his laptop. 'Art, what's your wi-fi password?'

'Fuck knows,' said Art. There was a hint of a slur in his voice. 'I may have written it down somewhere.' He got up clumsily.

'Hey Art,' said Peter. 'Come back. It's OK. Your network's unsecured. Well, in fact, it's not OK …'

'Peter, please don't,' said Virginia.

'Art, you need a password,' said Peter. 'Ever heard of hacking?'

'Isn't that what I do?' said Art.

'Peter, please don't look,' said Virginia. 'It's all rather distressing.'

He looked across at her - 'You sure?'- and closed down the browser. 'As you wish,' he said.

'What do they say?' said Harriet.

'Ohh.' Virginia seemed to be in two minds. 'They're just hateful and spiteful. Small-minded people who don't even know me. Ohh. Here. Peter, pass me your computer.'

He laid it on the table in front of her. 'Here. How does it work?' He knelt by her and pulled up the website.

'Look at this. Just - look at this.'

They read.

"Bourgeois bullshit. The normal Hampstead crap. Wealthy couples banging each other. Avoid."

> FictionGuy13
>
> "Tales from the one percent."
>
> CheLives

'I don't get it,' said Virginia. 'Is that good or bad?'

> **"Ms Ambrose writes prettily enough, but there is something dated about these drawing room dramas. One half expects the Mitford sisters to make an appearance at any moment.**
>
> **Worse still is that after half a century of multiculturalism one struggles to detect a single Black or Brown voice (apart from the waiters when the ladies lunch). This tawdry *Daily Mail* vision of England carries with it an ugly whiff of racism ..."**
>
> **Katinka Pryszka**

'Virginia, there are some good reviews as well,' said Harriet.

'What do they say about yours?' said Virginia.

They flipped over to Harriet's page.

'It's just me,' said Virginia, scanning the measured tone of the comments on Harriet's work. 'Thank goodness I used my maiden name. Honestly. Art, what do you think?'

'Don't look at me.'

'I mean, you're closer to these people politically, aren't you. Am I just a bigot?'

He said nothing.

'Do you know, if this is what it is like to have your work published, then I really think I don't want it. I really think I'll ring these people and ask to have my novel withdrawn.'

'Virginia, they're just ignorant morons,' said Peter. 'Rent-a-mob. Dave Spart.'

'Who?'

'It's like ... football fans calling the referee a bastard. Next day it's forgotten.'

She looked unconvinced. 'What's especially galling is that they know nothing about me, about the kind of person I am. My charity work, my family, my ...'

'It's a mark of success, not failure,' said Peter. 'I never even got to this stage.'

Harriet stood up. 'Virginia,' she said leaning forward over the laptop. 'You. Are. Not. Your. Characters.' She pressed down gently on the lid until it closed. 'Let's get on with Art's submission, shall we?'

*

Harriet and Virginia and Peter stood on the street outside as Art locked up.

Virginia said in a low voice, 'Do you think we should skip the pub tonight?' She tilted her head towards Art. He had rambled as he read. At one point he lost his temper over a comment Peter made, although he quickly apologised.

Art trotted down the steps towards them. 'What are we waiting for?'

'Just one then.'

They sat around a table with their drinks and Harriet and Peter tried to dissuade Virginia from giving up.

'I don't know. I just don't know.'

'Every writer gets it,' said Harriet. 'Even the very best.'

'Go on to Amazon,' said Peter. 'Just check the one star reviews.'

Art sat with his chin in his hand gazing into space.

Virginia sighed. 'OK Art?' she said.

His eyes focused. 'Must find the little boys' room ...' He got up and stumbled. 'Fuck.' His arm brushed his glass as he grabbed the table for support. His pint toppled and spilled.

'Whoa.' The others pushed their chairs back. Art was oblivious. He stumbled over to the loo.

They looked at each other. Peter got up and went to the bar. 'We've spilt a drink. Terribly sorry. Do you have a cloth?'

The barman, East European, was serving a customer. 'I come soon.'

Peter returned to the table. In a few moments the barman appeared with a mop. They waited for Art, but when he came out of the toilet he headed straight for the bar.

'Peter, you better help him,' said Virginia.

He walked over to join Art who leant against the bar to steady himself. 'Pint of Guinness,' he barked. The barmaid looked him up and down.

'It's OK,' Peter said to her. 'I'll pay.' To Art he whispered, 'Last one, eh?' She hesitated for a moment, but then began to pull the pint. It filled to its three-quarters level and she let it stand a moment. 'Come on, luv, it's an art. Pouring Guinness. An art. Ha ha. Or don't they teach you that in Poland?' She finished pulling the drink and looked at Art once more.

'What's that look s'posed to mean?' he said.

Peter handed her a five pound note. *I am the group's moneybags*, he thought. She placed the pint in front of them. 'Enjoy,' she said.

'Enjoy? What do you mean, fucking *enjoy*?'

'Come on Art, let's go.' Peter took him by the arm and led him away.

'Don't they know proper English?' Art looked over his shoulder and shouted, 'ENJOY - IT'S A FUCKING TRANSITIVE VERB.'

'Come on,' said Peter. He led him to the table. Art took one swig and then laid his head on the wooden surface. 'Fuckers,' he muttered. He started to snore lightly.

The barman came over. 'I'm so sorry,' said Virginia. 'Our friend's not feeling very well.'

'I know him,' the barman said. 'He comes every night. He's not a bad person. But swearing at staff - that's not allowed.'

'We'll be going in a moment.'

The barman nodded.

Art did not wake up.

After fifteen minutes they were beginning to get worried. His breathing became more laboured. The barman came over once more.

'What about his daughter?' said Harriet.

'Rosa?' said Peter

'Anyone have her number?' said Virginia.

Peter looked at them, and then at Art. 'Sorry mate,' he said to the sleeping form. He reached into the right inside pocket of his jacket and then the left. He frowned and tried the pockets of his trousers. Art belched. 'Here we go.' Peter was surprised for some reason that the phone he held in his hand was actually an up-to-date smartphone. 'Right, contacts. Here we are.'

'Read it out,' said Virginia, taking her own phone out of her bag.

'Got it. Rosa - 0 7 8 ...'

Virginia dialled. They waited. She looked away, and then turned to the others and nodded. 'Yes, hello, this is Virginia McCorquindale. From Art's writing group. I'm sorry to bother you, we appear to have a very slight problem ...'

After twenty minutes, when the pub manager was beginning to get a touch irritated, the twin doors juddered open and she swept in wearing a parka over a sequinned ankle-length gown, as though an evening of high glamour had been prematurely ended. 'Oh, Dad, Dad, what's happened to you?' she declared across the room to his inert figure.

'We were getting worried,' said Harriet getting to her feet. Peter had a strange sense that the two women took a moment to size each other up.

'Don't worry,' said Rosa. She turned to the hovering barman. 'I'll get him home.' She took her father by the arm. 'Dad, wake up.' And at the sound of her voice he began to stir. 'Come on, you're coming with me. Mmm ... ' She looked up.

'Peter.'

'Peter, hi. I may need a hand.'

Art managed to get to his feet and, with Rosa and Peter either side, they led him to the door and into her parked four-by-four. It took some lifting and folding but they soon had him, comfortable and snoring, in the passenger seat. Rosa shut the door. They all stood on the pavement.

'Will he be OK?' said Virginia.

Rosa sighed. 'I don't know whether you know - he got fired from his paper last week.'

'No, we didn't,' said Virginia. 'I'm so sorry.'

'I hear they're in financial difficulties,' said Harriet.

'You know -' Rosa turned to her '- we editors do actually talk to each other sometimes, even if I'm tabloid and that mob are, well, a bit la-di-da. I got a call a month ago warning me that Dad was *surplus to requirements*, as they say. Bunch of wankers. Always banging on about the cuts. Now they're downsizing like it's no one's business.'

'It's go digital,' said Harriet. 'Or die.'

'Not us baby,' said Rosa. 'Not us.' She moved round to the other side of the car. 'Dad's staying at mine tonight. I'll make sure he's OK. Eh Dad?'

The passenger window lowered as Rosa started the engine. She shouted out to them, 'Five hundred K. That's what his editor gets. Our man-of-the-people, Dad's boss. Makes you laugh. Or want to chuck up.' She engaged the automatic gears. 'D'you know he's written a book in his spare time. Might interest you lot. 'Bout being a concert pianist or something.'

The window rose and the car moved off.

'Charming,' said Virginia.

*

They met just once more. Just three of them. Peter, Harriet and Virginia.

Harriet read.

He knows without looking that the house is the one on the left. He has counted down, two by two, from the street corner. He knows it's the right place, though his eyes remain on the pavement ahead except to look once at his watch. He swears. Despite his careful timing, it is still five minutes before the hour.

He does not stop, does not look up to examine the house, or the door, or the curtains which he assumes are closed, but instead walks on. At the corner of the next street he looks at his watch again and sees that exactly two minutes have passed. He crosses the street, a further ten seconds, counts fifteen paces, turns a half-circle and begins to walk back. There is a woman in the far distance coming towards him, and it occurs to him that his nerve will fail if they pass outside the very house he is seeking. But she crosses the road well before.

Peter was following from his laptop. After a while he recognised the section. It was from the start of the narrative. He opened his email folder and flipped through Harriet's past submissions. He found the version she had sent all those months before and placed it side by side with the document from which she was reading.

It was the same.

It was exactly the same.

He remembered he had sent an email the day after with a full page of changes and suggestions and points to consider. She had ignored them all.

It was exactly the goddam same.

And he began to think about his own novel and whether he had ever changed the text after suggestions made in any of their meetings and whether anything that anyone said really made the blindest difference to him or to any of the others and whether they all just wrote whatever it was they wanted to write.

And whether they attended the group simply because they liked the sounds of their own voices.

'Anything wrong?' Harriet had stopped reading. Peter looked at her and then at Virginia.

Later he suspected that they must have been thinking precisely the same as him in the minutes leading up to that moment. 'It's over, isn't it?' he said to them. They were all silent for a few seconds. Virginia sighed. 'Well that's that then.' She began to fold up her papers. 'Shall I finish?' said Harriet. Peter shut down his computer.

They went to the pub, one final drink for old time's sake. Their untouched glasses lay on the table in front of them.

'None of us will make it after all,' said Virginia. 'Those glittering prizes. Not one of us. Will we?'

'So much for the long haul,' said Harriet. Her face was taut.

Peter said nothing. They left without finishing their drinks.

The three of them stood outside the pub. Harriet flagged a taxi.

'Stay in touch.'

'Sure.'

'Best of luck.'

Her cab pulled over. She climbed in without a word. Peter knew that she was in tears.

"If a member of the Writers' Group set dislikes the fiction of precisely, and only, those with the property of liking their books, does that member like his own book?"

The Writers' Group Paradox
(*pace* Bertrand Russell and the school of logical positivism)

For a while Peter looked to kickstart his writing with another group. He checked out a few on the internet but found one closer to home through a note, pinned up amongst the ads for puppies and bass guitars, on a board at the local Sainsbury's. He rang the contact number on the card and was invited to the next meeting.

It was explained to him they started *on the dot* at seven every second Tuesday. The hoster, who bore a disturbing resemblance to the deputy leader of the Labour Party, welcomed him at the door with a request for two pounds.

'To cover biscuits and drinks,' she said.

The drinks turned out to be a single flavour of low sugar-content squash which may or may not have been grapefruit. The other members of the group, four women, did not rise to greet him as he entered the living room.

There was a routine to which all were expected to adhere. Submissions were circulated by email the previous week. There were four slots during the two hour meeting. In each of the four someone would read for ten minutes, and over the following twenty the others responded one by one with their comments. The hoster referred to a large clock on the wall with a second hand and an amplified tick. Everyone was required to say something. This included newcomers.

Peter was exhausted at the end. He suggested a drink at the pub. The hoster seemed taken aback by the idea, while the others said they needed to get home. In the brief details they had given of themselves not one had mentioned a family.

Their vows were to literature, he reflected unkindly.

As she poured him a gin and tonic half an hour later, Janice was in fits. 'Macbeth's witches,' she shrieked.

Peter was not amused. 'Trouble is, there are five of them.'

'A whole coven. It gets better. Do you like their stuff?'

'Hmm.'

'Do they?'

'They seem to love it.'

'Think you'll stick it?'

After the second meeting he got an email at work - he had unwisely given them his business address - suggesting that his presence had had an unfortunate effect on the group's *ambience* (French *ambiance*?) and therefore, as he would surely understand, it might be better if his presence was discontinued.

'Disinvited,' he cried out to his workstation.

'Wassup mate?' said one of his colleagues. After Peter's holiday *sans famille* they were a touch curious about his extra-curricular activities.

'Say,' Peter said, 'what's that famous phrase of Marx's?'

'About losing nothing but your chains?'

'No, no. The other one. The funny one.' He tried to recall the words. *I don't care to belong to a club ...*

'History repeats itself,' his colleague intoned, 'first as tragedy, second as farce.'

Peter sighed. 'That'll do.'

Over the months that followed, Peter Pindar thought frequently about his writing project. Or, as he sometimes put it, his grand failure. And he wondered whether anything had been achieved over the previous two years.

But, as Janice pointed out, there was at least one positive consequence. He had started to read again.

He had rediscovered his love of literature, both the classics he studied at university and also the best of the moderns. He could discuss with her the shortlists for the prizes without sounding self-conscious or forced. She had herself started an informal reading group with colleagues from chambers, though he was not yet quite ready to go as far as to join that.

He thought frequently about the events in France and the madness that came to close to breaking up his marriage. And he thought, often and painfully, about Shelley.

He thought about things she had said and the things he knew of her past. Once, on the tube to work, as he recalled one by one the early group meetings, he remembered her talking about friends at university who had gone on the game. Later, at four in the morning, Janice asleep beside him, he awoke in a sweat with the certainty that the experiences she had described were not second-hand. He lay fidgeting for an hour, then kissed his wife on the shoulder and got up. After a cup of tea he returned to bed where he lay, for what remained of the night, with the woman he loved in his arms while he anguished over the memory of another.

He still hoped desperately that he might one day see Shelley again, yet he knew that if this were to happen it would have to be at a time and in a manner of her choosing. And before any such meeting he had to separate out, even box up, the various strands of his aching fondness for her - some sexual, some neutral and amicable, some protective as if for a younger sister he never had.

There was something in her that remained hidden and tangled, and he longed to believe he could be part of its unravelling. He kidded himself that in some obscure way he had offered her a way forward, even if it had come to nothing. Perhaps her writing had helped. But at this he could only guess. *Les flics* were still at her back.

Once, Janice asked about her.

'What happened to the Australian? The tall girl, the pretty one?' She gave him that look of hers as she said this.

'She was such a great writer,' he said. And then, with a sigh, 'She left us.'

Janice gazed at him across the breakfast table, but let the matter drop.

The tall one, the pretty one. It was days before he remembered that Janice had never met her.

He thought frequently about his brief incursion into the society of authors, though he looked back at it as he might do a visit to a foreign land.

He never spoke about it to colleagues or to his five-a-side mates, and he had abandoned attempts to solicit further agency interest. Someone had once asked whether you counted yourself a writer even when you were not published. He couldn't remember the answer. But the question had become academic.

On the other hand he believed, with absolutely no evidence to support the assertion, that he was a wiser husband and father.

And perhaps this was the real significance of his project. It wasn't that writing was therapy, as some supposed. It was more that it encouraged a certain way of thinking, a capacity to imagine another's mindset, to construct a *what-if*, to explore the possibilities of motive and desire without retreating into cliché. Indeed, to discover that the surface explanation, the cliché, was probably wrong.

But ultimately, and appropriately for a digital age, his failure lay in the weight of numbers. There were thousands of would-be writers out there - he sometimes thought the entire middle class of London was at it. And no doubt every other class and region of the country as well.

Maybe this was the problem. With this surfeit of personal statement in ebooks, books, twitter streams, blogs, there was no interest out there for any revelation other than one's own. Unless the tale-teller had two heads or had slept with Posh or Becks or indeed both.

His story was just one out of a million. And if every story's uniqueness gave it value, then that same quality made it valueless.

In bad moments, he feared it was inevitable that his own take would remain forever unheard, that his manuscript would remain locked inside that satchel in the attic. And it would stay there until it came to be burnt along with his dentures, his hip replacement and his corpse when the time came.

It had been so important to him. But to the masses beyond? Could they really give a damn?

*

Perhaps Janice sensed that Peter was adrift.

She began to arrange evenings out together when they could find a babysitter. One day she bought tickets for a performance of *The Dream of Gerontius* at the Royal Festival Hall. She told him a colleague was in the choir. 'Middle row of five, seventeenth from the left,' her friend had quipped.

Peter was early. The foyer and the ticket areas were crowded even an hour before the performance. He bought a newspaper, jostled at the bar for a glass of wine, and threaded his way across the sprawling mezzanine. Around a table in the far corner there was a group of eight people, young and old, dressed both casually and formally. They were each holding sheaves of paper, and a woman was reading. Amongst them was a man who looked like a youthful ringer for Barack Obama. Peter felt compelled to sneak a closer look. The man seated next to the presidential clone was staring at him, a worried, or perhaps embarrassed, look on his face.

'Hiya,' he called out.

Somehow it took Peter a few seconds to recognise him.

'Ben. It's you. You up for the concert?'

'Not exactly.'

And as the reader paused and the others looked up, Peter realised what they were all doing.

'Um. Everyone.' Ben rose. 'This is Peter. He's a writer too.'

The others around the table nodded an acknowledgement.

'Hey buddy,' a woman said - in her voice a trace of Runyonesque twang, 'join us.'

'Um. Excuse me for a second,' Ben said to them, and then to the reader, 'Just carry on.' He led Peter a few feet away.

'Peter, how are you doing?'

'You've dumped us then? For a smarter crowd?'

'I'm sorry,' said Ben. 'I should have told you, I know. It's just … it's just another writers' group.'

Peter laid a hand on his shoulder. 'I understand.'

'Look, do you have a second? Join us.'

Janice had texted earlier to say she would be arriving in twenty minutes. He found himself sat between the reader and an elderly gentleman dressed in pinstripe, with immaculately polished shoes and what he imagined was a club tie. The reader continued for another couple of minutes, and the group began, boisterously, to chew over and take apart what had been read.

Except for the old man. He was silent. After a while he turned to Peter and said in a soft voice, 'You're a writer as well?'

Peter hesitated. 'Not exactly.'

'What does that mean?'

The two of them twisted their seats away from the others. 'I used to be.'

'Given up?' the man said.

'I gave it my best shot. No one out there was really interested.'

'I'm sorry. What were you writing about?'

Peter sighed. 'Oh. Me. People like me. My family, similar families. The things we do, the problems we face …'

'And …?'

'I don't know. That's it. I don't really know what I was writing about. Perhaps that was the problem. Perhaps that was why no one was interested.'

The old man watched him.

Peter took a sip of wine and said, 'How about you?'

The old man shrugged. 'Nothing much. The same really. Me. My past. My friends. People like us.'

'I hope you're joking.'

The old man studied him and took a deep breath. 'I'm Henry, by the way,' he said. 'Manners. You must excuse me for not introducing myself.'

Peter waved away the apology.

They stared at each other. 'Do you know' - the man took another deep breath - 'I was an attaché at the British Embassy in Buenos Ares during the 1970s. I was a young man …'

'The Falklands?'

'Before all that business. But Argentina was still a military dictatorship. And we, the British, were in something of a delicate situation. So …'

There was a trace of dandruff on the man's shoulders. As he spoke Peter noticed a minute tremor on his right upper eyelid, and he had an intuition that his writers' group were the only people the old man ever spoke to apart from the home help and his GP.

'So to what extent does one support an unsavoury regime? One had British companies one had to represent. Should that have blinded us to what was going on? Our American cousins had no qualms. Better dead than red, they insisted. But we Brits were never quite as ... rigid.

'I was not married. I was a young man. And outside my official duties I had, let me tell you, a lively social life. Not just embassy people. But locals. Writers, artists, thinkers.' The old man's gaze shifted to a distant point over Peter's left shoulder. 'We were a gang. A real gang. And then. And then ... They started to be picked off. We'd meet, in a bar, in a café, and I would hear that Enrique, Pepe, Maria had not been seen for a while. One by one our numbers diminished. Their families would be distraught, but I'd tell them Enrique or Maria would turn up soon enough. I'd tell them it was some peccadillo. Some trifling affair. A new girl in the frame, a new boy. These people trusted me. I was their figure of authority, the man with the contacts.

'But of course they never reappeared. They were never seen again. And of course the people to whom the families complained, the police, the army, the priests, sweet heavens, the Church itself, these were the very people responsible.

'I was a young man. Naïve. God, god, so naïve.' A snigger. 'But so were my friends. These people weren't lefties, or agitators. They were ordinary folk. Like all of us at this table today. Some were conservative. I tell you, some even supported the generals. Scant difference it made.'

Peter said, 'The Disappeared?'

'*Los Desaparecidos*?' Peter saw the man's cheeks momentarily tense. 'I never use that term. It has, like all clichés, lost some of its resonance. The reality is, those bodies were never recovered and the families never properly grieved. We don't know where they are dumped: at sea, in mass graves, in the mountains. Their lives were erased. The disappeared ones - if I may paraphrase - if I may re-boot, as you young people say - these are the erased ones. The ones whose stories were struck right out of the history of this world.'

The old man's eyes came into focus once more. 'Do you know - Peter, it's Peter isn't it - I will never find a publisher. Never. My wife's dead, we have no children. I no longer have the energy for such things. But I have relatives in Australia, and they tell me there's a whole clan out there. My DNA is alive and well. Perhaps one day one of them will read my old nonsense. Perhaps one day one of them will even print it. I understand you can do it quite cheaply on the internet these days.

'Do you know, this is something I can cling on to. I ... I, who stood by and did nothing, I can cling to this. That the stories of my friends, the ones who were erased, might one day be retold.

'Do you understand what I'm saying? Do you? Or does it all sound just a bit silly? Like the ramblings of an old man?'

The others around the table were arguing and laughing, drinking and cursing.

And Peter had a sense of the weight of time, of the accumulation of small lives, lives whose importance had so often been sacrificed by the powerful and ignored by those who could shout the loudest. And also of the precariousness of such small voices. And of the necessity of letting them speak out. Of giving form to that which men and nature would crush to dust.

*

He felt his phone buzz and got up from his chair.

'Henry, it's been a pleasure to meet you,' he said. 'A real pleasure. And it's not silly. It's not silly at all.' He nodded one by one to the others at the table. 'Ben,' he reached for his hand, 'stay in touch. Won't you.'

Peter walked back towards the bar. Crowds of people swirled. He saw Janice in the distance waving her arms. He hurried over and they kissed.

'Where have you been?' she said.

'I met someone. He's a writer. Like me.'

'What's he writing about?' She took his arm.

My old nonsense, the old man had said. 'Oh, nothing.' They entered the auditorium. 'Nothing. Everything.'

Eighteen Months Later

"A Breathtaking New Talent."

The Huffington Post

"Un Nuevo Talento Impresionante."

El País

"A Parable for Our Troubled Times.

A chance visit by a mythical giant to a lowly Peruvian family kicks off a magical journey by our modern-day everyman, taking him by way of Lima and Rio to the fleshpots of London in a journey which becomes a quest for love, spirituality and just about everything else which is important to us in this, our sublunary world ..."

Kristy Dork, *Sentences & Sensibility,* **BBC4**

"Just occasionally the hyperbole is justified.

In prose both limpid and lapidary, this astonishing novel, at times whimsical, at times literal and diamond hard, has exploded like a supernova into the modern literary consciousness ...

... Its hallucinatory realism merges folk tale, history and the contemporary into a seamless mélange both classic and hip, both timeless and achingly modern ...

... Eschewing the conventions of plot, yet displaying a command of form other novelists can only dream of, this fine piece of fiction is written with a virtuosity which takes it beyond the remit of the Booker and those other prizes which increasingly cater for a jaded audience of bookgroups and middle-brow creative writing workshops ..."

Professor Dilwyn Foot, The Guardian

"Paulo Coelho meets James Joyce!"

Zadie Eisenberg, The Daily Mail

"Congratulations to Phyllida Fowst for nurturing this rare talent."

The Telegraph

"All hail Raúl Olivera ..."

Phyllida Fowst writing in The Bookseller

*

A community of email links which has lain silent for a year and a half sputters into life in the hours after the Saturday editions of the papers land on the nation's doormats.

Peter Pindar carries a stack of them, supplements and flyers and shrink wrap included, into the bedroom where his wife Janice lies propped up in bed after a mild attack of dizziness. On the table at her side are a jug of water and a mug of weak tea.

'It was never like this with those two,' she says as Peter walks in.

'Those two?'

Janice nods her head towards Emily and Katie, still in their pyjamas. who lie sprawled out on Peter's side of the bed with pencils and writing pads in their hands.

'If it's a boy ...' says Katie, 'What about ...'

'... Darius, Launcelot, ...' says Emily.

'... Rupert ...' says Katie.

'And if it's a girl?' says Peter.

'Mummy, Mummy, I like Scheherazade.'

At that moment Peter's phone sounds. He has half-a-dozen messages backed up.

'I don't believe it,' he repeats to Janice. 'That bastard.'

'Language.'

'That bastard.'

'Here, let me see.'

He passes her the Review section of the FT. 'Look. The pink 'un as well.' His phone, discarded at the bottom of the bed, pings once more. 'Emily, let Daddy have it,' he says. 'No, No. You can't look at my texts.'

He leans across and takes the phone from his daughter. 'Hmm,' he says to Janice. 'Remember Art? Listen. "really, REALLY sorry. Even the dash-dash-dash-dash-ing Gaurniad's running it."'

'Daddy, what's *dash-dash-dash-dash-ing*?'

*

Five days later, at seven in the evening, Peter stands outside the front door of a house in Islington. He has not yet pressed the bell, and is wondering whether he actually has the courage to do so, when he feels a hand on his arm. He turns.

'Harriet,' he says.

'Peter, how are you?'

'You look ... different.'

'You look nervous.'

'I am.'

'Here, let me.' Harriet reaches past him to press the bell. But he stops her.

'Wait,' he says. 'Just a moment.' They face each other on the door step. 'You're looking ... great ... but where's the ...?'

'The Prada?' Harriet is wearing jeans and trainers. 'I packed it all in.'

'Wow.'

'I'm at UEA. Creative Writing masters programme. After *The Writers Launchpad* ...'

'You won?' His voice rises an octave.

'No.' She shakes her head. 'No. But I got an honourable mention.'

'Wow.'

'So if I'm going to do it, I'll do it properly. And that means being taught by the best.'

At that moment the door opens. Virginia stands in the light of the hallway. 'Peter. Harriet. I knew there was someone there.' They kiss on the cheek. 'You're in good time. I'm just opening a bottle of fizz.'

'Who's here?'

They walk into the living room. Art, Kathryn and Lucy stand to greet them. 'Hey.'

Plus ça change ..., Peter thinks, as another round of hugs and greetings takes place. But some things really have changed. He notes the mineral water that Art is drinking as Virginia pours the champagne. And Kathryn has cut her hair short and looks suntanned and somehow weathered. At some point she will explain she has been in Haiti for six months with *Médecins Sans Frontières*.

'Ben sends his regards,' Virginia shouts out. 'Perhaps you read the email. He's moved to Boston.' She hands a fluted glass to Peter. 'And Shelley,' she says more quietly, looking Peter in the eye. For a moment his heart races. 'She's jetlagged and just back from Australia. I don't think we can expect her tonight, but who knows, perhaps next time.'

Peter nods his head a fraction.

Virginia turns to others. She raises her glass. 'To us.'

'To us.'

'To us.'

And as they talk, as the conversation turns to Raúl whom Kathryn has not seen since before France, as they discuss the craziness of it all, the injustice, the luck, the imperatives of money and big business, the egos and the hypocrisies, the superlatives and the clichés, as they discuss all these things, Peter is aware that he has missed them all and that in truth he would rather be in this room with these people than just about anywhere else in the world, with the small exception of …

'So Peter, you have some news?'

'Well, our foursome is about to become a fivesome.'

… And as his realisation grows a hibernating thirst begins to uncoil in his stomach, a craving to imagine, to dream, to plant that first step once more on some yellow brick road; a desire to open a word document, place his fingers on a keyboard, and type just whatever comes into his imagination. And he knows nothing yet about plot or character or genre or style. But he guesses that the title might not be a million miles away from a phrase which has popped into his head as he gazes at his friends -

'So is *The Writers' Group* back in business?'

'Do you remember that day,' Art is saying, 'when Raúl first read?'

'I was so embarrassed,' says Virginia. 'Sorry, Kathryn, I know you and he …'

'Don't,' says Kathryn. 'I felt the same.'

'I had to bite my lip,' says Lucy.

'The silence that followed was unbearable,' says Harriet.

'What could one say?' says Peter.

'Such drivel.'

'How can they have such poor taste?'

'Have publishers gone mad?'

'And the papers. Taken in by this guff.'

'Bastards.'

'So unfair.'

'Gentlemen,' says Virginia.
'That guy was such crap.'
'Ladies,' says Virginia.
'Simplistic.'
'Ungrammatical.'
'Gentlemen, Ladies,' says Virginia.
'What?'
'Please,' says Virginia.
A chorus of voices - 'WHAT?'
'Please, all of you,' says Virginia. 'Don't be mean. We should drink.' She raises her glass. 'To Raúl. After all -'
She pauses to sip.
'- it's only fiction.'

Printed in Poland
by Amazon Fulfillment
Poland Sp. z o.o., Wrocław